BLOODSHED

weaver

Bloodshed by Weaver

© 2018 by Weaver. All rights reserved.

No part of this book may be reproduced in any written, electronic, recording, or photocopying form without written permission of the author, Weaver.

Books may be purchased in quantity on Lulu.com

Interior Design, Cover Design, and Editing by Chris Borghese

Cover photo obtained from Pixabay.

Weaver, 2018 - Bloodshed
ISBN: 978-1-387-75118-1
1. Science-Fiction 2. Adventure
First Edition

Printed in the United States of America

Dedicated to Eve,
because your weirdness
and desire to pretend to be
a mermaid gave me an
idea for a plot.

prologue

As the young Felid girl, Kailena, got closer to the swampy green water of the oasis to get a drink, Odessa saw her opportunity. She swam to the surface of the lake and waited for the panther-like shapeshifter to get closer, her gills pumping in excitement as her moss-green hair spread through the murky water like a fan.

The second that the girl leaned towards the water to drink, Odessa shot upwards and grabbed the large catlike creature by around her neck, yanking her towards the water. As she splashed heavily into the pond, the shapeshifter girl saw the mermaid and she frantically tried to lash out at the vile creature, but it was to no avail as the water made her large, black-furred paws move slowly.

Odessa pulled Kailena down further towards the bottom of the lake and as the water filled the girl's lungs, her movements became more feeble and sluggish while she tried to escape from the mermaid's clutch. Odessa saw her chance. She pulled herself towards the large black cat's neck and sank her teeth deeply into the skin, injecting the girl with the venom that would let the mermaid control the Felid's body. Kailena's body fell limp as she went unconscious, and Odessa quickly swam her to the passageway underwater that led to the cavern under the desert, tugging the large body behind her.

As Odessa glanced around, she saw her brothers and sisters looking at her in confusion.

Why isn't she just eating her prey? Maybe she isn't hungry at the moment. One of her sisters, Jaelin, made it her goal that as soon as Odessa left her prey, she would go and steal it from her. If she wasn't going to eat it, then why should she let it go to waste?

Odessa pushed the body out of the water and onto the dry rocks of the cavern. She knew that soon enough, the Felid's body would be hers to control, and from there, she would be able to lure more of the shifters to the pond. It was a known fact that if a merperson injected their venom into another creature, they were able to control the creature's body, almost like a puppet. From there, she and her siblings would be able to control their bodies and ultimately destroy the shifter village. They were getting much too close to the oasis, and none of the merpeople wanted them there. The only good thing they brought was food, but if they started feeding primarily on the shifters, she knew that they would soon to be trying to exterminate the merpeople.

Moments later, she knew it was time, so she swam back into the main underwater cavern to talk to her siblings.

"Why are you not eating your prey, Odessa?" Jaelin asked, snaking closer to the cavern where the unconscious Felid laid. Odessa hissed sharply at her sister, blocking her path.

"Fool," she spat. "I envenomated it."

Keki shook his head in daft confusion. "I do not understand."

With a hiss of annoyance at their stupidity, the mermaid explained her plan. The others quickly agreed that it was ingenious, and she swam back to the cavern.

She saw that the Felid girl had shifted back to her human form as she was unconscious, and Odessa tugged the shifter's body back through the tunnel, and onto the sandy ground around the oasis. She would allow the Felid enough time to get to the village, waiting patiently until it was in view, and then she would take control in order to lure more of the creatures to her siblings.

Within the hour, Odessa, while possessing Kailena's body, managed to lure three more Felids to the lake for her siblings to take control over. Soon enough, there were four of the possessed Felids working to get more of their kin to the oasis, where the merpeople's deadly trap was set. When each of the merpeople had a shifter under their control, seventeen in total, they started their attack. They barricaded the rest of the shifters in their houses and set fire to each and every one of them. A few of the shifters managed to escape the houses and tried to fight back against the "rogue shifters," but the merpeople always came out on top.

Odessa looked around her in the chaos and smiled in satisfaction. This was all her doing. All of the destruction, all of the death, the peace that would follow soon after, it was all her idea. She sighed happily and turned back towards the oasis. She might as well take Kailena's body for food. She glanced to her right, just ahead of the oasis and saw a couple of young boys running away from the town, the light glinting off of the necklace that dangled from the younger one's hand.

Oh well. They are young enough that a night in the desert will kill them, and we have more than enough food for the time being. There is no reason to go after them, they will be dead by morning, she thought grimly in satisfaction.

chapter one

quivlie

I woke up still tied to the chair, blinking my large, yellow eyes. I was in the same human clothes from the night before, in the same small room hidden inside the same human government base. I sighed.

It's funny how the humans think they can keep me here, tied to a chair, I thought. I flexed my arms experimentally, and felt the bindings loosen slightly.

Easy.

In one fluid motion, I ripped them from my body, the thick ropes snapping off of me. I rubbed my arms, trying to bring the circulation back to them.

After I could feel my arms again, I untied my waist and then my feet, making sure that my blood was circulating properly before trying to stand. When I stood, I realized that my tail had been bent awkwardly to the side, and I frowned in pain, my skin slightly flushing a darker shade of green. I swished it back and forth a few times.

That's better, I thought. *Now, to get out of here.*

I scanned the room, seeing that it was completely empty except for the chair and me. I smiled slightly and went to the door, softly rapping my knuckles along the wood. Fairly strong door. I tried the knob, but as I had expected, it was locked.

I traced my moss-coloured hand across the wood, and immediately felt it stir slightly.

It's a relatively new door. Finally, some good luck, I thought.

I closed my eyes and rested my hand on the door.

Open.

In my mind, I felt the wood of the door parting, loosening the structure. My skin lightened slightly in pleasure and I stood again, taking a few steps backwards. I braced myself and ran quickly towards the door, slamming my shoulder against the wood. I felt it give way immediately upon impact and I stumbled into the hallway.

A human man stood beside the door, hastily reaching for his gun. I shot my leg into his ankles and he stumbled to the floor. I grabbed his Xeran taser gun from his belt as he went sprawling, quickly shooting him in the back. I leapt over his convulsing body as I raced down the hall, picking a direction at random. In front of me, another human stood, this one wider than the other. I quickly raised the clunky, silver gun and fired the weapon, again leaving my target heaped on the floor. My skin brightening more, I hurried to find the door to the outside of the building.

"Drurida! Halt!" a deep voice bellowed from behind me. I spun around, taser raised. A man stood at the end of the hallway. Before I could even think about what I was doing, I fired the taser towards the human and kept running. Quickly rounding a corner, I almost slid into the adjacent wall, but caught myself with one hand, pushing myself back upright and onto my feet.

My skin flushed darker green as a pair of humans came running down the hall towards me. The bigger one was too close for me to use the taser, and drew his arm back to punch me. I ducked out of the way, and dove towards his midsection, bowling him into the ground. I quickly rolled to my knees and shoved him backwards as he started to stand, his head smacking against the ground. As I started to get to my feet, the smaller human hauled me off of him. I called out in annoyance, a rare thing for a Drurida to do, and I slammed my foot on top of the guard's as hard as I could. The human tripped backwards, and I quickly spun around and fired the taser towards my opponent. As the guard fell to the ground, I turned and fired at the other human again.

A loud blaring sound wailed through the speakers on the wall, and my hands flew up to cover my large ears. Despite the pain of the loud wailing, I saw the silver metal door down the long hallway and quickly slammed the door open, nearly throwing myself outside the building as I ran towards the nearest town, the taser still clutched in my hand.

alison

As I blinked awake, I realized that I was still at the restaurant, the wooden table underneath my head and the bright lights glaring. What woke me up was a strong hand on my shoulder.

"Alison, we're closing up for the night," Peter said. I nodded groggily and stood.

"Yeah, sorry, Pete. I'll see you tomorrow," I replied, my voice tired as I turned to leave. He nodded and walked me to the door.

"Here, before you go," he said, thrusting his closed hand to me. I extended my hand, and he dropped a crumbling fortune cookie into my palm.

"Thanks," I said, smiling. He smiled back to me as I walked out the door, locking it behind me. I looked around the streets, seeing the similar houses and shops, none of them mine. I sighed and started back to the apartment. I tore open the small package to the fortune cookie and broke it in half. I pulled the little piece of paper out of the cookie.

> It is honorable to stand up for what is right, however unpopular it seems. Your lucky number is 13.

I rolled my eyes slightly, but ate the cookie despite the unappealing fortune, putting the small slip of paper into my pocket.

Ten minutes later, I turned the small key to the room and swung the red door open. I flicked on the light and stepped inside, kicking off my shoes and tossing my jacket onto the chair as the musty smell of the apartment washed through the room.

I walked into the small bathroom, and grabbed the toothbrush from the counter. As I squeezed a small dab of mint flavoured toothpaste onto the brush, I heard light footsteps from the bedroom of the small apartment. I turned on the tap, leaving it running as I stepped softly into the living room, my stocking feet making little to no noise against the ratty brown carpet. I quietly made my way into the bedroom.

Glancing into the room from around the doorframe, I heard a drawer squeak close. A hooded figure stood by the end table of the bed, hurriedly looking through the second drawer. I mentally cursed myself as to how stupid I had been.

My knife is still in my coat pocket, and my crossbow is under the bed. Oh well, I thought, *guess we'll have to do this the old fashioned way.*

I softly padded closer to the hooded figure, slightly readying my hands to fight. He suddenly straightened up, and I froze still.

He spun around so fast that I barely had time to react before he lunged at me, but I spun out of the way and shoved him as hard as I could, causing him to go tumbling to the ground. As he fell, he quickly rolled backwards into my legs, making me tumble to the ground. Grunting in surprise, I fell onto the carpet, pain blossoming in my side, but regained I composure as he stood and raced out of the room.

Groaning irately, I rolled to my feet and raced after him, but by the time I was out of the room, the front door was wide open. I ran after him, but he must've already been down the stairs, because I didn't see him in the hallway. I sighed in defeat, and went back to my bedroom.

Damn it! What did he take? I asked myself, turning the tap off in the bathroom before reentering my bedroom. I went to the dresser and saw that the contents of the top drawer were slightly scattered, but he had left my gold bracelet and ring. In confusion, I opened the second door, and realized with a start that the brooch was missing. I rifled through the drawer, and cried out in exasperation as my search turned up empty.

I quickly spun around as I heard the window slam open, and a soft thud outside. I scrambled back to the living room, and saw that the window was wide open.

He tricked me! Tricked me into thinking that he had ran out the door, but had really hidden in the room, then escaped through the window. No! I mentally cursed myself in annoyance at my naivety. I sighed and bolted the door and windows shut, drawing the curtains tightly.

Maybe I should tell the authorities. I laughed aloud at the thought. *What's the point? They wouldn't care about what of mine was stolen. God only knows where he is now!* I glanced around the room again, and groaned when I realized that the extra pair of boots I had stashed near the bed was gone too.

So that's why he tricked me. To steal my freaking boots.

What the hell. Never going to get any of it back, I decided, not bothering to change as I laid down in the bed.

dot

My green eyes flickered open and I lifted my silver metal head as the human connected me to the charging cord. I wasn't very aware of the humans that stood around me talking, but I saw them and saw their mouths moving.

"Now, this Android is a house care robot. This kind of 'droid is made to be able to follow simple instructions, lift heavy objects, and pay close attention to details. To test if it works or not, it is put into a room with markers and paper. If it cleans them up as we instruct it to, it passes. If not, it is considered a failed attempt and is destroyed," he said. The children listening looked excited at the prospect of destruction. "The 'droid hasn't been hearing what we've been saying so far, so it can't cheat, but I'll turn on its auditory microphones. Those are so it can listen to what we say."

I heard all this, and didn't understand why he said my auditory microphones weren't on. I saw the human step forwards and reach his hand towards me. I flinched away and skittered backwards slightly. The human frowned, and roughly grabbed ahold of the back of my head, bringing it forwards and turning a small knob before flicking a hatch down. I didn't know what he thought had changed, because there was no difference from before.

"Hello, Dot. Follow me," the man said.

Dot.

That was my name.

I stood obediently as he unplugged me. The man started to walk, and both the children and I followed him. A room awaited me, and I took in my surroundings as the man went inside.

"Repeat after me: I will clean the room."

"I will clean the room." I repeated, my voice slightly less robotic than the other Androids that the man had heard before, although he put the slight difference to the side and pointed towards the room. I started towards the room, and began picking up the markers from the floor and around the table.

My eyes landed on the paper, and a thought came into my mind. Tilting my head slightly to the side, I took a thick black marker and made a few quick lines across the paper. After a moment's thought, I took the thin blue marker, and quickly transformed the lines into the beginning of an elegant boat. After barely more than a minute, I took ahold of the finished drawing and left the room with it clutched in my hand.

The man and children were waiting in the next room over, and they turned to me as I neared. Seeing all of their eyes on me, I became suddenly aware that they were all wearing clothing and I wasn't. Doing a quick mental Internet check, I found the reason that humans wore clothes and two small groups of pixels on my screen turned red near my cheeks. Frowning in confusion, the man went towards me and took the paper from my outstretched hand.

"You made this?" he questioned. I heard small amounts of anxiety and anger in his voice. Ignoring it, I nodded.

"Yes, sir, I did," I replied quietly, my voice somewhat sheepish. His face turned bright red, and he immediately pressed a small button on his belt. Almost immediately, the blaring of sirens cut through the air. I whirled around in alarm as a large swarm of humans surged towards my, pushing the children and man back.

Fear flew through me as they aimed their guns towards me. The millisecond the first shot was fired, I reacted on mechanical instinct and dove to the side. I quickly rolled to my feet and started running through the large building, using an image I found on my internal computer to guide me through the maze of hallways. Finally, I reached the exit, shoving the door open and running away from the large factory. As I hurried by, I passed a sign reading *Hofferson Androids Inc.*

jaret

I ran through the dense woods, my four strong legs pushing me forwards as I raced towards the town. As I reached the edge of the forest, I felt my skin morph as I returned from my canid form to my human form. I quickly raced out of the tree line and towards the town. I slowed as I reached the rows of houses, walking down the street as if taking a leisurely stroll down the road, keeping my head lowered slightly towards my chest as I walked.

The hunters burst through the forest moments after I had, guns and bows drawn, ready to shoot the large black dog they had seen earlier, but realized that it was nowhere to be seen. It must have gone back into the forest, outsmarted them and gone behind their backs. Sighing about the loss of meat and fur, they tiredly decided to head back to their hunting cabins that were nestled in the woods, although still far away from the Drurida territories. They didn't want to have to consort with the strange creatures more than they already had to, which was admittedly very rarely.

I sighed in relief as I rounded the corner onto a slightly busier road, a few people walking along the sidewalks and two or three carriages being drawn down the road. When I was in my canid form, I was still the same in heart and mind, same thoughts, same emotions, although with different views on the world. When I was human-like, I felt more like prey, waiting for the predator that was undoubtedly lurking somewhere close in the shadows. When I was dog-like however, I knew that I was the predator, at the top of the food chain. Nothing could stop me. I was nearly invincible. But when I changed back into my human form, I was always exhausted, tired from the strain of lugging around the heavier body, the burden staying with me, even when I turned.

Shaking my brown hair out of my eyes, the image of me shaking the water from my fur earlier in the day slammed back into my memory. The wave of tiredness washed over me as I passed the fountain in the centre of town. I contemplated the timing wearily as I neared my caravan. The tiredness was being delayed for longer now. Not by much, but by a little more, a few seconds maybe, every time. I shook the thoughts from my head as I unlocked the door to the small caravan that doubled as my home.

I grabbed an apple from the counter and bit into it, the juices from the slightly overripe fruit dripping onto the floor. Almost immediately, a small swarm of ants ran towards the residue. In disgust, I brought my foot down on top of the insects, grinding the ants into the floor of the caravan.

chapter two

quivlie

As I neared the town the next morning, I realized that there weren't many Druridi horses in the outskirts of the town. Probably not many community-dwelling Druridi either, I reasoned.

The sun blazed overhead, but the cold wind that whipped around the buildings cooled me down. I had not slept all night, and now I was starting to feel the effects. My skin was dulling and my vision started to swim. I needed to find somewhere to rest for an hour or two, and soon.

The side effects of lack of sleep were far worse for a Drurida than for a human. If a Drurida did not sleep for more than twenty hours, their body would start to shut down, first starting with skin-dulling and hallucinations, then continuing to worsen until they could not walk without thinking they were going to fall down a nonexistent pit. By the end of the twenty hours of being awake, the hallucinations become so intense that nothing would exist and yet everything would exist simultaneously, ultimately leading to brain malfunctions, possibly seizures and then death. It had been eighteen and a half hours for me, and so far a dragon had soared overhead, a large snake had wrapped itself around my leg and a bolt of lightning struck down towards me from the cloudless sky.

I virtually stumbled into the town, the taser gun still clutched tightly in my green hand. A sign came into view, an arrow pointing towards the buildings. As I got closer, I could see the words written on the sign. *Traiton*. I knew that Traiton was a trader's town, lots of apartments and hotels to stay in, and lots of people to trade with.

I wondered how much I could trade the taser gun for. Probably at least enough to buy some food, maybe rent a hotel room for a few nights. Heading through an alley, I saw the fountain in the centre of the town, the clear water pouring down the statue in the middle. I made my way to a shop that had a sign outside: *Weaponry Trading*. I opened the door and stepped into the small building.

A human woman stood on the other side of a counter, talking to a man on the other side, also presumably human. He handed her a thick knife and she handed him a small pouch of coins in return. As he turned to leave, his gaze rested on me for a moment longer than would be considered respectful. My skin darkened, but I walked to the counter, placing the taser gun on the table.

"Speak English?" she questioned. I frowned slightly.

"Just as well as I speak Druridish," I replied, my harsh accent a definite contrast from the human's softer voice. The shopkeeper nodded. "What can I get for the taser gun?"

The shopkeeper picked it up and inspected the gun. "Does it work?" she questioned. I nodded. "Know which model it is?"

"A Xeran thirty-four," I replied.

The shopkeeper nodded, somewhat impressed with my knowledge on Xeran weaponry. "Then I'd say fifty-four pieces," she said. I scowled slightly.

"New it'd be bought for almost four hundred pieces," I responded, my skin darkening.

"Used, I'm saying fifty-four," the shopkeeper countered. I shook my head slightly.

"The human that was just in here. That was an Ardelian knife, not very strong, yet you gave him a hundred pieces, at least," I replied, a slightly irritated edge to my voice.

"Take it or leave it, Drurida," she replied. I plucked the gun off of the counter and left the store, my skin darkening again. Looking around the square again, I saw another weaponry trader, except this time the sign was translated into many different languages, including Druridish. Sighing in relief, I made my way towards the other store. I entered the shop, and a Drurida shopkeeper was standing behind the counter talking to a Xeran man. They both looked up as I came in, the shopkeeper's skin lightening slightly in happiness. Mine lightened in response and I nodded to him. He nodded back and signalled for one minute. I looked around the shop. Weapons of all sorts lined the walls, sorted by the make and type of weapon.

The Xeran man started out of the store, raising his scaly hand in greeting. I nodded as he passed me.

"How may I help you?" the shopkeeper asked, speaking in our native Druridish.

"I have a gun to sell. A Xeran model thirty-four, barely used as far as I can tell," I replied, also in Druridish.

He nodded, impressed at the gun as I handed it to him for inspection. "I'd be willing to offer you two hundred fourteen pieces."

I nodded immediately. He rifled in his drawer and put a large handful of coins into a small draw bag, handing it to me over the counter.

"Across the square the human was only willing to buy for fifty-four," I said. He nodded, but his blue skin darkened noticeably.

"The humans here are less likely to sell to Druridi for reasonable prices lately. Some community had hunted too close to a human town and one of their horses escaped, ran through the village, accidentally knocked a few humans over as it ran. Luckily, it didn't hurt any of them too badly, but they trust us even less now. News travels fast through their world. Be careful consorting with them," he warned.

I nodded. "Thank you," I replied gratefully.

"Not a problem. Good luck," he responded. I nodded my head and turned to leave the store, heading back into Traiton.

dot

I slumped against a large rock, feeling the battery drain slowly from me. I knew that if I didn't find a power source soon, I would not be able to continue for much longer. I had been running for nearly a day now, getting away from the factory, following a mental map towards the town of Traiton, a small trading town in the district of Hapling. I stood again, knowing that I had to get closer to the town in order to be able to find power.

alison

The second I woke up, I knew that something was different. I quickly changed into clean clothes and hurried out onto the street. The fountain remained in the centre of the the square, the same species walked around the sidewalks as always. Nothing appeared to be different. But I knew better. I ducked back inside and grabbed my jacket off the chair, walking out as I slipped my arms into the sleeves, shrugging it the rest of the way on.

I went down the stairs, heading towards the restaurant to get breakfast. Almost at the same time, a Drurida girl and I reached for the door handle. It made my stomach churn slightly as the Drurida's green skin darkened, seemingly studying me with her piercing yellow eyes. I reached the door first, however, and I pulled it open, standing back and holding it so that the Drurida girl could enter first.

"Thank you," she said, her voice gravelly as she stepped inside the restaurant. I entered after her, and headed towards my usual seat. As it came into view, I saw that a human was sitting in my usual spot. He looked to be about twenty years old, and he had shaggy brown hair that reminded me slightly of a wolf's fur.

I sighed and picked a different table to sit at, closer to the wall. A few minutes later, a waitress had taken my order, and I was carefully studying the painting in front of me.

A large dog stood by the edge of the forest, a man standing with a shotgun pointed toward it, a woman and small child standing behind him. The dog was jet black, and huge, its teeth pulled back in a silent snarl. The chair across from me scraped back, and as I looked over, the man that took my table was sitting there, his green eyes twinkling as he studied me.

"Yes?" I asked irritatedly. He smiled at me slightly and I rolled my eyes.

"It's not a dog. It's a Cainan. You can see its eyes if you look close enough. Human eyes. It's too big to be a normal dog. Its ears are too pointed, muzzle is too long, it's too thin to be a normal dog, or a wolf, for that matter," he told me. "It's a reminder to the other races that humans are still at the top of the food chain. Still more important than the others," he added.

I nodded slowly and raised my eyebrows. "And you felt compelled to tell me this, why?" I questioned. He shrugged his shoulders and leaned back in the chair.

"You looked like you would want to know," he replied simply. I frowned slightly. "I'm going to go back to my table now. Have a good day," he said, standing.

I slowly shook my head in wonder. *Humans are more confusing than any other race I know of,* I mused.

A few minutes later, Beth, one of the waitresses at the restaurant, another human, came to the table with my waffle and coffee.

"Thanks, Beth," I said. The waitress smiled and nodded, placing them on the table before she left.

chapter three

quivlie

As I went towards the restaurant with my newfound coins, a human woman and I nearly collided by the door. Before I could open it, the human did first, letting me enter the building before her, but not before she averted her eyes from mine. My skin darkened slightly as the human stood there, clearly uncomfortable in a Drurida's presence.

"Thank you," I said to the human, in English, as I entered the small building. She nodded curtly and went in after her. I headed to the right, and towards a table in the corner, sitting in the slightly too-small chair. I scanned the room and saw the human sit across the room by a large painting. A second later, a human waitress came to my table.

"Hello, I'm Anabelle. Here's the breakfast menu," she said in a high-pitched voice, placing a menu in front of me. I averted my large ears, not so much as to be rude, but just enough to somewhat quiet the shrill pitch of her voice.

"Good morning. I'll have water to drink, and a small sandwich platter," I said.

The girl nodded and jotted the request down on a pad of paper. "Is that everything?" she asked. I nodded. "Okay, I'll be right back."

"Thank you," I said as the human left. I scanned the room for any potential threats, my instincts taking over as I started to feel slightly claustrophobic. A man sat alone at a table, but he wasn't human. Not entirely anyways, but I couldn't quite put my finger on why I felt like I should avoid him. A second later, he stood and sat across from the human who had come in with me.

I averted my eyes and continued looking around the room. Nobody else especially caught my interest, except for a small bearded dwarf with an axe who was seated near the door, but that was only because he was talking loudly to a Terin girl, her long green hair nearly hanging to the floor. I reached up and touched my thick, chin-length black hair thoughtfully, comparing it to the vibrant colours of the Terin's. Not a second after, my skin darkened slightly in disgust. Drurida girls kept their hair cut always shorter than their elbows, and the men had shaved heads or very short hair. It was so that they didn't get tangled in the trees. In their communities, Druridi had their houses built in the trees and came down to hunt and scavenge.

A moment after I was finished inspecting the other patrons, the waitress came back with my food and water.

"Thank you," I said as Anabelle set my order on the table in front of me.

"No problem," she replied and walked back to the kitchen. I inspected a quarter-sandwich, and realizing that it was ham and lettuce, I took a bite. As soon as I swallowed the mouthful, I realized how hungry I had been.

After finishing nine quarter-sandwiches and drinking my water, my vision swam again, reminding me that I had to find somewhere to sleep, soon. The wall morphed and churned, and I tried to get to my feet, stumbling back onto the chair. I reached into my small bag and put enough for my meal onto the table, plus a tip. I again stood, and, head swimming, I left the restaurant, heading towards one of the hotels in the square. I braced myself against the counter as the human at the desk looked over at me.

"May I help you, miss?" he asked.

"I need a room, please," I said, the wall behind him contorting.

"That'd be fifty pieces for the week," he said. I nodded and quickly counted out the correct payment, shoving it towards him. He traded the handful of coins for a key, handing me the small metal skeleton. I thanked him and hurried to get up the stairs to my room.

Nearly collapsing onto the bed, I sank into sleep immediately.

dot

I saw the town and picked up my speed, running as fast as my metal legs could carry me. As I neared the town, a quick Internet search made me stop in my tracks. Androids with any independence or creativity were destroyed, and if one was seen it was to be destroyed.

Scanning the dusty terrain around me, I saw a cloak and a blanket lying half-buried in the sand. I quickly unburied them, and slipped the cloak over myself, tearing the blanket into pieces and wrapping them around my hands and feet, hiding my metallic exterior from view.

I just had to buy a Housekeeper Android power cord, and find somewhere to charge. Doing another quick scan of the sand covered terrain around me, I found a backpack containing a small handful of coins, a wrinkled map, and an empty water bottle. I put the coins into a pocket in the cloak, and started towards the town.

As I entered the town called Traiton, I immediately saw a building with a sign hanging outside, saying *Android Accessories and More*. Hopefully they'd have a charging cord for my make. I felt the battery percentage tick lower, a mere fraction of a percent, and I was fully aware of it. I opened the door and stepped into the shop, seeing a human standing with a male Android beside her. I walked closer to them, and the house care android looked my way, although its expression was blank, as if it wasn't completely aware as to what was happening. My screen changing to a look of slight confusion, I went to the human behind the counter.

"I am in need of a charging cord for a Housekeeper Android, version H14," I said, keeping my head lowered. The shopkeeper nodded and turned around, grabbing a cord from behind him.

"Is that all that you need, ma'am?" he asked.

I nodded, the cloak moving up and down slightly. "Yes, thank you, sir."

The shopkeeper nodded and put the cord on the table. "That will be seventy-three pieces."

I nodded again and handed him the change. He handed me the cord, and I left the shop immediately after, not wanting to give the human more reason to suspect my identity as an

Android. Drawing the hood over my face slightly more, I saw an inn and headed towards the building.

A bell chimed as I opened the door, walking forwards towards a man behind a counter.

"I would like to rent a room please, sir," I requested.

"Fifty pieces for the week," he said, his monotonous voice almost sounding robotic, but a quick scan of his skeletal structure told me that he was human. I nodded and fished the coins out of my pocket, handing them to the innkeeper. He took the coins and passed me a key, telling me how to get to my room. I nodded, thanked him, and started to ascend the stairs. Looking at the numbers on the signs, I navigated my way to the hotel room.

Turning the key in the lock, I entered the small room. I took the cloak off and placed it neatly on the chair, unraveling the cloths on my hands and feet and putting them beside the cloak. After I unpackaged the cord, I scanned the room for a power outlet, finding one near the bedside. Perfect. I plugged one end into the wall, set the timer on the cord, sat down on the bed, and plugged the other end of the cord into the charging slot on my leg.

My screen became blank for a moment before a percentage flashed up. *12.2%. 12.3%. 12.4%.* The numbers slowly ticked by as the minutes passed.

jaret

After I had told the girl about the true form of the dog in the painting, I went back to my seat, leaning back comfortably in my chair. I sighed deeply and looked around the room.

A Terin girl was sitting a few tables away, her long green hair nearly reaching the ground and her delicate pink wings moving slightly, a red-haired dwarf sitting across from her. I drank the remainder of my coffee and left the restaurant, heading towards the forest again.

If I could catch a deer or elk I could sell it to be able to buy a horse, if I could find a fair game trader.

Then I'll finally have enough to get out of this town, I thought. *Find Charlie back in Walkton.*

Since I had gotten there seven years ago, when I was twelve, I had been trying to earn enough money to buy a horse so that I could get out of the small traders' town. Me and my family had lived in a small shifter village between Walkton and Traiton.

My brother Charlie and I were two of the three survivors of the attack that had been conducted by a few of the shifters that had lived in the village. The two of us had escaped and started to run. Me and my brother had gotten into a fight halfway between the towns, and my brother started towards Walkton while I went to find Traiton. I had gotten to town dehydrated and hallucinating, but an older couple let me live with them until the husband passed away three years later, and the wife got sick and had to be taken to the big city to be healed. That was two years ago.

Since then, I had made a living by hunting game to sell to the traders, searching for trinkets in the forests, trading with the Druridi people in the forest and selling the items back in the town. In the outskirts of the forest, I stripped out of my clothes, and started to feel my skin morph.

Seemingly expanding from the inside, my skin started to shrink into my body, being replaced by the thick black fur. I felt my face start to change shape, my nose and mouth elongating into a muzzle, and my tailbone starting to lengthen and grow fur. I felt my ears reaching upwards and reshape into points, my arms and legs growing and becoming thinner. Soon the transformation was complete, and instead of the human that was there moments before, there now crouched a large dog-like creature, its green eyes blazing in the shadows of the looming trees.

Hunting in the daylight was risky, I knew that, but there was more game in the forest. I started running towards the centre of the forest, sniffing the air for prey. The faint scent of elk wafted past, and I changed my direction slightly to be heading closer to the marshes, also more dangerous, but also more plentiful in prey.

What I had to be careful of were the Druridi, crocodiles, and macrogators. Macrogators were exactly what they sounded like: big, deadly, fast. They were the main point of concern for hunting in the marshes. The crocodiles were like bumblebees compared to hornets in relation to the macrogators. Still not good news, but not nearly as dangerous, or persistent. The Druridi's goddess was Mielikki, the goddess of the forest and of the hunt, and they mainly hunted deer as well. They proved as less of a threat, though, because if they thought me to be just a large wolf, they wouldn't harm me. Mielikki was frequently depicted as a wolf, so they were sacred animals to the Druridi.

As I neared the marshes, the scent of the elk grew stronger, so I slowed my pace and headed towards the denser part of the forest, keeping myself hidden in the undergrowth. Watching through the bushes, I saw a large male elk pass in front of me, barely two metres away. I took this opportunity to lunge, and landed on the creature's back, quickly biting its neck and snapping it to the side. It gave a final bleat when I landed on it, but it was silent as it fell, dead, to the ground.

I always tried to kill as quickly and painlessly as possible, not wanting to make the animal suffer.

I awkwardly managed to drag the elk to the edge of the forest near where I had hid my clothes. I shifted back to my human form, getting dressed again and going into town to get the wagon from behind my caravan. Nearly running through town to hasten my return to the elk, I made it to my caravan quickly and hurried to bring the wagon back to my prey.

alison

When I was finished my breakfast, I started back into town. Passing the fountain, I started back towards my apartment. After a quick reach into my pockets, I realized that I was running low on coins.

Ugh.

Going up the stairs to my apartment, I passed a Terin, who glared at me in disgust, like I was a maggot on a half-eaten sandwich. This was part of the reason why I was more cautious around other species, especially the Terin people and Druridi. You never knew what they were thinking. I shuddered as I quickly ascended the stairs.

Pulling the key from my pocket, I opened the door, grabbed my crossbow, gloves and knife, and headed back downstairs, starting towards the forest. Maybe I could catch something and sell it to the traders. If not, I could try to find something different to sell, maybe a bunch of wolfsbane. It sold for a lot those days. Apparently, some of the more superstitious people liked to keep it around their homes to try to ward off Cainans. Nobody liked having them around.

Too unnatural, I guess. Like everything else is these days, in my opinion at least. And most other humans.

As I started towards the alley to go towards the forest, I saw the same guy from the restaurant that morning wheeling a large wagon ahead of me. I sighed and angled myself away from him, not wanting to have to talk to anybody more than I absolutely had to.

As the forest neared, the sounds of the wildlife did too. I knew that I shouldn't get too close to the marshes, but there was always good hunting there, and wolfsbane grew close to the wetlands that spread throughout the forests, so, despite the feeling that I shouldn't, I started towards the closest marsh.

My crossbow slung over my shoulder and my knife in my pocket, I carefully made my way through the forest, keeping an eye out for valuable plants or any game. I pushed aside a large, gnarled group of vines, and continued through the dense forest.

Someone should really cut a trail through here, I thought. *But then again, the animals would be more cautious, and the plants would be scavenged more often.*

The thick plants and trees was a perfect natural protection for most of the other plants and animals through the forest.

Stepping around a thorny bush, I saw the plants beside me rustle. Quickly grabbing my crossbow from my shoulder, I loaded and raised it. Stepping towards the shrubbery, a rabbit darted out of the bush. I fired after it, but quickly realized that I was too slow as it rushed to safety. Sighing at the loss, I continued making my way through the forest. My foot sunk slightly into the ground, and with every step, I grew closer to the marsh.

Finally seeing the clearing of trees, I started going back a few paces. I scanned the area for wolfsbane or prey. I saw the vivid purple flowers through the dense forest, reaching towards the tree canopy. I carefully picked a few with my gloved hands, wrapping it gently in cloth before I put it in my pocket.

Wolfsbane in right jacket pocket, I noted where I had stashed it to avoid potentially losing it in the future.

I looked around again, and through the veil of green, I saw a crocodile lazily climbing ashore. If I didn't bother it, and it didn't see me, I wouldn't get hurt. There was no way that my arrows could pierce its thick hide, so I quietly made my way around it, staying in the tree line. Soon it was out of sight, and I was closely watching a rabbit, slowly drawing my bow as not to scare it. I fired the bow, and at the exact same millisecond, a hawk dove towards the rabbit. The arrow missed the rabbit, but buried into the hawk's shoulder as it grabbed the rabbit. It screeched in pain, and dropping the rabbit, it quickly landed in a nearby tree. It frantically tried to pull the arrow out with its beak, but twisted it deeper into its shoulder.

Giving a small cry of pain, it frantically looked around the area. Suddenly, a massive eagle could be seen from above, slowly descending towards us. The hawk spread its wings, and tried to fly away, but only made it a few metres before landing on the ground. Its wings were supported by its shoulders, and it couldn't fly without moving its shoulder, making the arrow go deeper every time it tried.

I quickly hurried towards it, expecting it to hop away from me, or at least try to fight me off, but it stayed still, not realizing that I was there. Quickly grabbing ahold of it, it obviously became aware of my presence, and it started trying to break free of my hands. After a moment, I got it to calm down slightly, and I took my chance to inspect the burgundy feathers where the arrow was lodged into its flesh.

Knowing that it would try to escape the second after the arrow was gone, I took a firm hold of the arrow, and pulled. It pulled easily out of the bird, and as I had expected, the hawk tried to wrench itself out of my grasp. I gently released it, and quickly backed away as it hurriedly spread its wings and flew back to the tree. Smiling slightly, I continued through the forest.

chapter four

```
quivlie
```

I opened my eyes and sat up in the bed, looking around the small room. I glanced around, seeing the small bag of coins sitting on a table. Rubbing my eyes, I stood, and grabbing the bag, I left the hotel. If I was going to get back to me family in Walkton, I'd need to get some sort of transportation, preferably either a horse or hovercraft of some sort. It was a three day's journey on horse, almost five days on foot, only a day on a small hovercraft, six hours on a big one. Walking wasn't worth the risk, especially for a lone Drurida.

Between the two towns was desert, nothing more, nothing less, except for the creatures. Most of them attacked when their prey was sleeping, paralyzing them as they awoke, rendering them powerless as they devoured them alive.

I shuddered as I thought about my son and mate. I didn't remember anything about the few days before the government base. I didn't even know if my family was still in Walkton, or even if they were still alive. My skin dulled dramatically. It was worth the risk to find them though. If I had to scour half the globe to find them again, I would.

My son, Paulto, had turned three a few weeks before. I smiled slightly as I thought of him, walking towards the restaurant to get breakfast. Opening the door, I headed back towards the corner where I sat yesterday, quickly choosing and sitting at a table. A moment later, the same waitress from the day before came to my table to take my order.

"Hi again! Welcome back!" she exclaimed happily. I smiled slightly and nodded, although the smile was insincere. "Here's your menu, I'll be back in a few minutes," she put the menu on the table.

"Thank you," I replied. Anabelle nodded and walked away, practically skipping to the next table. I shook my head slightly in wonder, and looked down at the menu. A moment later, the perky waitress came back to her table.

"Have you decided yet?" she asked.

"Just a glass of water and a fruit platter, thank you," I said, my gravelly baritone an extreme contrast to the waitress' high pitched voice. She nodded, grinned and left.

Mielikki, this person is exhausting, I thought, running my hand through my thick hair.

After I ate my breakfast, I left the restaurant in a haste, trying to escape the distractions that the loud group of people brought. I stepped outside, and, looking around, I started towards the desert again, hoping to find something I could sell to the shopkeepers. As soon as I had enough money, I could buy a hovercraft and I could make it to Walkton without having to worry about the desert creatures at night while I slept. A small hovercraft would probably cost nearly seven thousand pieces, if it was used. A new one would cost almost fifteen or sixteen thousand.

No matter what, however, I knew that I would get back to my family. Back to Paulto and Haishin.

dot

The timer on the charger went off and it detached from my leg. My screen blinked back to life and I stood, my human eyes refocusing to the light. I stood and, going to the chair, took ahold of the cloths and wound them around my hands and feet again, positioning the cloak over me so that I wasn't visible to other people. I grabbed any of the things I thought I might've needed for the day, money, the charger, the backpack, and headed out of the room.

Descending the stairs, I left the hotel, trying to avoid the areas I knew would be crowded with people. As I walked through the town, I felt a soft rumbling under my feet, but judging by the other citizens' behaviour, I realized that I was only able to feel it because of the extra sensors that were built inside of me. A second later, the rumbling intensified, and that was the point that other people started noticing.

A Xeran mother took her daughter's hand and ran hurriedly away from the fountain in the town square, where the water was starting to spill out of the large concrete bowl.

"Earthquake! Everybody get to the restaurant basement!" I heard a human man shout.

Almost instantly, the majority of the people in the town square frantically started to run towards the restaurant and file indoors, but a few of them ran out of the town and towards the woods instead. I suspected that they were part of the shapeshifting races, as they found they were better off in the forest just in case they accidentally shifted. Shifters would sometimes accidentally shift under stressful situations, and if there was suddenly a large wolf or tiger in the middle of the safety room, it was certain that panic would spread quickly. None of the people there were huge fans of the shifters being in the towns, and many of the more spiritual citizens, which was a large percentage of the population of Traiton, would use wolfsbane and other herbs to try to ward them away, but only worked if the shifter came into direct contact with the herb.

I contemplated going with the humans for a moment, but decided against it as I would take up room that might be needed for somebody else, and there would be a higher chance of somebody finding me out in a more crowded space, so I started to head out of the town, but as soon as I turned somebody grabbed my hand in theirs and started hurriedly leading me towards the restaurant. I glanced over and saw that it was a younger man. Doing a quick scan, I found out that he was nineteen years old, and was a Cainan, a shapeshifter who had a wolf-like alternate body.

"Come on, you should get inside," he said to me as they got closer. I nodded slightly, not wanting to be rude, but as the crowd of people surged towards the doors they got pulled to the back of the group. The ground gave a violent rumble as the earthquake intensified, and there were a few screams and calls of fear from inside the restaurant basement.

As I looked around, I saw a Drurida girl hurry towards the restaurant after them, a shopkeeper running behind her. I was almost certain that the Cainan boy was sure that I wasn't human based on the texture of my hand, but he gave no indications of noticing.

The last people to reach the restaurant were a younger man who was accompanying an elderly woman, and a human woman coming after them. Doing another scan, I found that the man was yet another shifting species, a Felid, his black hair nearly falling into his piercing green eyes. Felids had cat-like alternate bodies, and were only slightly more accepted than Cainans. The woman was a Terin lady with dark yellow wings and waist long grey hair, the skin around her dazzlingly twinkly yellow eyes crinkling with age. The human woman wasn't very old, twenty two years old, and the bow clutched in her hand told me that she was a hunter, most likely in addition to being a scavenger. The two were common traits to be found together in the citizens of Traiton.

The restaurant owner quickly bustled the people inside and down the set of stairs that was adjacent to the door, and as the last of the group made it inside he shut the door behind them and started down the dark stairs behind them. In the basement, I could still feel the ground rumbling and churning around her and the other people. The earthquakes in the area usually lasted pretty long, between thirty minutes and an hour.

The basement under the restaurant was used as a safe room because there was much less clutter that could fall and harm the civilians. Three of the four entrances to the basement were located outside, so in the event that one of the caved in, there would be three more to evacuate from, and the three outside were much less likely to become blocked than the one inside the restaurant. When they had first began building Traiton, they knew that earthquakes were common in the area, but despite that fact, they built the town, deciding to make an extremely strong place for the civilians to take cover in the likely event of an earthquake.

jaret

As soon as the earthquake hit, I ran towards the town square and saw a person in a cloak looking around, as if confused as where to go, so I ran to them and helped them to the restaurant basement. I noticed that their hand seemed slightly less human-like than what would be considered normal, but I put it aside and hurriedly helped them to the safe spot to wait out the earthquake.

As I was in the crowd to get in, I saw the woman that I had told about the Cainan painting earlier that morning came in behind them. When they reached the bottom of the flight of stairs, the larger safety room had been nearly filled to capacity.

"Three or four people need to go in the smaller room!" Peter called. I started towards the smaller room, the hooded stranger following after me, along with a couple other people - the woman from the restaurant this morning and a Drurida girl. The four of us stepped into the smaller room, and Peter slid the door shut before I secured it tightly, making sure that the door wouldn't fly open. The small wooden room was empty, except for the small light attached to the corner of the wall and the few benches secured tightly to the walls. The four of us sat down as the ground around us continued to shake violently. The Drurida girl was the first to speak up.

"How long do the earthquakes usually last?" she questioned.

The hooded stranger was the one to answer her. "They typically last between twenty and forty minutes, but it isn't uncommon for them to last for closer to an hour," they replied, their voice sounding almost robotic. The human girl gave a small frown, but the Drurida nodded slightly.

"Thank you," she replied, her accent harsh in comparison to the tone of the hooded stranger.

"Not a problem, miss," the stranger responded. Now I was starting to realize the sound of their voice more clearly.

"Who do you belong to, Android?" the human girl questioned. I frowned and the Drurida's skin darkened slightly in irritation. The stranger faltered before they answered.

"I'm not…" they paused, "I don't belong to anybody."

The human's frown deepened. "What do you mean? You have to belong to somebody, otherwise you wouldn't be out of the factory." she seemed annoyed. The Drurida's skin darkened more dramatically and the human gave her an uneasy glance. I frowned again. This human sure wasn't being very nice to the Android - even if they were a robot, they were still programmed to have feelings and such.

The Android shook their head and pulled the hood back. As I saw their face, I realized that the Android had chosen a slightly more feminine appearance in which face they chose to appear with. They bundled the cloths that were wrapped around their hands and feet and put them on the bench beside them.

"I escaped the factory. The man who was to make sure that I worked properly said that I was a failure because I didn't clean the room like I was supposed to," they explained.

The human's face paled. "Wait, so you have independent thoughts?" she asked. The Android nodded. I was getting slightly anxious about what the Android was saying. Well, more so about how the human would react than to what they were saying. I knew that many of the humans would prefer to have towns of just humans, none of the other races, and also that there was a large reward for turning in an Independent Android to the authorities, and why would she be any different?

"You're thinking of turning her in," the Drurida stated.

The human turned her head to her. "You would understand if you were human," she replied calmly and then glanced to me. She thought I was human, too. I shook my head slightly and she gave a small frown.

With a glance over, I saw the Drurida's skin darken dramatically again. She was pissed, and rightfully so. I decided that it would be a good plan to try to change the subject.

"What's your name?" I asked the Drurida girl. She looked over, her skin lightening a tiny bit, and she offered a small smile.

"Quivlie. What is yours?"

"Jaret," I replied and looked to the android.

"Dot," they answered and the three of us glanced to the human. She scoffed slightly and I rolled my eyes.

"Alison," she responded tersely. I nodded.

"Where you from, Quivlie?" I asked, trying desperately to keep the subject changed. She seemed slightly confused as to where I was going with this, but simultaneously intrigued at my approach at the situation.

"Walkton," she replied, although I had a mildly difficult time trying to find out what she said because of her accent. "You?"

"Traiton, for most of my life. What about you guys?" I asked Alison and Dot. Alison sighed.

"Nowhere really yet. I was finished in production two days ago and got here yesterday," Dot replied.

"Woodbarrow," Alison said. "I had to move here with my parents when I was fourteen, though, and I haven't been able to afford to go back yet."

chapter five

quivlie

As I went into the basement of the restaurant, I immediately realized that I was being roomed with the man and woman from the restaurant this morning, along with a hooded person who I hadn't seen before.

With a sigh, I knew that the humans were more likely to be judgmental of me because of my association with the other Druridi, but I was willing to deal with it for an hour at most. When the human girl started questioning the Android's story, I got quite annoyed. Why didn't she just believe her? The way she talked about Dot was a big reminder of how Alison had looked at me that morning. Like she would be happier if I didn't exist, or at the very least wasn't there. It didn't really matter what she thought, though. The only thing that really mattered a whole lot to me at the moment was being able to afford to get back to Walkton to see Paulto and Haishin again.

"Where's your family, kid?" Alison asked, her question directed towards Jaret.

He shrugged. "My parents are dead, my half-brother's either dead or in Walkton, my adoptive father is dead, my adoptive mother is either dead or in Otteran," he replied. "But I'm nineteen, I don't need anyone to look after me, I'm not exactly a little kid anymore." He was clearly anxious to not let the awkward silence continue for any longer than it already had, as he kept asking questions. "You?" he asked Alison.

"Parents were killed by a pair of shifters," she replied tersely. Both Dot and Jaret noticeably stiffened. Hm. That could be what he was. I couldn't tell just by looking at him, but my instincts told me that he wasn't human.

"I'm sorry," Jaret apologized a few seconds later. Alison shrugged. "What about you?" he asked me.

"My son and my mate are in Walkton. If they're still alive, that is," I replied, smiling slightly. Alison frowned, but Jaret smiled.

"What's your son's name?" Dot asked.

"Paulto. He turned three a couple weeks ago," I responded. Jaret and Dot both smiled, but Alison wasn't warming up to the situation very well. In fact, she looked mildly irritated, as if the thought that a younger Drurida existed was bothering her. My skin flushed a slightly darker shade as I looked to Alison. The room gave a violent shake as the earthquake rumbled on, and Dot skidded against the bench and nearly landed on Jaret.

"My apologies, sir," she said, scrambling back to a seated position. Jaret shook his head.

"No, don't be sorry, it's fine," he responded.

Dot shook her head. With the next quake, a small pile of sandy dirt fell from above and onto the bench beside Alison.

"What the hell?" Alison exclaimed, moving to the side. I quickly looked up, and saw a small crack near the top of the wall. I immediately leapt to my feet and got on top of the bench, using my strong tail to push against the wall behind me to brace myself so that I wouldn't fall.

I placed my hand on the wall, over the crack, and felt it creak slightly under my hand. It was older wood, so it would be a lot harder this time to make it comply, especially this much.

"What are you doing?" Jaret questioned, standing. I ignored his inquiry, and closed my eyes in concentration.

"Druridi have the ability to manipulate and slightly control the way that plants grow and move. Because the room is made out of oak wood, she is most likely trying to fix the crack in the wall so that the room won't continue to fill with sand and we won't be suffocated," Dot answered. "Well, more accurately, you. I don't have to breathe," she corrected herself.

My skin suddenly went very dull as the wood lurched back to rejoining itself, and my knees buckled as I virtually collapsed onto the bench below me, exhausted. Dot immediately leapt to her feet and helped me into a better position to be laying in. Jaret moved closer towards me, and Alison sat, watching in shocked silence.

"Are you okay?" Jaret asked, helping me sit up. I pushed myself into a sitting position and leaned breathlessly against the wall before nodding my head.

alison

As soon as the Drurida girl got onto the bench with me, I immediately inched away from her. It wasn't that I didn't appreciate her trying to help us, just that she had gotten awfully close to me when she had jumped onto the bench.

"Miss Quivlie, are you sure that you are alright?" the Android asked skeptically. Quivlie nodded slightly and took a deep breath as her skin grew slightly less dull. I leaned back against the wall and sighed deeply in irritation.

"Where are you guys heading off to after this? Staying in Traiton for a while?" Jaret asked, his question directed towards Dot. She shrugged. I rolled my eyes. A robot shouldn't be able to choose, it's supposed to be owned by someone, not trying to decide what to do with its life.

"I am unaware as to what I'm going to do next. I think that it would be wise to try to talk to the head of the Law Enforcement Officers and try to convince them that I'm not dangerous and I'm not going to hurt anybody. That would make the remainder of my existence much easier," the robot answered. Jaret nodded.

"Yeah, he's in Walkton. What about you, Allie?" Jaret asked playfully. I scowled lightly.

"Don't call me that," I said firmly. Jaret raised his eyebrows slightly but nodded.

"Okay, sorry," he replied, a slightly indignant edge to his voice. "Where do you want to go, Alison?" he asked again, saying my name pointedly.

"Probably Woodbarrow, maybe Walkton. Any bigger city, really. Hell, even Hyarsh would be better than Traiton," I replied with a short laugh. Jaret smiled and nodded.

"What about you?" he questioned, this time directing the question to Quivlie. She sat up a little straighter as she regained some of her energy.

"I don't know. I don't have enough money to buy any sort of transportation back to Paulto and Haishin, and I can't exactly make it to Walkton on foot, so I'll have to stay here until I can afford to buy either a horse or a hovercraft," she replied. "What about you?"

"Eh, I kinda want to go find my brother. Find out what he's up to and all that," he answered. Suddenly, a look of realization crossed over his face. "Hey!" he exclaimed excitedly. I raised my eyebrow.

What does he want now?

"What?" I asked. He looked as if he was a little kid sitting under the Christmas tree on Christmas morning.

"We all have a similar goal here; get to Walkton. We all also have a similar problem: lack of transportation. If the four of us were to put our money together, we would have enough to buy a couple Hybrid Bikes and enough food to make it to Walkton. It would make a lot more sense than just all splitting ways," he explained. I bit my lip.

He was suggesting that I give all of my money to a couple of strangers so that we could get to the city? Yeah, but I only needed enough to pay for a quarter of the bikes, a quarter of the weapons, a quarter of the food. It did make sense, he had a point there.

"I'm in. That would make the most sense, especially seeing as that we would only need enough food for three of the four members of the party," Dot said. Jaret grinned excitedly and looked to Quivlie. She smiled back at him.

"As am I, the sooner I can see my family, the better," she stated. The three of them looked to me.

I ran my hand through my hair. Sure, I would have to spend a couple days with these freaks, but there were probably more humans compared to the other species in Walkton. After a moment of silence, I made my decision.

"Sure."

dot

As soon as Jaret had the idea, I immediately knew that it made much more sense than trying to get there on my own. For one thing, if I didn't get to Walkton fast enough, my battery would die long before I got to any town. Another, if I was to be seen by one of the Law Enforcement Officers, one of my fellow travellers could pretend that I was their property as to avoid me being destroyed. I would also be helpful in place of a physical paper map, because that could easily get lost. I quickly did a calculation of the duration and intensity of the earthquake.

"My calculations predict that the earthquake will last approximately seven more minutes," I stated. Alison nodded and Quivlie tried to fully sit up. Jaret went back to his bench and picked my cloak and cloths off the ground, handing them to me as they had been thrown off during on of the shakes. I smiled thankfully and started reclothing myself so that nobody outside the room would know that I was an Android without a master or mistress with me. I said as I started binding the cloths around me. He smiled in return.

"When the earthquake stops, I'll go buy two Hybrids. You," Alison started, gesturing to Jaret. "Can you speak Certic at all?" she questioned.

He nodded. "Yeah, my adoptive parents were teaching me for a few years."

I was slightly skeptical of this. Certic wasn't an extremely common language, but it was relatively similar to English, so I didn't object as I thought that Jaret would be able to figure it out.

"Good. You're going to go get fuel for the Hybrids," Alison said. Jaret nodded. "You're in charge of getting enough food and water for the three of us," she said, nodding towards Quivlie. "You're in charge of getting weapons for you three. Remember, we'll be driving for at the very least two days, so grab anything else you think you might need," Alison added, talking to me but talking about weapons for Jaret, Quivlie and I. I nodded affirmatively.

"Yes, miss," I responded. The four of us sorted out the money that they would need. 10 pieces each for fuel, 250 pieces each for the bikes, 50 from Jaret, Quivlie and I for weapons, and 50 from Jaret, Alison and Quivlie for food and water.

There had to some deal-making and exchanging of goods for everybody to be able to spend at least 310 units, seeing as that both Quivlie and I had less money available than Jaret and Alison did. Quivlie promised to pay Alison back for what she didn't currently have when they got to Walkton (she reluctantly agreed), while Jaret said that I didn't have to pay him back so long as he got to drive one of the Hybrids. I was fine with not driving; in fact I preferred that I wouldn't have to drive. Seeing as that I hadn't experienced much of the world in person yet, I would much rather use the time to look around while somebody else drove.

Within the next few minutes, the earthquake came to a rumbling halt, and after waiting a moment to make sure that it was actually over, Peter came to help us out of the room. Soon enough, the flood of people were out of the restaurant basement, and they were all parting ways to ensure that their shops and homes were still intact, and to replace anything that had fallen or broken during the earthquake.

"Okay. I need to go home first, take care of some things. How about we meet up by the fountain in an hour and a half with the stuff we're each supposed to get?" Jaret suggested. Alison nodded.

"Alright, that's fine. Work for you guys?" she asked me and Quivlie. We both nodded.

"Yeah, that would work fine," Quivlie replied.

"As would it for me," I added.

"Okay, good. See you guys then," he said as he started against the grain of people, heading back towards the restaurant. Without a word, Alison left too, heading towards the apartment complex. Quivlie turned to me.

"How charged are you right now?" she questioned me. I did a power-check.

"Ninety-six percent. I have enough power to last me approximately four days, which should be enough to get to Walkton. Just in case it isn't, though, I was going to go to the

Android Accessories store and buy a portable charger. Do you think that is a wise decision?" I asked.

Quivlie nodded. "Probably a good idea. I'll see you again in an hour and a half," Quivlie responded, nodding her farewell as she started towards the hotel that I had been staying in.

"Goodbye, miss," I called after her. I did a quick check, and I found that the best-priced weapons could be found at a weaponry store across town, so I started on my way.

jaret

As soon as we split ways, I headed towards my caravan to get everything that I would need for the trip. I decided to grab what little food I had, a few throwing knives, my jacket and a change of shoes. I didn't know what the weather would be like out there, and I just wanted to make sure that if it was cold during the nights, I would at least have my jacket to keep me warmer.

I should have told them that I'm a Cainan.

If they find out halfway there, they might freak out at me. Oh well. It's too late now, we already started doing this.

That was pretty much anything of any value that I had. Except for the necklace. It was my mother's. As soon as the rogue shifters started attacking the village, she gave it to me and told me that when I got somewhere safe, I was supposed to sell it so that I would have enough money to survive. She gave Charlie her bracelet. I grabbed the necklace from my drawer and slipped it over my head, the heavy pendant resting in the middle of my chest. Taking one last look around my caravan, I sighed deeply. It had been my home for the last five years.

I had a sudden idea. Marley didn't have anywhere very good to live. I could give it to him. He was only twelve years old; his parents went into the forest to hunt one day, and never came back out. When he didn't have enough money to pay the rent on his apartment, he was evicted.

I grabbed the key and clambered out of the caravan, heading towards the restaurant where I knew that he would be. Sure enough, he was sitting in the alley beside the restaurant, fiddling with a rock that he held in his hands. As I got closer, he looked up and raised his hand in greeting. I nodded back to him and crouched down beside him.

"Hey, Marley," I greeted.

"Hi, Jaret," he replied. I smiled faintly.

"Here," I said, thrusting the hand with the key in it towards him. He looked at me in confusion, but put his hand under mine, palm facing up. I opened my hand and the key dropped into his.

"What's the key for?" he questioned. I gestured back towards the direction of my caravan.

"The caravan. I don't need it anymore; I'm going to Walkton with a couple other people to find Charlie," I responded. Marley's eyes widened slightly in disbelief.

"Really? You're giving it to me?" he asked, clearly confused. I laughed lightly and nodded. "Wow," he mumbled, a grin starting to form itself on his face. "Thanks a lot, dude," he said, suddenly pulling me into a hug. I laughed and hugged him back.

"No problem. Just try not to get it broken in the next couple years," I responded. He nodded. "Oh, the back left wheel's already broken, has been for a couple years now, so if you need it for transportation you'd need to get that fixed beforehand, but otherwise it works fine," I explained.

"Thank you," he repeated himself.

I smiled and shook my head. "You don't need to thank me. I'll come back to see you when I find Charlie."

"Promise?" he asked.

"Yeah. I should get going though, I still need to go buy fuel. I'll see you. Stay safe," I said.

"Okay. Good luck with finding Charlie," he nodded.

"Thanks. Bye," I said, standing up. He waved as I went around the corner, towards the fuel station. Within the next couple minutes, I was standing at the counter, trying to talk to the Certic woman who worked at the station.

"I need fuel for two bikes," I said, in Certic.

"Where to?" she asked.

Well, I was pretty sure that was what she asked.

"Walkton," I responded.

"You need ten gallons for the two," is what I thought she said. I was pretty sure. I nodded, thanked her, grabbed two five-gallon canisters and went to the register. A different person was working there, and as I paid for the fuel he looked at me in slight confusion.

"I thought you told Ferida that you were going to Walkton?" he questioned.

I nodded. "Yeah, I am." I responded.

He nodded slowly and handed me the receipt. "Well, good luck."

I smiled and started towards the door, the fuel canisters in my hands. "Thanks," I answered.

chapter six

quivlie

When we left, I started towards the food vendors near the middle of town square. As I walked, I thought about what I should get. Mostly food that wouldn't go bad fast, although we did need some fresh fruits and vegetables. I couldn't really buy much food that needed boiling, as we would need to use the water that we would being for drinking, so that would exclude any pasta or rice or anything like that.

I sighed and went up to the first vendor. She was selling fruits and vegetables, so I grabbed a couple of the more under ripe ones that I could find, paid for them and put them in my bag. Next vendor was selling cakes and other baked foods, but those wouldn't stay good for very long, so I continued walking. I figured that I should buy some dried meat, dried fruits, nuts, maybe a loaf of bread or tortillas.

If I got much more water than we'll need, then we could probably make rice or pasta if we could get a fire going. I could probably make a fire if we could find enough wood. Then if would be relatively easy. And if I couldn't, I'm sure that one of my travelling companions would be able to. It would also be a good plan to get granola or something similar. I went into the larger store that sold foods. The cashier looked to me when I walked in.

"Hello, miss. What would you like?" the young Drurida girl asked me, in English, from behind the counter. I looked around behind her.

"Hi. A container of assorted nuts," I started. She nodded, turned around and grabbed it off of one of the shelves before plunking it down on the counter between us. "Three containers of different dried meats, it doesn't matter which three," I said next. She scrambled to grab the containers before tossing each one onto the counter beside the nuts. I smiled as she got back to the counter, her hair completely askew. I noticed that she had grown her hair down to the middle of her waist, so I knew that she had most likely lived in human villages all of her life, and that her parents probably had too.

"Anything else?" she questioned breathlessly. I paused but continued a second later.

"Also a medium-sized bag of rice," I said.

She raced through the shelves to collect the last item. "Is that everything for today?"

"Yes, thank you," I replied.

She really reminded me of myself when I was younger. Very determined to get everything done as quickly as possible, trying to keep people happy.

"Okey dokey," she said, starting to add the prices together. She bit her lip as she double checked her answer. "That would be one hundred and fifteen pieces," she said. I nodded and got the correct amount of money out of the bag to pay her. She slid the money off of the counter and put it in the register. "Thank you," she said, sliding my purchase towards me. I smiled to her and put everything in the bag that I was using for food.

"Thank you. Have a nice day," I said to her.

"You too," she responded. I turned and walked out of the shop, heading towards a shop where I assumed they would sell water canteens.

alison

I started across town, towards the Hybrid Vehicle Dealership. As I got closer to it, the pungent scent of metal and fuel grew stronger as it washed over me, the wind carrying it closer to the town. I sighed and pulled my long blonde hair into a ponytail as I walked through the gates. In the entire area, except for a lane in the middle that led to the store, used, new and broken Hybrids lined the laneway on both sides and almost all around me. As I neared the store, a short human woman came out to meet me.

"Hello," she called to me, raising her hand in greeting. I nodded my head in response.

"Hi," I replied as I got closer to her.

She grinned. "So, how can I help you?"

I glanced around at the Hybrids around us. "I need to buy two Hybrid motorbikes. They just need to be able to get to Walkton within a couple days, the faster they can get there, the better."

She started towards the left side of the store, gesturing for me to follow her.

"Alright," she said, stopping beside a line of different motorized bikes. "New or used?" she questioned.

I thought for a second before answering. "Used would be fine, they just need to be able to get there quickly," I replied.

After a second of thought, she unchained a rusty bike from the others. The paint was starting to chip, and the leather seat was cracking slightly, but overall it looked like a pretty decent bike.

"How many people are going?" she inquired.

"Two humans, an Android, and a Drurida," I replied. She nodded curtly and pushed the bike towards me.

"You can fit two people on this one, preferably one of the humans and the Android," she stated.

"How much?" I questioned. She glanced down thoughtfully at the bike.

"Four hundred twenty pieces," she replied. I nodded. That would be fine; I would still have five hundred eighty pieces left to buy the other bike with.

"Alright, that would work fine," I responded. She smiled and wheeled the bike towards the store. She braced it against the wall.

"Would you like to take it for a test drive, see how it works first?" the employee asked.

"Yeah, sure," I shrugged. She nodded and went inside the store. I followed a few steps behind her, and she grabbed one of the many sets of keys off of a wall covered with little hooks, a key dangling off of each of them. She headed back outside to the bike, and handed me the key.

"You know how to work it?" she asked. I took the key from her, smiling.

"Yep," I replied. I got onto the bike and put the key into the ignition. Before I turned it, I pressed my left hand down onto the button beside the wheel, and as I turned the key, the bike sputtered to life. Although the engine rattled as it lurched forwards, it did so with surprising speed. Surprised at the sudden movement, I had to quickly find a good path, as I didn't want to drive the bike into another one, or a building, or a fence.

As I turned the bike around, I realized that although the bike sounded like it wouldn't get very far, it could go a long while without breaking down. I slowed the bike and pulled back up to the employee again.

"Yeah, this'll work fine," I said to her.

"Okay, that's good. Now for the other one," she said softly, pausing. She started to a different row of bikes and after a few moments pulled a bulkier, blue bike out of the lineup. "So, this one is equipped to handle heavier loads, so the Drurida and one of the humans would be able to drive on this one, as long as the Drurida is sitting at the back, so if you stop too suddenly the bike won't tip forwards," she said.

"How's the traction on the tires for them?" I asked.

"Very good, they're made to go across the deserts," he responded. "I'll get the key if you want to try this one out too."

"Yeah, that would be great," I responded. She gave an affirmative nod and quickly went back inside the building, bringing the key out a second later. After I tried this bike out too, I found that both of them went relatively fast, and we would have no problem getting to Walkton, so I went and paid for both of the bikes, having sixty-four pieces left.

dot

As I walked to the weaponry store, thoughts were whizzing through my mind. Since Jaret was a Cainan, he would already have sufficient melee weaponry - his teeth and his claws - so it would make the most sense to get him some sort of weapon with projectiles, probably some sort of gun, maybe a bow. It would make sense to get either kind of weapon for Quivlie. Druridi were skilled hunters, usually hunting with bows in their communities, so Quivlie would be evolved to be good at shooting. Then again, because Druridi were larger than most humans, her size and strength would be a good asset in close combat. I would prefer to use a melee weapon, because there's less distance between my opponent and I, less time for them to dodge my attacks, so I would likely be more accurate, especially considering my programming. Housekeeper Androids are also programmed to be able to protect their Masters if they are in danger, mostly how to use regular objects as weapons if needed.

As I entered the weapons trading store, I immediately looked around at the many guns, bows, swords and axes lining the walls. I saw the cashier at the store raise his hand in greeting. I waved back to him and looked back to the walls.

"Do you need help finding anything, miss?" he asked me.

"No thank you sir, I'm sure I can manage," I responded. He nodded and turned back to the blade he was sharpening. As I glanced around, I saw a particular gun that caught my eye. It was a Xeran gun, model 360-T, and Xerans were quite adept weapon-makers. It was small enough to hide if need be, but big enough that its bullets would make a powerful impact. By doing a quick check on my internal computer, I found that most Xeran guns were very easy to use. Even if Jaret didn't have a lot of experience with guns, this one would be relatively easy for him to handle, so that was definitely the best gun for Jaret that was available at this shop.

Within the next six minutes and forty-two seconds, I found a set of throwing knives that the four of us would be able to each use a few of, and a human katana that I would be able to use. I just needed one more weapon, one for Quivlie to use. Druridi weren't the most agile creatures, so it would probably be best to get her a blunt melee weapon, because it could be effectively used as a shield while still being able to used in offense. Because Druridi were much stronger than humans and most other species we had the potential to encounter in the desert, it would be especially effective if Quivlie used her strength against them, and any blunt weapon would be useful for disabling them. The cashier came around the counter to me.

"Have you found anything of interest yet, miss?" he asked. I smiled slightly to myself.

"Yes. I would be interested in purchasing the set of throwing knives, the katana and the Xeran 360-T please," I replied. He raised his eyebrows in an impressed manner and grabbed the key from his belt to unlock the weapons. As he unlocked them, he went and put them behind the counter.

"Do you need help finding any else?" he questioned. I tilted my head in thought.

"Actually, would you be able to recommend a weapon that would be suitable for use by a Drurida?" I asked him. He nodded and started further left down the wall, gesturing for me to follow him.

"Would this one here work well enough?" he asked, pointing to a sword higher up on the wall. I gave it a second of thought and then nodded. I could tell that it was made by Druridi, and was specially crafted for their larger hands to be able to hold easier.

He unlocked the mesh wiring on the wall and pulled the large, machete-type sword out of its brackets, putting it behind the counter with the gun, knives and katana. "Would that be everything?"

"Yes, thank you," I responded. A few minutes later, I was carrying them down the street, towards the fountain where I figured that somebody would probably be waiting, earning a few odd glances from the other civilians along the way.

jaret

As soon as I was done getting the fuel and meeting up with Marley, I started to the fountain. When I got closer, I saw that Quivlie was waiting on one of the benches, playing with a rock that she had picked off of the ground. She looked up and her skin visibly brightened. I smiled and sat down beside her, putting the bags on the ground by our feet.

"Hey," I said to her.

She smiled back to me. "Hello."

A second later, Dot came walking out of one of the shops, a gun slung over their shoulder, a belt of throwing knives around their waist, and a sheathed sword in each of their hands. As they saw us, they raised their hand in greeting, and, nearly stumbling, they gave one of the swords to Quivlie and the gun to me. Woah. It was a pretty big gun, especially considering I'd never fired one before.

"Don't worry, they're easy to use; I'm sure that one of us can teach you how to use it if you don't know how," Dot told me.

"Okay, thanks," I replied. Just as Dot went to sit down on the bench on Quivlie's other side, I heard the whirring of an engine and the clunking sound of something being towed. Quivlie's ears turned towards the noise, soon followed by her turning her head in the same direction, right as Alison came around the corner of the street, towing a motorbike behind the one that she was on. As she saw us, she pulled up beside us.

"Alright, got the bikes," she said, hopping off of it. "You and me will be on this one," she said, gesturing to Quivlie and then pointing at the larger of the two bikes. "And you and you will be on the other one," she said to Dot and I. I nodded excitedly.

"Okay," Dot replied. Quivlie bowed her head slightly in a nod.

"Wait a minute," Alison said shortly, turning to me, a mildly condescending tone to her voice, "do you even know how to shoot that thing?"

I shook my head. She sighed and rolled her eyes in exasperation, and grabbed my arm, half-dragging me towards one of the alleys going out of town. I shot a look back to Quivlie and Dot. Dot was frowning slightly, and Quivlie's face was expressionless, although her skin seemed a bit duller than it was before.

As we went behind a line of stores, she shoved the gun into my hand and went to get something off of the ground, gesturing for me to stay where I was. A second later, she put a piece of wood on top of a large rock behind an apartment building about twenty feet away from where I was standing. She came back to me, took my forearm, and dragged me about fifteen feet further away from the rock before she grabbed the gun from my hand. She virtually pushed me behind her while she raised the gun, pointed it at the wood, and pulled the trigger. The small log blew apart as a soft, deep *fwud* sound thudded through the air, following shortly with the sound of splintering wood.

She gave a smug smile and passed the gun to me, going to get another piece of wood from by the apartment. I looked over the gun, and a second later, she came back and took it from my hands again, putting it back into my hands but in the proper position to hold it.

"Okay. So, just aim it at the log, look through the scope, pull the trigger," she ordered, her voice bored. I looked through the scope as she said to, but I got confused as to how to aim it. There were four lines, all different colours, all very close to the same spot in the middle of the lens.

"Um, which of these lines am I aiming with?" I questioned.

"Blue ones," she replied shortly. I nodded and aimed the gun back at the log, aligning the blue line to the wood. I put my finger on the trigger, and I gave it a gentle squeeze, but when the gun didn't go off, I pulled the trigger harder. Suddenly, something in the gun started to work again, and there was another soft thudding sound as the bullet shot out of the gun, the wood falling backwards off of the rock as the corner of it was barely hit.

"Good enough, let's go," Alison said sharply, grabbing my arm again and leading me back towards the town.

Dot and Quivlie had wheeled the bikes closer to the edge of town, and were in the process of loading the bikes with the supplies we would need for the trip. I was nearly bouncing in excitement again as Alison and I helped them with the last of the supplies.

chapter seven

quivlie

While Alison and Jaret were doing impromptu gun training, Dot and I were discussing the trip.

"It should take us about forty two hours to get to Walkton on these bikes," Dot said.

"So we should be there by morning in two days," I replied. She nodded and handed me the bag of peanuts that I had bought. I secured them to the back part of the bigger bike, Alison and mine, as Jaret and Alison came back around to us. Jaret was eyeing the gun in his hand, and Alison came over to us and helped us finish loading the bikes.

"Okay," I said, "are we ready to leave?"

I questioned my travelling companions. Dot nodded, followed shortly by Jaret's 'yep' of agreement and Alison's accompanying 'mhm.'

"Come on then, the sooner we leave, the sooner we get there," Alison said grumpily, mounting the front of the bigger bike, the motor purring to life as she started the engine. The three of us quickly scrambled to get onto the bikes in an attempt to slightly alleviate her angry demeanor. As Jaret fumbled with starting the bike, Alison made an exasperated noise and virtually pushed him out of the seat so that she could start it. As soon as the other bike's motor was purring softly, we got on the bikes and started out of Traiton, into the desert, towards Walkton.

As the bikes bumped across the dirt and sands, the wind whistled by the four of us and the various creatures who dwelled in the desert watched is with curiosity as we sped past them. My eyes wandered as Alison drove, taking in the mostly unfamiliar surroundings. For the most part, everything looked exactly the same. Sand covered, flat, and dusty. The ride was quiet for the most part, except for the sounds of the motors, which weren't extremely loud. Jaret and Dot were talking, but even with my advanced hearing I couldn't make out what they were saying very well. Something about camping, I was pretty sure.

"So…" I started, the awkwardness audible in my voice. She turned her head slightly towards me. "You've lived in Traiton most of your life?" I questioned, trying to make conversation. I saw her ponytail move up and down as she nodded.

"Yeah. We moved there when I was fourteen, eight years ago," she replied, loudly because of the wind. That would mean that Alison was twenty two, two years younger than I was.

"When did you move to Walkton?" she asked me, her voice bored. I knew that she was just talking to alleviate her boredom, and that she didn't really care what the answer was, but that didn't bother me.

"I was twelve. My parents, my brother, and a few of the other Druridi in our community all moved to Walkton, including Haishin and his mother," I responded. Us leaving was the reason that they left. The elders in our had village betrothed Haishin and I when we were born, so when we wanted to move, they agreed to come with us. The elders were all extremely relieved that Haishin and I became friends right away when we were children. If we weren't betrothed, the two of us probably would have ended up together anyways. He was both my best friend, and the one I loved. That was half of the reason why I needed to get back to Walkton. Him, and Paulto. Our son was the other half.

"And Haishin is who, exactly?" she called back to me.

"My mate," I replied. Her blonde ponytail bobbed as she nodded again. We continued talking about nothing in particular, and her tone began to lighten and she acted less like I was an annoyance to her. Well, at least it was progress.

Dot and Jaret were a couple metres behind us and to the right, so when Alison started to slow down, they followed suit, the motors quieting to a soft purr instead of a medium-loud growl.

"We should get set up for the night. Soon it'll be too dark to keep going," she called to the other bike. We rode for a little bit longer until we found a decent place to camp, a shallow pit in the sand, about three feet deep, and approximately ten feet wide by ten feet long.

"I can take first watch shift," Alison volunteered.

Dot nodded a second later. "So can I. We'll wake you two up in a few hours."

"Alright," I responded. Jaret and I brushed makeshift beds into the sandy pit, each of us using a jacket as a pillow as we drifted into sleep, Alison and Dot kept guard, and the animals of the desert rustled through the sand.

alison

Within a few minutes, both Jaret and the Drurida were asleep. Dot and I positioned ourselves outside of the pit, one of us on either side, each of us holding our weapon as the cool wind drifted past.

"Why do you dislike Quivlie?" Dot asked me, after about half an hour of silence on both ends. I turned to her. She was fiddling with her katana.

"It's not that I don't like her or anything. I would just prefer that her species would keep away from mine. Everybody should just mind their own business, in my opinion," I responded.

She nodded and I turned away from her, looking around the desert for any potential threats. The night was surprisingly calm, and the only noises were the wind and the breathing of our sleeping companions. I felt a stray strand of my hair tickling my cheek, so I reached back and undid my ponytail, before regathering my hair and pulling it into a better one.

"I don't think I quite understand, Miss," Dot started, "you say you don't not like her, and yet you constantly act disgusted or annoyed at the things she does. I would have thought that that would have been a sign of you disliking her."

I frowned slightly. "I don't dislike her, I just don't particularly like her," I replied stubbornly. Dot sighed and turned away from me. I rolled my eyes. *Why am I even arguing with a robot?*

I grabbed my flask from out of my jacket ad took a quick drink from the vodka as Dot looked on in confusion.

dot

I could tell that Alison didn't like Quivlie very much. I didn't need to be an Android to notice that. She always looked uncomfortable when they were talking, or annoyed that Quivlie was even talking to her. I assumed that if she knew that Jaret was a Cainan, she would like him a lot less than she did.

I scanned around the desert, my sensors indicating what were rocks, what were animals, and what the other distant shapes in the dark night were. The moon case a pale, silvery glow on the sandy ground around us, barely noticeable.

"Why do you dislike Quivlie?" I asked Alison, running my hand lengthwise down my katana. She turned her head to me, her brow furrowed.

"It's not that I don't like her or anything. I would just prefer that her species would keep away from mine. Everybody should just mind their own business, in my opinion," she explained, her voice tense with annoyance. I cocked my head to the side. That sounded very much like dislike to me. It's not like a horse can comprehend its dislike for the flies buzzing around it, it just knows that it doesn't want them there. The horse would dislike the flies, even if it had no concept of disliking something.

I pressed her on her response, and she turned her head back to me, frowning. She didn't seem to be the happiest of people. In fact, I didn't think she had smiled once since we had met her.

"I don't dislike her, I just don't particularly like her," she responded, sounding angry. I sighed and turned back to the direction that I had previously been facing: west. She was too stubborn to admit that she disliked Quivlie, even though it was clear that she did. I shook my head in confusion. Humans were by far one of the most difficult species to comprehend.

There were only another three hours and it would be time to switch guard duties with Quivlie and Jaret.

About half an hour later, Alison scrambled down into the pit, careful not to wake Jaret or Quivlie, and untied a container of nuts from one of the bikes. She grabbed a handful and tied it back onto the bike before climbing out of the pit.

Suddenly, my eyes focused on a shape in the distance, coming slowly and vaguely in our direction. My vision switched to its higher power night-vision setting, and I looked closer at the animal. It was a kailito, a small deer which primarily ate nuts and seeds, but would catch and eat birds and lizards if food was scarce. It wouldn't pose any threat to my companions, but I worried that it might wake them up if it got any closer.

As quietly as I could, I quickly slid into the pit and grabbed a handful of the same nuts that Alison had, before starting towards the deer, keeping low to the ground as to not startle it. Alison watched me, frowning, either in annoyance or confusion; probably both. The deer turned its head towards me as I got closer, its small wings tucked close to its body and its large horns making its head seem unnaturally small.

When it saw me approaching, it cocked its head slightly to the side and stepped towards me, lowering its head and putting its impressive horns between us. In an attempt to scare me off, it bared its teeth and opened its wings, displaying the multi-shaded brown colours on the undersides of its wings. I held my hand out and stopped moving. As soon as it ate, the kailito deer would retreat back to its den and sleep for the rest of the night. It reached its head out towards me and cautiously sniffed my hand before taking a few of the nuts in its mouth, moving them to the ground between its legs. It proceeded to do that with the rest of the nuts, and I backed away.

As soon as I was about three metres away, it quickly ate the nuts. It bowed its head to me, and opened its wings again - this time in appreciation instead of fear. It turned away and started to retreat back into the direction that it had come from. I stood and began to head towards our makeshift camp, turning my back to the deer. Suddenly, I heard a thump a few metres behind me, and a squeal of panic from the deer.

I spun around and quickly drew my katana from its sheath as I saw the deer frantically trying to throw a small, carnivorous gopher-like animal, called a hendrelin, off its back. As the deer bucked its hind legs into the air, the hendrelin went flying in front of it before it quickly scrambled to its feet and hissed loudly at the deer.

The deer immediately started running as fast as it could in my direction. I drew my katana as it ran past me and blocked the hendrelin from following it as it ran towards us, careful not to accidentally harm it. The kailito stopped behind me and turned back to the hendrelin, its horns level to the creature as it charged towards it. The hendrelin growled loudly in aggravation and turned away, running back towards where its den was most likely located. The deer turned to me and bowed its head once again. I bowed back to it, and it made a small noise of content. I smiled as it started back towards its den, flying close to the ground, seeing as flying any higher would require a lot more energy.

I returned back to where Alison was waiting with Jaret and Quivlie. She raised her eyebrows at me. "What was that for?"

"If the kailito got any closer, it might have unintentionally woken them," I replied, pointing to our sleeping travel companions. She nodded slowly.

jaret

I woke up as Dot gently shook my shoulder.

"Hm?" I groaned tiredly.

She smiled. "Your turn."

I got to my feet, stretching my arms. My back cracked. *Ow.* Sleeping on the ground hurt more than it seemed it would.

"Okay. Everything go fine?" Quivlie asked, standing. Dot nodded, and Alison rolled her eyes. I could tell that she was tired. Her ponytail was coming undone, her hair looked like it was trying to escape the hair tie, and there were dark bags under her eyes.

"Yeah," Alison grumbled. Well, I guessed something happened - she seemed more annoyed than usual.

"Okay. Get some sleep; we'll be driving for most of the day tomorrow," Quivlie said. Alison nodded and brushed the area of sand that Quivlie had been sleeping on into a flatter shape again. Dot had taken the portable charger off the bike and had positioned herself sitting up by the edge of the pit.

"I set the timer to automatically unplug in three hours. I'll become functioning again after that. If you need me before them, press this button-" she explained, pointing to a small circular button by the charging port in her leg, "-and I will awaken again."

"Okay."

I rubbed my eyes. Soon, Alison had fallen asleep and Dot's screen went black as she plugged the charger in. Quivlie and both grabbed something to eat from the bikes and climbed out of the pit.

"When we get to Walkton, you're going to find your family?" I asked Quivlie. She nodded, eating a piece of some kind of dried fruit from the container.

"Yes. Haishin, Paulto, and Ella should be in our home when we get there. Haishin won't have left for work yet by the time we get there."

"Who's Ella?" I questioned.

"A family friend. She takes care of Paulto in the morning when Haishin and I have to go to work, and then she drops him off at his school in the afternoon," she answered. "You're going to try to find your brother?"

"Yeah. I have no idea where he'll be, though."

"What did you say his name was?" she asked.

"Charlie," I responded.

She bit her lip and smiled. "I don't think that I know him. There are a lot of people in Walkton."

"Yeah, I didn't really think that you would," I laughed. She smiled, and her skin briefly went lightly.

"Why did you and your brother split up in the first place?"

I shrugged. "Well, it's kind of a long story," I said hesitantly. If I told her, she would know that I was a Cainan, and if she knew that and told Alison, she wouldn't let me go with them.

"We have time if you want to tell," Quivlie replied, her skin lightening by another tiny measure.

"Basically, we were in the middle of nowhere. We got into a fight about whether we should go to Walkton or Traiton, so he went to Walkton and I went to Traiton," I said, deliberately being vague.

"I had one sibling when I was growing up as well. It was just him, me, Haishin, and a few other Druridi about our age when we were still in our community, but nobody really wanted to be friends with the strange Drurida kids when we moved to Walkton," she replied, sighing wistfully.

There was a sudden screeching noise from somewhere in the distance, and Quivlie jumped, her hand flying to her sword, her skin darkening dramatically. I grabbed my gun, just in case. She laughed airily a second later, as a large, bat-like animal flew overhead a few metres away from us.

"Mielikki, that scared me," she said softly.

I smiled. "Mielikki is the goddess of the forest, right?" I asked. I didn't really know much about that kind of stuff.

Quivlie smiled and nodded her head. "Yes. She's the goddess of the forest, hunting, Druids, and the wanderer. She will be watching over us on our journey. Making sure that we do not get lost."

"What happens when a Drurida dies?" I questioned. Quivlie glanced back in the direction of where Traiton was. Or, more accurately, the forest.

"We are cremated. Then our ashes are put into a bowl of water that is made out of birch wood," she said, brushing a strand of her hair out of her face. "A tree seed is planted, and the water, which we call Mielikki's water, is poured over the seed. It will be easier for them to find Mielikki in the afterlife if they are a part of the forest that she protects."

chapter eight

quivlie

After I explained the cremation process to Jaret, he was even more interested in learning about Druridi and our lifestyle in the communities.

"What do you do about marriage and stuff like that?" he asked me. "Like, you don't refer to Haishin as your husband, like humans would, but as your mate. Wait, it is the same concept, right?"

I smiled, and my skin lightened. "If we were humans, then yes, we would count as being married," I replied. "When we are born, the elders betroth us to another Drurida close to our age. When the two are growing up, the community does its best to try to get us acquainted."

He cocked his head to the right in slight confusion. "What do you mean?"

"As in, they make sure that we're in a lot of activities together. They basically try to get us to like each other when we're young, so that when we are older and essentially get married, we're compatible," I replied, doing my best to explain it in a way that a human would understand.

"Cool."

"That's why a lot of us usually end up being close friends with the ones that we are betrothed to," I added.

He made a noise of approval at the answer. "How does the 'elders' thing work?"

"When a Drurida turns eighty, is in good mental and physical health, and has passed all or most of the training tests when they were younger, they have the opportunity to become an adult," I started.

"Mhm," Jaret nodded in encouragement.

"The elders are in charge of betrothing members of the community, deciding what to do in times of distress, etcetera. They are essentially each community's government."

"What are the training tests like?" he asked.

I laughed. "You're very curious as to how my people live, aren't you?" I smiled, and he grinned in response. I continued: "When a Drurida turns ten, they have to do a series of tests to find out which area or areas they excel at. When they are done the tests, they, the elders, and their parents have a kind of meeting to figure out which job would best suit them."

"So, sort of like a job interview?"

"Sort of. More like an interview to find out what you should be studying," I replied. "For example, if the Drurida excels at hunting, farming, and baking, they could decide which of the three interests them the most. That decides what they will study, so that they can improve upon the subject that they already excel at. That way, by the time they're older, they would have nearly mastered the subject and they can do the corresponding job well enough to keep the community healthy," I stretched my legs out in front of me.

"That seems cool," Jaret said, making me smile. "What were you studying to be?"

"I was excelling at hunting and communications, but I was more interested in becoming a hunter, and Haishin was studying to be a hunter - the two of us were training to become the same thing. When our families moved to Walkton, our parents made sure that we continued our studying there."

Jaret nodded, his eyes widened with excitement. "So you're, like, a master hunter?"

I smiled. "Not a master, but I was training to become a hunter, so I'm a better hunter than, say, a medically-excelled Drurida would be."

For the next two hours, he continued asking me questions about the Drurida lifestyle until the sun rose above the horizon.

alison

When I woke up, Jaret was poking me. On the forehead. Repetitively.

I slapped his hand away and sat up, directing an angry glare at him. He just smiled innocently at me and went to get the bikes out of the bit.

"You're such a pain in the ass," I grumbled in his direction.

"I know," he responded, wheeling his and Dot's bike out of the pit. Quivlie had rolled the other one out, and Dot was standing out of the pit, surveying the desert around us. I stood and brushed the sand off of my clothes before climbing up to join them.

"Here," I heard Jaret say from behind me. I turned, and he tossed me a bag of dried fruits. I caught it easily and fished a few out before grunting my thanks and tossing it back to him, making sure that it was tied tight enough so that the food wouldn't go spilling out. He gave some to Quivlie, grabbed a few for himself, then secured it back to the bike. Jaret sat as he ate, Quivlie leaned against one of the bikes, and Dot stared into the distance while she waited for us.

"Alison," Jaret said, to get my attention. I looked over to him, and he tossed me one of the water bottles that Quivlie had bought. As I caught it, I nodded to him.

"Thanks," I said, taking a drink from the bottle. I threw it back to him, and a few minutes later, the four of us were once again on the bikes, following the mental map that Dot was using to guide us towards Walkton.

We had been driving for three of four hours, the scenery not changing much - mostly consisting of sand, dirt, the occasional rock and some sort of animal about every half an hour. Dot and Jaret were a few metres in front of our bike, so that we could follow them and Dot's directions. That was also the reason why I knew something was going wrong with their bike. Every few seconds, it would shudder and make a sort of whining noise; I was certain that our bike would be soon to follow. I pressed down on the gas pedal and our bike sped up beside them.

"It's almost out of gas!" Jaret called over to us. I glanced at the fuel gauge on our bike and saw that the red arrow was teetering dangerously close to the E, signifying 'empty.'

"So is this one!" I said back to him. "Pull it over!"

He nodded and slowed the bike, and I followed suit, pulling the bike up behind him. The idiot didn't get enough fuel. We weren't even halfway there yet! I swung myself off the bike and stormed to where Jaret and Dot were getting off theirs.

"Are you fucking kidding me?" I exclaimed angrily at him. His face went pale.

"I thought that I-" he started.

"You thought that you got enough gas? Well, you didn't!" I interrupted him. "And now, we're stranded in the middle of the fucking desert!"

"Alison," Quivlie said shortly, her skin darkening as she put her hand on my arm. I shrugged away from it. "It is not like he meant to not buy enough fuel."

I frowned and glared at Jaret. He was looking ashamedly down at the ground.

"It's alright Sir, Miss," Dot said. "There is an oasis that isn't very far away. We can sleep there for the night, you can get some water, the trees will provide enough of a cover from the sun and the animals."

"Fine," I replied abruptly, "we're bringing the bikes and our stuff. You, because it's your fault, you're wheeling that one," I said to Jaret, gesturing to the bike that he was closer to. "I'll get ours."

He nodded, avoiding my gaze. "I'm sorry."

I rolled my eyes.

"It's alright, you didn't mean to do it, it isn't your fault," I heard Quivlie say as I walked back to the bike I shared with her.

I frowned. It was his fault. If he had gotten the right amount of fuel, then we would have been able to get there probably about five days sooner. We wouldn't be stranded in the middle of nowhere, and we'd have enough fucking food.

"Come on. If we start walking now, we'll get there before it gets dark," I snapped, wheeling the bike past them. The three of them started after me, Jaret pushing the other bike at his side.

dot

Every few minutes, I would check the map to see how close we were to going in the right direction, changing our course slightly if we ever started veering off of our path.

"It really isn't your fault, Jaret," Quivlie was saying to him, reassuring him for the seventeenth time.

He shrugged. "I know it is. If I had actually understood what they were saying, I would've gotten the right amount, like I was supposed to," he replied, his voice full of disappointment and regret. I slowed so that they were closer to me when we were walking.

"Certic isn't an extremely easy language to understand, or to remember if you learned it a long time ago," I lied. It actually was fairly easy, but I knew that saying that would not help him feel any better. "Anyone could have made that mistake."

That part was mostly true.

Jaret gave a small nod, and Quivlie's skin brightened in thanks. I did another check of the map, and adjusted our course slightly more to the right, realizing that we were walking too far right.

"How much longer do we have to keep walking for?" Alison grumbled.

"Approximately twenty-two minutes," I responded after checking.

"Here," Quivlie said to Alison, taking the bike from her.

"Thanks," she said, reluctant to show appreciation. Quivlie smiled at her and the four of us kept walking.

"Jaret, I could take the bike for the rest of the way if you wanted me to," I offered. He glanced over and gave a small smile.

"Thanks," he said.

I smiled and took the bike from him. As his hand brushed against mine, there was a soft hissing noise.

"Ow!" he exclaimed, pulling his hand away quickly.

"Oops. I'm sorry, I should have warned you," I said apologetically.

He shook his head and inspected the mildly burnt part of his finger.

"No, don't be, it's fine," he replied, laughing faintly.

Because I was made of metal, I felt more physically hot than any of my companions did. That was one disadvantage of being made out of that shiny solid: being such a good conductor of heat.

Nineteen minutes later, we could see the oasis over one of the sand dunes.

"We're almost there," Quivlie stated.

The further we walked, the more annoyed Alison seemed to be getting. "As I can see," she said irritably.

The oasis was relatively large, ten metres and thirteen centimetres long, eight metres and seventy-two centimetres wide, and the light foliage and twelve trees around it protected most of the water from the sunlight.

jaret

As soon as we got to the oasis, Dot went to go and see if they could find any forms of civilization near where we were. I shrugged my jacket off and tossed it onto the bike, which was closer to the lake.

"Jaret, could you help me fill up the canteens?" Quivlie asked. I turned around and nodded as she handed one of the canteens to me.

"Is the water safe to drink?" I questioned. She went to the side of the pond and put her hand in it, swishing through it a few times. She was probably using her magic-stuff to check.

"Yes, there isn't very much pollution here," she responded. I knelt between the pond and the bike, dipping the canteen into the water and letting the cool, clear liquid fill the small metal container. When it was full, I handed the canteen to Quivlie and she handed me the next one. I submerged my hand and the container into the pond.

I glanced back to see what the others were doing. Alison was sorting through the contents of her bike, clearly looking for something specific. Dot was on the other side of the wall of trees, staring into the distance. Suddenly, I felt a cold, wet hand wrap itself around my wrist.

I quickly looked back to the lake, and saw the pale, aqua-coloured face of a mermaid staring back at me, her swampy green hair clinging to her face and her dark blue eyes piercing into mine. She gave a devilish smile as she tightened her grip and yanked me towards the pond. I cried out in panic and reached out with my other hand, frantically trying to grab onto something. When my hand found something, it was, unfortunately, my jacket, and I was pulled into the lake. I tried to break away from the mermaid, but her grip was too tight.

Opening my eyes, I quickly saw that the lake was filled with creatures. I kicked at her arm, but my feet were moving too slowly in the water to do anything but nudge her away from me. She struggled to force me further under the water, but another one of the merpeople grabbed onto my leg and started to drag me down. One tried to bite me, but I quickly avoided their teeth and kicked at the side of their head, which effectively pushed them away.

There was a loud splash near the surface of the lake, and with a feeling of alarm, I saw that Dot had jumped into the water. They grabbed onto the mermaid holding my wrist, and with inhuman strength they pried its hand off of me. My lungs were starting to burn as I frantically tried to make it to the surface of the pond to get air, but more of the merpeople swarmed Dot and I, making it nearly impossible for that to be accomplished. I felt the hand around my ankle released me as a dark colour filled the water and I shot to the surface.

As soon as I got to the surface, Quivlie and Alison were trying desperately to pull me onto the sand. I helped to push myself onto land, and not a second later, Dot shot to the surface. I laid on the ground, gasping for air, and Quivlie and Alison scrambled to help drag Dot onto the sand by me. I glanced to the pond to see that one of the merpeople was trying to grasp for one of us. In a sudden movement, Dot brought their sword down just a few feet from my head and the mermaid gave a shrill shriek of pain as Dot's sword severed its head. Their sword dropped to the ground, and Dot stepped away from the lake, staring at the mermaid's blood staining the sand.

"Are you okay?" Alison asked me, extending her hand to help me up.

I nodded as she pulled me to my feet. "Yeah, I'm fine."

We looked at Dot. Suddenly, Dot gave a small twitching movement before slumping to the ground.

"The water-" Dot started, spasming again, "-is causing me-" they gave another twitching movement, "-to slightly malfunction."

Quivlie helped the Android to their feet. "You'll be fine, though, right?" she asked.

Dot nodded. "For the most part, yes. Although-" another spasm interrupted their sentence. "Although I might not be able to use my internal computer as well as I could before."

"Merpeople can't get out of the lake, right?" Alison asked.

Dot shook their head. "Like fish, they need water to survive, unless possessing a body that doesn't need to be in the water."

"So as long as we stay away from the water, we can still stay here tonight, right?" Alison questioned. Dot gave a nod of confirmation. "Alright."

Alison exhaled deeply.

chapter nine

quivlie

The four of us started gathering wood for making a fire as a cold wind starting blowing through the desert. Soon enough, we had gathered enough wood to make a fire. A small one, but it would provide warmth and light nonetheless. Dot and I were going to take first shift, and then Alison and Jaret would. That way, by the time it was their turn, the fire would be hot enough to keep them warm. Dot didn't need to keep warm, and Drurida could endure more dramatic temperatures than most other species.

The Android had, by now, stopped most of the glitch-spasming, but every few minutes she would give another involuntary lurch. I glanced towards Alison and Jaret. The two of them were asleep a few metres away from the water. Alison was using her jacket as a blanket, but I had given mine to Jaret seeing as that the mermaid had pulled his into the water.

Dot looked at me as I poked the sticks in the fire around with another branch, trying to move them deeper into the flames. She looked over to the lake, and a second later, there splash of water as one of the mermaids tried to claw itself out.ND Dot and I immediately skidded to our feet and hurried towards the lake, our swords at the ready. A second after the mermaid slipped back into the water, its head resurfaced.

"It would have been best if you would have let me take the boy," it hissed.

I frowned, and my skin flushed half a shade darker.

"They can talk?" I asked Dot.

She cocked her head to the side in confusion. "Hence it talking: yes, they can talk."

The mermaid narrowed its light blue eyes at us and bared its teeth in aggression, hissing softly.

"They are dangerous. They will not hesitate to kill their own kind. I've seen it before. Witnessed it. Possessed it," it said, slipping under the water for a brief moment before resurfacing.

I could feel my skin darken more, and Dot's frown grew. "What do you mean?" I demanded.

It smiled slightly, and spat: "His kind."

Dot and I both glanced back at our sleeping companions.

"Humans?" I asked, confused. "It is no secret that they can be dangerous. No secret that they will not hesitate. But not all of them are like that."

In way of an answer, the mermaid gave another small smirk before slipping under the surface of the water, its scaly green tail appearing momentarily above the water as it slipped back into the depths.

"What did it mean by that?" I asked.

Dot shrugged. "Apologies, Miss Quivlie, I do not know what she meant."

I nodded, and the two of us returned to the campfire. Seeing that the fire was starting to dissipate, I took a small handful of sticks from our pile and put them in the middle of the flames. I looked to our sleeping companions. Jaret was snoring softly, sprawled on his stomach, and Alison was laying on her side, using her hands as a pillow.

"What time is it?" I asked Dot.

Her face went blank for a split-second. "Two forty-seven."

Alison and Jaret had gone to sleep just over two hours before, so another hour and we'd have to wake them up.

alison

I felt a hand on my shoulder and I lurched awake. The Android had gently shaken me out of my slumber. I rolled onto my back and sat up, brushing the sand off of my hands before rubbing my eyes. I glanced to Jaret, and he was sitting up, his teeth chattering slightly. I sighed and stood, stretching my back and legs as I did so.

"I will set me timer for three hours. When it unplugs and I am activated again, you have to wake Quivlie up, and then you three could eat something for breakfast, and then we would have to continue moving. Alright?" Dot reviewed. I nodded and she returned the gesture, grabbing her charger off of one of the bikes and propping herself upwards in the sand before she plugged herself in, and her screen went blank.

Quivlie was arranging herself a bed when Jaret and I went to sit by the fire that they had built. He sat cross-legged and rubbed his hands quickly together, putting them close to the fire but not close enough for them to burn. I sat across from him and a few moments later, I saw that Quivlie had drifted into sleep. I sighed deeply and glanced around. The wind had gotten cold in the past few hours while we slept, and now the breeze was piercing through our skin, the fire our only protection from the bitter cold. I glanced at Jaret's bare arms and shook my head. He glanced up to meet my gaze.

"What?" he asked, his teeth chattering.

I shook my head and gave a small shrug. "You seriously lost your jacket."

"I didn't mean to, I just grabbed whatever was right there, and it was my jacket," he said indignantly, but he was blushing. I saw him give a quick glance to the jacket that I had on the seat of my motorbike. I rolled my eyes and stood, walking over to the bike and grabbing it. I tossed it over to him, careful to avoid the fire. He grinned.

"Thank you-u-u," he sang, shrugging my jacket over his shoulders.

"Whatever," I replied. He sighed and leaned backwards, using his arms to keep himself upright.

"So, do you have any siblings?" he questioned.

A sudden stab of pain shot through my chest. "I-" I paused. "I did."

He looked at me, confusion written all over his face. "What do you mean?"

I scowled. *How stupid is this kid?*

"My twin sister was killed at the same time that my parents were," I answered tersely.

A look of realization washed over his face. "Oh. I'm sorry," he said, running his hand through his shaggy brown hair. I rolled my eyes. He stood and grabbed another handful of twigs from the 'to burn' pile and tossed them into the fire. The flames reached higher as they grabbed the sticks with their fire-y grip, and one of the logs in the fire popped.

"Grab me some water, will you?" I asked him, gesturing towards the bike. He nodded and walked over, grabbing a canteen from the closer of the two bikes and tossing it to me. I caught it and took a drink before throwing it back to him. He put it back on the bike and sighed softly, putting his hands into the pockets of my jacket as he walked out of the ring of trees, his gaze focused upwards on the stars.

Jaret pulled my flask out of the pocket and looked at me. I shrugged and held out my open hands. He half-smirked and tossed it to me. I caught it easily and took a drink before tucking it into my pocket. His hands moved slightly in the pockets of my own jacket as he walked, and he suddenly let out a yelp of pain, quickly pulling his right hand out and cradling it with his other hand.

"What?" I asked. I stood and walked over to him, glancing at his injured hand.

"Something burned me," he responded hastily, looking his hand over. I looked closer and immediately saw the red welts starting to form along the back of his fingers and hand.

Right jacket pocket.

The wolfsbane was still in that pocket. It only burned shifters. I immediately looked up to his face in shock. It made sense, then. Why he had told me about the Cainan in the picture. Why Dot had gotten him a gun instead of some sort of melee weapon even though he had no experience with guns of any sort. He met my gaze, eyes wide, as the unravelled bundle of wolfsbane fell to the sand.

"You're one of them," I said bluntly, stepping away from him.

His brow immediately furrowed in worry. "I'm not like some of them. I'm sorry I didn't tell you, I knew that you-"

Rage flooded through me. "Not like them? You are one of them!" I exclaimed angrily.

They killed my parents. They killed Amelia.

"Your kind killed my family!" I said. "The only people I ever cared about are fucking dead because of your kind!"

He shook his head urgently. "No, it isn't like that. We're not all the same, I would never do anything to hurt anybody unless they were trying to hurt somebody else first," his voice was panicked, and he reached towards my arm to calm me.

"Don't fucking touch me," I fumed, stepping back another few feet.

"I'm sorry, I just-"

"Stop. Talking." I snapped.

Jaret lowered his head in submission and apology. "I'm sorry, Alison-"

As soon as he started to talk, I immediately loaded and raised my bow. His eyes filled with fear as he saw the arrow pointed square between them.

"Please don't, I'm sorry!" he pleaded, raising his arms in surrender.

jaret

"And tell me, why the hell shouldn't I?" she demanded, her tone full of anger.

"I never did anything to hurt anybody, I swear," I explained as terror flowed through my body. I started to feel something inside me stir.

Oh, no. Not now.

If I shifted now, she would definitely see that as a threat.

"Alison, I'm so sorry, I should have told you," I apologized, hoping she didn't hear the strain in my voice.

"Why didn't you, then?" she cried, the bow staying level to my head.

"I was scared that you wouldn't let me come with you," I responded, "I need to find my brother. I don't even know if he's alive. I need to try to find him."

Her eyes flashed. "What the hell is your problem? There's a reason I wouldn't have let you come!"

I saw Quivlie stirring. As soon as she saw what was happening, she scrambled to her feet and scurried towards us.

"What's going on?" she asked tiredly.

"He's a fucking shifter!" Alison explained, her voice nearly hysterical. Quivlie looked to me and nodded slowly.

"And why is your bow raised?"

"Because he's a shifter! Why the hell do you think?"

Quivlie raised her hands and stepped between Alison and I. I started to slowly back away from the two of them as I started to feel the shift coming. I shook my head to clear it, tightly shutting my eyes and reopening them a few times to get myself refocused.

"I'm sorry that I didn't tell you, I know I should have, but-" I began, trying again to apologize.

"There are no 'but's!" Alison shouted, steadying her bow again.

"Alison, hurting him will get us nowhere. He has not done anything to hurt any of us so far, and he will be a good asset if we are in danger. Please, just think," Quivlie pleaded.

Alison wiped at her eyes with her sleeve and I realized that she had started crying. "It would be safer for all of us. We would have a better chance of getting there," she said, her voice cracking.

"Alison. What would your parents want you to do? What would your sister want you to do?" Quivlie asked.

Alison gave a little shudder and I could hear her breathing become louder. "His kind were what killed them. If it weren't for them, we could have made it to my sister's wedding and she wouldn't have left her kids behind. She would still be alive right now."

I could feel my heart start to beat faster, and I started to shake. Quivlie took a few steps towards Alison, keeping her hands raised. Alison's bow slipped marginally lower, and Quivlie took the chance to move a tiny bit faster towards her. I could see that Alison had started shaking by the time that Quivlie reached her, and by then, her bow had dropped so that it was pointed vertically at the ground.

With a quick step forwards, Quivlie wrapped her arms around Alison and pulled her into a hug. Alison's crying intensified immediately and she slumped against Quivlie's shoulder. I didn't try to hold back the inevitable shift any longer when I felt my body start to morph, the familiar feeling of being ripped apart flooding through me. I gave out a soft, involuntary whimper and Alison and Quivlie's heads both snapped back to me, their eyes wide with fear and curiosity.

I saw Alison raise her bow, but I hastily started to run away from the oasis, my four legs carrying me swiftly across the sandy rocks. Pain shot through my back leg, and I gave a yelp of pain, realizing that she had shot me. I struggled to keep running as panic and pain flooded through me.

chapter ten

quivlie

When Jaret started to shift, I immediately tightened my grip on Alison, but she managed to shrug away just enough to fire her bow towards him as he started running. I couldn't see where it hit him, or how badly he was hurt, but we both heard the cry of pain proving that the arrow hit its mark. Alison pushed away from me and started walking briskly after him.

"Alison, don't," I said, grabbing onto her wrist as she passed me. She pulled her arm away from me, and, saying nothing, continued in his direction. I knew that she was a hunter and could easily track him - that's what I was worried about. His safety. I knew that Jaret would come back. That, I was sure of. Alison, however, was a different case. I couldn't tell whether or not she would even try to come back to the camp.

I sighed deeply and sat beside Dot. I knew that it wouldn't do me any good to leave the campsite to go after them, especially because I couldn't just leave Dot here alone. As I waited for at least one of my comrades to return, I gazed up at the night sky.

My family and Haishin's mother were standing in front of the council of elders, the four of them sitting on the long benches of the treetop home, the brown cloth from their cloaks billowing slightly as they reached towards the ground.

"Both of your families wish to depart the community to live among the humans?" the head of the council, Aislin, asked our parents.

My father and Haishin's mother, Yenstim, both bowed their heads in affirmation.

"Yes, Gloria Aislin. The six of us would be living in Walkton. It is not extremely far from the community. We will ensure that the children will continue with their training, especially Quivlie and Haishin, seeing their potential, that is," my mother said.

Gloria Aislin turned her head back to the rest of us. She gave a small nod and her greying blue skin lightened as she offered a smile.

"The community is sure to miss you after you leave. Your departure ceremony shall be held tomorrow at dusk," she responded. My parents and Yenstim all bowed their heads in thanks, and Haishin, Brendel, and I all followed our parents' example, bowing our heads to the elders.

I could remember the day that Haishin's family and mine had told Gloria Aislin that we were going to move to the human town. It was not frowned upon, but it did not happen very often in our community, so it was a sort of special occasion. The next night was full of the departure festivities as we all formally said goodbye to our friends and family. For the most part, the only other people we had talked to. Most of us, especially the Traders, of course, rarely talked to any of the other races. We mostly kept to ourselves, as the other races found it uncanny that we rarely showed much facial expression.

The shade and brightness of our skin was our indication to our mood. If our skin was to brighten, then we would be feeling love, curiosity, or happiness. If it were to lighten in shade, usually excitement, happiness, or attentiveness would be the emotion behind the change. Darkening in shade or brightness would be sadness, anger, fear, aggression, or frustration.

Typically, a general rule was that, the darker a Drurida's skin fluctuated from its normal shade or brightness, they were feeling a negative emotion. If it lightened or brightened, the Drurida would normally be feeling a positive emotion or an emotion that showed interest, usually in what they were looking at or what somebody was talking about. We adapted that way so we would quickly to be able to communicate without words, and so that we wouldn't have to rely on seeing each others' faces to recognize that we were in danger.

Druridi were fairly high on the food chain, but humans were above nearly all of the other races. While hunting, it was important that we would be able to communicate with each other without making much noise.

I sighed deeply and glanced around the campground. The water was still, and none of the merpeople had resurfaced yet. It was about twenty minutes before Alison came trudging back, her hands shoved deep into her pockets as she dragged her bow behind her.

"He's gone," she stated, slumping down on the ground beside me.

I nodded once, and then yawned. She turned back to look at me.

"You can sleep. You need to. I'll keep watch until morning," she offered.

I bowed my head in thanks. She nodded in response and I found where I had been laying before, drifting back into an uneasy sleep once more.

dot

The charger unplugged itself from my leg and my eyes refocused to the light as I rebooted again. While my eyes were refocusing, I stood and started to pick up the charger from off the ground, but as I stood, I quickly realized that something was off. I looked around the oasis and saw that Jaret was nowhere to be seen. I walked over to Quivlie, who had started repacking the bikes.

"Where did Jaret go?" I asked her.

Her skin darkened in regret and I cocked my head to the side.

"He left. He's a Cainan," she replied, brushing her hair out of her face. I nodded, because I knew that already.

Is there something important today involving Cainans?

When I tried to find Cainan traditions, I felt a static buzz in my head and I quickly stopped trying to gather the information. The water must have broken me more than I had anticipated. At least I could figure out which way we would have to go based off of the sun and where we had come from.

"Yes, I know that he is a Cainan. But why did he leave? Is there a kind of celebration or gathering that he is included in that is happening today?" I asked.

She shook her head. "When Alison found out, she wasn't very happy with him. He ran the first chance he got, because otherwise she probably would have shot him worse than she did."

"What do you mean 'worse than she did?'" I asked.

Quivlie's skin flushed significantly darker. "When he ran, she shot at him, but seeing that he kept running, it couldn't have hurt him too badly."

I nodded slowly, worry piercing through me. "But, Miss Quivlie, why did she shoot him?" I prodded.

"You should know that humans aren't very accepting of many of the other races, but especially shapeshifters. They see them as unnatural. She was scared," she answered. I understood what Quivlie meant. Alison was surprised, and she acted on instinct, fear, and anger. She had seen her family killed by shapeshifters, and she didn't trust them. She was scared that he would try to hurt her; angry, both because he didn't tell her, and about her family dying.

I didn't fully understand the concept of fear. Even with my advanced programming, I never felt it. I found that I could, however, feel happiness, embarrassment, worry, and anger. Happiness when my companions were happy. Embarrassment when I initially realized that I wasn't wearing clothes, although I quickly realized that that was irrational embarrassment.

I started to worry about Jaret in that moment, about whether or not he would be okay. Anger at Alison for being so angry at him. As far as I could tell, those were close to the only things that I had felt so far. I just tried not to let the rest of the group know, because that would alienate me even more. I tried to act more robotic than I was, because I worried about what their reactions would be. The more I acted like an Android, the more they saw me as an Android with some independent thoughts, instead of a human in a body that belonged to a machine. I pretended to be who I wasn't so that they would accept me more.

"I understand," I answered, going to help her repack the bikes. I looked around for Alison. She was standing just outside the ring of trees, looking into the distance. Quivlie followed my gaze.

"That's where he ran. She is regretting making him leave, I can tell. If he comes back, she won't hesitate to let him come with," Quivlie said.

I nodded my agreement. "Let's hope she won't. I like him."

"Yes, he is a nice person," she answered.

Alison came walking over to us. "Ready to go?" she asked. I looked to Quivlie. We were going to leave without Jaret? If he couldn't find us, he would have a hard time getting to either Walkton or back to Traiton without a bike, even if he was in his canid form while running. He would have to sleep halfway in-between either of the cities, and that left him in a very vulnerable state.

Quivlie nodded slightly. "Yes, we are ready," she answered for the two of us. I didn't understand why she was okay with leaving Jaret, but I didn't want to disagree with my companions and cause another argument.

The three of us got the bikes and started in the opposite direction of where we'd come, towards Walkton.

jaret

I stopped running and sat down, my tail momentarily getting squished between the sand and I. I twisted my head around and took ahold of the arrow in my muzzle. I gave it a sharp pull and I yanked it out of my leg. I yelped in pain as the blood started to tint my dark, grey-brown fur a deep red. I rasped my tongue along the gouge to clean it and tasted the familiar metallic taste of blood.

I quickly looked up and sniffed the air. She was following me. I immediately struggled to my feet and started away from their direction in a limping sprint. After the ground was flying beneath me for what felt like hours upon hours, I figured that she was far enough away, so I shifted back into my human form and, breathing heavily, leaned against a rock.

I carefully rolled my pant leg up and over the gash, wincing in pain when it brushed against the tender area. I bit my lip and looked at the cut. It was about a centimetre or two deep, and about four centimetres long - deepest in the middle where the arrow was the longest. It was bleeding profusely, and have to run right after wasn't helping at all. I pressed my hand against it in an attempt to slow the bleeding, but the pain came shooting back, except much worse this time.

I grimaced and suppressed a whimper of pain, but it did nothing to stop the blood; it just started to seep out from under my hand. I wiped my hand on the leg of my pants and took a cloth from my pocket, wrapping it tightly around the cut, making a sort of tourniquet to try to at least slow the bleeding. Pain shot through my leg again as I pulled it tighter and tied it firmly.

A sudden thought came to me: I couldn't shift back, because if I did, the cloth would get much looser, seeing as that in my canid form, I had pretty small legs. Most Cainans were pretty lanky, unless they were heavier of very muscular in their human form as well. I was pretty lanky in both my canid and human forms, but I was especially small in my canid form. The cloth would fall off, and probably into the sand, and then get dirty and unusable. I didn't have any water, so I couldn't just wash it off. I didn't have any protection - I didn't have my gun with me when I ran, or any of the throwing knives, and I couldn't shift. I was completely defenseless; just like when I was a kid. Except then, I could at least shift to protect myself. That's what I ended up doing, running most of the way to Traiton in my canid form. I wondered what Charlie did. If he even made it to Walkton, that is. What if he hadn't?

What if this trip is for nothing on my part?

Quivlie and Dot still needed to get to Walkton. So did Alison, but it was more for recreation than anything, I was pretty sure. What if Charlie had never made it to Walkton? He had less protection than I did, and he would have gotten there slower than I had gotten to Traiton seeing as that he wasn't able to shift.

Our dad was married to somebody else, Megan, before he married my mom, Emily. Megan was Charlie's mom. They got divorced when Charlie was two, and he married my mom a year later. I was born the year after that. Megan was a human, and our dad, Tyler, was a Cainan. So was my mom. Despite him being half-Cainan, Charlie wasn't able to shift into a canid form. Megan had to live in Otteran for work, so Charlie had lived with us.

Despite having had a few hours of sleep, I was still very tired. I barely even noticed that I was tired before I drifted off into sleep, leaving my sleeping body completely vulnerable to any threats.

alison

About five minutes later, I changed our course to the right. I was still mad at him. Very. But I knew that it was irrational to make him leave like that. And shoot him... I hadn't told the Drurida or the Android, but that was why we were going the way we were; to find him. Well, either him, or his body.

"Miss Alison, I don't mean to question you, but why are we going this way," Dot said, gesturing back to the left of the oasis, "so wouldn't it make sense to continue moving in a straight line?"

"I know what I'm doing," I replied shortly. She nodded, but I could see that she was hesitating. I looked downwards at the ground, and saw the dog-like markings in teh sand. Good, we were going the right way.

A few minutes later, I saw something further in the distance, and I sped up my pace to get to it faster. My arrow, the end tipped with dried blood, the same dark crimson staining the sand beneath it.

"We're going the right way," I said, handing the arrow to Quivlie. She looked at it, showing it to Dot before returning it to me.

We were walking for almost another thirty minutes, following his trail, before I saw him in the distance. I automatically felt my heart skip a beat when I saw how still he was. I ran over to him, skidding to a stop a few feet away, Quivlie and Dot right behind me. I gentle nudged his side with a toe, and I sighed in relief as he jerked awake. As soon as he saw us standing over him, he scrambled away from me and to his feet, his face turning white. His green eyes met mine and they grew with fear.

"Let me see your leg," I ordered. He frowned in confusion.

"Bu-but I thought you didn't want me to come with you?" he stuttered.

I rolled my eyes. "I didn't. But I know I wouldn't forgive myself if I left you in the middle of the desert to die, not to mention with an injured leg."

It was barely a second before I quickly realized that he had scrambled to his feet and was hugging me. I pushed my arms between us and forced him away from me, glaring slightly.

"Thank you," he said, grinning.

"Never lie to me again. Ever." I snapped.

"You are okay?" Quivlie asked him.

"Yeah, I'm fine, for the most part. Well, my leg, not so much, but asides from that, I'm fine," Jaret answered.

"Jaret, may I please see your wound?" Dot asked. He gave a short nod and sat down in the sand, gingerly unwrapping the bandage around his leg and holding it carefully in his hands so as to not let it touch the sand. He winced as he pulled the cloth of the cut. I quickly realized that it would need stitches. It was big enough that it wouldn't be able to heal adequately before it got infected, and we didn't exactly have the resources to accommodate those conditions at the moment.

"Do any of you know how to do stitches?" Dot questioned. "I am afraid that I do not, because I did not know how before the mermaid pulled me into the water, and I cannot search for that information now."

"Yeah," I said, giving a short laugh. I briefly searched through my pockets, and quickly found the first-aid kit I always kept in my pocket. I pulled the small box out and popped it open. I then grabbed the thin plastic gloves out and slid my hands into them before I took out the small container that held the needles (which had been sitting in vodka to sterilize them. I changed the vodka every few days, just to make sure they would stay clean in case somebody got hurt).

"You seriously just have a first-aid kit in your pocket twenty-four seven?" Jaret asked, the impressed tone in his voice easy to hear.

"Yeah. I've needed it a bunch of times but I didn't have it handy, so I just decided to bring it with me everywhere," I replied, taking the small bottle of disinfectant spray from the box.

"This'll hurt," I said, just a very brief second before I sprayed it on his cut, making sure to completely cover it. He immediately tensed up and choked back a noise of pain."

"Thanks for the warning," he said, his teeth gritted.

I laughed. "Not a problem at all," I responded sarcastically. "Okay, this shouldn't hurt too much, because the skin around the cut should be mostly numb by now. The nerves around it are pretty much dead, so you should be fine," I said, taking the thread and poking it through the needle. I could see both Quivlie and Dot watching me, clearly surprised that I actually knew what I was doing. As I started to stitch up the cut, Jaret relaxed as he realized that it wouldn't actually hurt that much, and that I wasn't just lying to him.

"Why do you know how to do this?" he asked.

"When my sister and I were fourteen, she moved to Walkton with our aunt, because she wanted to learn how to become a doctor, and they had much better facilities there than they did where we were living. The few times I saw her after that, she would almost always have to give at least one person stitches; usually me. After the second or third time, she taught me how to do it myself so that I wouldn't need to rely on her or pay another doctor to help me all the time if I got hurt," I answered.

I put the last few stitches in and then tied the loose strings together. I took the cloth bandage from in the box and wrapped it tightly around his leg. I gave him a finalizing nod.

"There, you're done," I said, peeling off the gloves and shoving them into one of my pockets. He stood and looked down at his leg.

"Hm. Cool. Thanks," he said.

I nodded and finished packing up the first aid kid before returning it to my pocket. Quivlie handed him one of the canteens of water, which he gratefully took.

"Are we ready to continue moving?" Quivlie asked us. I nodded, and Dot and Jaret followed suit. We made sure that we had everything that we needed, and we continued walking.

chapter eleven

quivlie

The four of us were walking for about four hours before Jaret's leg started bleeding again. We stopped, and Alison was very exasperated that she would have to redo the stitches. They had started to come undone while we were walking, and the cloth had started to stain a dark red. While Alison was redoing the stitches, Dot and I started making a fire.

It was probably best to have Jaret rest for longer because his leg was hurt.

The two of us took the wood that we had brought off the bikes, and we started to make the base for the fire. It wouldn't be overly big, but it would be big enough to keep us warm throughout the night.

"Seeing as that Jaret's leg is hurt, I think it would be best if he could sleep for the entire night tonight," Dot said. I looked up at her.

"As long as I get at least one or two hours of sleep tonight, I will be fine to keep going tomorrow," I replied.

"I am charged enough that I would be able to continue walking tomorrow without having to charge tonight. We didn't walk a lot today, so I'll be okay."

I made a soft noise of agreement. I realized that, as we were together for longer, the less robotic her voice started to sound - almost like she was forgetting that she sounded differently than the humans.

The Androids were programmed that way, so one would be able to hear their voice if it was a human or an Android while talking to them. That was one of the many things that were different about Independent Androids. Their voices sounded much more human-like than the vast majority of Androids. They were practically the equivalent to human brains being put into Androids' bodies, except for the fact that they had all of the same capabilities as Dependent Androids.

I had a very sudden, and quite random thought. If the hotel payment was only fifty dollars for the week, then why did it cost so much to buy food, or to buy fuel, or anything, really? It seemed like everything in Traiton was overpriced except for the hotels and residential fees. My skin dulled in confusion.

"Dot, are you aware why everything in Traiton is so much more expensive than the living spaces? I was able to rent a hotel room for a week for fifty pieces, but the food for the trip was more than twice as much," I asked.

She looked up at me and shook her head lightly. "My apologies, Miss Quivlie, I am unaware as to the reasoning, although I would guess it to be-"

"It's so that you'll stay there because it's a good price, but then you'll end up spending all your money buying other things," Alison called over to us. Dot nodded, indicating that that was what she had been thinking.

"Pretty much the only things that people know about Traiton are that they have cheap hotels there, and a lot of stores and traders," Alison continued. "People assume that if you can stay there for an affordable price, that you'll be able to buy things for an affordable price, too. It's basically to trick you into staying for longer so that you have more time to buy stuff, and then you'll spend more money. A lot of the hotels in town are at least partially owned by merchants and shop-owners, so it helps those businesses get more money. Pete, the guy that owns the restaurant, also co-owns parts of a lot of the hotels, so that helps the hotels stay in business without having to charge much for being able to stay there."

That actually made sense. The people would stay there because it was a good price, but because the food was so expensive, they'd have to use more of their own money to be able to eat, which was very important to the majority of the species. They'd be forced to spend the money that they didn't use on hotels on food, and since most of the hotels were rented by the week, they'd want to stay there for at least a week so that they weren't wasting the money that they already spent, but in turn, they'd have to spend that money on food, and they'd spend some more of that on entertainment or other necessities.

While Alison was explaining and finishing up with Jaret, Dot and I had finished building the fire, and now the small flames were starting to spread through the small, fort-like pile.

"Exactly my thinking," Dot stated. If I wasn't mistaken, I heard a slight tinge of annoyance in her voice; the first that I had heard. She was annoyed that Alison had interrupted her theory, but she didn't want to question her authority.

Because Androids were built by and for humans, they saw them as authority figures, more important than themselves. I guessed that trait carried on to Dot, despite the fact that she had mostly independent thoughts.

The idea was interesting to me. It was reminding me of how we wore our head with the Druridi. Even though those of us who lived in the cities didn't have to worry about our hair getting tangled in the trees, the vast majority of us still wore it as if we did, out of either tradition, or, rarely, out of convenience. That was why I had never grown my hair past my shoulders; because when I was growing up, it would have impacted my ability to do what I needed in order to survive, to hunt.

Even though Paulto hadn't ever had to do anything of the sort, he never wanted to have longer hair than Haishin did, which, like me, he kept to the acceptable standards of a Drurida hunter's in the community. Paulto didn't want to be the odd one out in the family, even though we made it very clear to him that he didn't have to keep his hair short.

Dot didn't want to seem annoyed because she wanted to stay as stereotypically like an Android as possible while still trying to stay true to herself, even though she should have known that none of us would have a problem with her having emotions, with the possible exception of Alison being mildly passive-aggressive about it.

Neither of them wanted to be alienated, but neither of them understood that being unique had nothing to do with how much we cared about them.

Paulto didn't want to be "weird," and neither did Dot.

dot

Shortly after Quivlie and I finished constructing the fire, Alison was done stitching and re-bandaging Jaret's leg for the second time that day.

The sun was starting to set, so the three of them started to eat their version of dinner as the fire grew and continued to devour the sticks that we were feeding to it, the flames licking upwards in the darkening sky.

"What's your job like in Walkton?" Jaret asked Quivlie.

She looked up at him and spoke, "Haishin and I own a weapon shop and repair centre. His mother and my parents opened it when we first moved to Walkton, and when they retired, they passed it on to Haishin and I. We're planning on passing it onto Paulto and his mate if he has one when we retire."

"Cool. So, you sell and fix weapons? Do you fix them and then sell them, or do people ask you to fix them for them?" he questioned.

"Both. Some people sell us broken weapons for not very much money, and then we fix them and then sell them," she replied, "some of them pay us to fix them, and some of them sell us weapons that work fine but that they just don't want or use very often."

He nodded again, interest evident in his eyes. As they continued to talk, I tuned out of their conversation and tried to use my mental computer again, to see if the water had maybe just not fully drained yet when I had tried to use it earlier. I closed my eyes in concentration, and tried to access the map that we had been using before. The static returned, pushing against my efforts, and I quickly stopped trying. When I opened my eyes again, I saw that Alison was looking hopefully at me. I shook my head.

"I'm sorry, Miss Alison. It still isn't working," I stated, trying not to let the frustration and embarrassment creep into my voice. She sighed in exasperation. Quivlie's eyes met mine for a second, and I knew immediately that she had picked up on the frustration that I was trying to hide. Despite the fact that Druridi didn't show much emotion other than their skin changing shades, they had become quite adept at picking up on social cues from other species. I felt another emotion tingle through me, and I quickly realized that it was, again, worry. I was concerned that by not meeting the specifications for a normal Android, I was further alienating myself from the three of them.

Her skin briefly lightened very mildly and the corners of her mouth turned up in a smile. I returned the faint expression. It was her version of telling me that it was okay, that she wouldn't tell the others. I knew that she was much more adept at understanding emotion than I was, and I knew that she wouldn't purposely do anything to put any of us in harm's way.

"How should we arrange the night shift exchanges?" Alison asked, turning towards Quivlie and I.

"I can take the first half of the night. You need to sleep so you don't get all seizure-y, and you need to charge," she said, nodding towards Quivlie and then me.

"I could take the first half with someone, I'm still goo to stay awake for a while," Jaret offered. The three of us all immediately shook our heads.

"You aren't on duty tonight. No. The more rest you get, the faster your leg will heal. Besides, if you move around too much too soon, I'll need to redo your stitches, and I am not doing that again tonight," Alison said sternly.

"Fine," he grumbled.

"Good. Actually, Miss, I have charged enough that I will be able to continue moving until tomorrow night, so I would be able to take the whole night if the three of you want to sleep," I offered.

Quivlie shook her head. "Will that not quickly become boring without someone to converse with?"

"It isn't a problem; the three of you need to rest more than I need to charge at the moment," I answered.

Alison shrugged. "All right, then."

Quivlie looked to me and smiled slightly. "I'll keep you company for the first half of the night, Alison can do the second."

Alison groaned. I smiled and shook my head.

"It will be fine if you want to sleep. It's your decision in the end, but I think that it would be wisest if you took advantage of the opportunity to rest."

"You can sleep, I will keep her company," Quivlie said to Alison. She nodded happily, one of her rare smiles forming on her face.

Within the next hour, both Jaret and Alison were asleep, a jacket thrown over each of them to act as a blanket as they slept, the fire adding to their warmth as the desert grew cold in the night.

jaret

That was probably the longest I had slept in the previous month and a half, despite only having been out there for a few days. When Dot woke Alison, Quivlie, and I up, the sun was shining down on us, the warmth seeping through our skin.

"Let me see your leg again," Alison ordered, walking over to me. I unwrapped the cloth from my leg. It hurt a lot less than it did the day before, but it still didn't look very okay. However, Alison seemed happy with it.

"Okay, we'll wash it tonight, and then tomorrow morning, and then tomorrow night, and so on like that," she said, rewinding the cloth around my calf. I didn't know how we would do that, but I wasn't about to argue.

After the three of us ate something and Dot stomped out the fire, we started on our way again.

It was mine and Dot's turns to wheel the bikes for the first half of the day, and then Alison and Quivlie would take over for the second half.

I was still limping, trying not to put too much weight on my leg, because that was probably why my stitches had come out the day before. Having the bike was actually helpfully, because I could brace myself on it a bit and I didn't have to put any more weight on my right leg than I absolutely needed to.

The strong wind was against our backs, and Alison kept on having to irately retie her ponytail, as her blonde hair kept on whipping out and getting in her face. My hair was doing that as well, but I didn't have very much control of it. When I glanced to Quivlie, who was on my left, her dark hair was doing something similar, except for the fact that it was doing so less violently. As the wind grew stronger, one of the emptier bags of food on my bike went flying forwards. Dot ran ahead and grabbed ahold of it before the wind could blow it any further.

"Here," they said as they thrust their hand out towards me, almost having to yell because of how loud the wind was getting. I took it and put it back on the bike, trying to ensure that it wouldn't fling off again. Soon enough, the wind was getting so strong that it was whistling past us and we had to fight against it as to not go hurling forwards. I felt something tickling against my feet, so I looked down and saw that the strong wind was causing the sand to start whipping faster over the ground. Quivlie's eyes met mine and I saw her skin darken slightly in fear.

"Soon, we will not be able to see because of the sand," she stated. I made a noise of agreement. She was right. The stronger the wind got, the more sand would start to blow around, and the less visibility we'd have. But if we wanted to get to Walkton, we would have to keep moving. The longer we stayed in the desert, the longer amount of time we had to be attacked by something. Alison was a few metres to the left and in front of us, and within five minutes, I couldn't see her due to the sand flying through the air.

"Miss Alison!" Dot called, their voice all but getting lost in the howling winds.

"I'm right here!" I heard her call back, and a second later, she blindly stumbled in our direction again.

"Stay close to the others! It would not be productive if we lost one of our members," Dot said.

When I glanced to Quivlie, I saw that her large ears were turned backwards, either to try to lessen the harsh sounds of the wind, or to try to keep sand out of them. With the sand swirling through the air, both breathing and seeing became difficult. I couldn't open my eyes very wide, because if I did, the sand would quickly collect in them and block my vision, and if I opened my mouth for more than a few seconds, the sand would swirl inside and start diving down my throat, trying to suffocate me as it did so.

I raised my arm so it was partially shielding my eyes, but it didn't do much to aid my vision aside from the fact that I was no longer blinded by the sand. All I could hear was the wind howling as it raced past, the steps of my footsteps in the sand barely audible as the wind overpowered its soft noise. The only thing I could smell was the dirty stench of the sediment as it went whipping around me. The sand grinding against my body, the smaller grains stinging as they slammed into my skin and the wind pushing me to the side as it raced ahead of me was all I could feel. A hand grabbed my forearm, and I saw that

Quivlie was steering me back in the right direction. I hadn't realized that I had been veering to the right.

"Thank you!" I shouted to her.

We continued to walk, making sure not to lose the others as we walked. I felt the nose of the bike bump into something, and I saw that Dot had planted themself in front of us, their hand clutching Alison's arm.

"We should stop! We will only get more lost if we keep trying to go like this!" they called to us.

We nodded our agreements and waited for the wind to die down.

alison

As soon as the wind died down about an hour later, the four of us were all but covered in a thin blanket of sand.

"Alright," I started, brushing a few grains off my face, "we're going that way?"

I pointed to our left and coughed.

Quivlie frowned in confusion. "I thought we were going that way," she said, gesturing to our right. I groaned inwardly. We were lost. Dot and I simultaneously looked upwards and she grimaced. The sun was blocked by the clouds; it would be setting in a relatively short amount of time.

"Well, the sooner we start walking, the sooner we get somewhere," Dot stated. She started off in a seemingly random direction, the landscape looking completely different than it had looked before the sandstorm had shifted everything. The other two and I followed, trusting her.

As I stepped onto an apparently loose pile of sand, my foot sunk downwards before I slid to the side, down the small hill it was on. I scrambled back up the hill, regaining my composure while we kept on walking. Quivlie turned her head to me, her large yellow eyes blinking in the brightness of the day.

"Are you alright?" she asked.

I nodded, but rolled my eyes. "I'm fine," I replied, hastening my pace so that I was a few steps ahead of the group.

Wait, the sunlight!

I quickly looked upwards, but as I expected to be nearly blinded by the blazing sun, only a thick blanket of clouds greeted me, floating in front of the sun, weaving together so that not a ray of sunlight peeked out of the grey mass. I groaned and caught up with the rest of my group.

How is the sky so impossibly bright if the sun is behind the clouds?

After walking for nearly another few hours, I had to check Jaret's leg again, but the darkening sky left me little time to do so.

"Okay, sit," I said to him, gesturing towards a rock protruding from the sand. He sat down, shifting himself into a more comfortable position. I rolled up his pant leg and started unwinding the cloth bandage, carefully placing it in his hands so that it wouldn't get all sandy. None of the stitches had come out while we had walked, so I wouldn't have to redo them again; thank God. That was getting ridiculously tedious.

"Yeah, you're fine for now," I said as I started to rewrap the bandage around his leg. He nodded lightly. I could tell he was still wary of my intentions, although he had no reason to be. I was initially mad at him, but I could understand why he had lied.

"Thanks," he said, standing as I backed away. Dot and Quivlie hurried over to the two of us. As they neared, I recognized that Quivlie's skin was brighter than it had been before, and Dot looked… happier, more excited.

"I saw a building over the hill," Dot said, voice full of excitement. My eyes widened in disbelief, and Jaret and I followed after them to the top of one of the sand dunes. Sure enough, the roof of a large, silver building was visible from the top of the hill, a few pillars of smoke rising into the sky.

"Let's go, then," Jaret said excitedly, grabbing the motorbike and starting to wheel it forward. Dot grabbed the handles of the other bike and the three of us hurried after our most enthusiastic companion.

chapter twelve

quivlie

We hurried our pace as we realized how close we were to somewhere, excited at the prospect of getting closer to civilization, not including the Xeran people who made their villages under the sandy ground of the desert.

When the four of us neared the large building, I spotted a silver metal sign directing us to the towns, including the title of the building, *Hofferson Vehicle Manufacturing & Repairs*. On the sign, there were various arrows indicating the routes to multiple different towns and cities, including Traiton, Walkton, Otteran, and Hyarsh. Jaret was also looking at the arrows, as he turned to me a second later.

"What's that?" he asked, pointing to a name which I hadn't noticed before, the arrow aiming in the same direction as Traiton's did: Kai'id.

"It is the Drurida community close to Traiton, the same one that my family lived in before we moved to Walkton," I responded.

"How do you pronounce it?" he asked, sounding confused.

"Kah-i-eed," I answered, trying to enunciate it carefully.

I quickly realized that this was a factory, and as the sun started to set, the four of us got to the door. A button for an intercom system was beside the locked door, so Alison pressed her finger to it. A soft buzzing noise rang through the air as the intercom connected to somebody inside the building.

"Hello?" a human woman's voice came through the speaker.

"Hi. My three companions and I were traveling to Walkton, but we got lost in a sandstorm and ended up here. We were wondering if we could stay the night so that we could get to Walkton by tomorrow?" she said.

There was a pause before the lady who had answered the intercom said anything back.

"Who are you?" she asked shortly.

I immediately winced. I could tell by that question that I would be much less welcome here than my companions. Alison glanced back at us and saw that Jaret's face had gone pale.

"Two humans, a Drurida, and an Android," she answered. Jaret automatically relaxed his shoulders as he exhaled softly. There was another pause.

"Alright," the human said, a loud beeping sound coming from the speaker as the door started to slide open.

"Act like any other Android. Only respond to 'Dot' or 'Android,' and only do anything that either Jaret, Alison, or another human tells you to," I said to Dot, purposely keeping my voice quiet. She gave a tiny nod of agreement, and straightened her posture to become more rigid. Both Dot and Jaret leaned the bikes against the side of the building before we grabbed whatever we would need for the night.

We walked inside the building and started down a large hall; the walls, floor, and ceiling were all covered in metal paneling. Footsteps echoed through the hall and a moment later the woman who we had been presumably talking to met us halfway down the hall. I immediately recognized that she was not human, although I could not tell what species she was, similarly to when I saw Jaret in the restaurant. She gave a sharp nod as she met Alison's eyes.

"What are your names?" she asked Alison, automatically presuming that she was our 'leader.'

"Alison Hawthorne," she said, gesturing to herself. "Jaret…" she waved to Jaret, her eyebrows furrowing as she realized that she didn't know his last name.

"Jaret Faolan," he supplied.

The woman gave a small scowl of skepticism and she started to turn to walk inside the building. I felt my face contort into a minuscule frown of offense.

"Quivlie Deshnerim," I stated loudly, keeping my voice strong and confident to ensure that I wouldn't be overshadowed by Alison and Jaret, primarily by the fact that they were 'human.'

She stopped and gave a short nod. "Tala Yawker," she replied, turning and gesturing for the four of us to follow after her. I glanced to Dot and I could see the slight nervousness in her eyes. She was worried about them finding out.

"You can sleep in the residential part of the factory, we can give you dinner tonight, breakfast tomorrow, and then we'll get you transportation to Walkton in the morning," she explained while we walked down the hall.

"Thank you, we appreciate your hospitality," Alison said, fixing her ponytail. That was definitely the most polite thing that I had ever heard her say. Tala turned her head back to us and nodded once.

As she turned her head back to the front, I saw Jaret look at me and raise his eyebrows slightly before furrowing them. My skin darkened from its natural colour - in question - and he slowed his pace to fall into line beside me. He put his arm a bit in front of mine and walked slower, causing me to slow down as well.

"She's Cainan too," he said quietly.

He stepped back so that he was walking beside Alison and behind Tala again. That was why I had felt that she was not human. Druridi typically could not distinguish humans from a shapeshifter's human forms, but we could instinctively tell that they weren't human when we were in their presence.

dot

The four of us followed Tala through the maze of hallways leading through the building, and we eventually made it to a hallway which had twenty different doors leading off the sides, a smaller, bunker-like room behind each door, with two bunk beds situated in each room; the residential unit of the factory. She led us to the end of the hall and stopped by one of the doors.

"The four of you can stay here for the night. Turn right at the end of the hallway, then the banquet hall is four doors down on the right-hand side. Dinner will be served at seven-thirty. I would advise against snooping around the factory; if we find any of you doing so, we will be forced to evict you immediately," Tala said.

"Again, thank you for your assistance," Alison replied.

Tala nodded and started down the hall, leaving the four of us at our room. I immediately relaxed my shoulders, relief flooding through me. All I had to do was make it through sitting with them at dinner, and then until she sent us off to Walkton in the morning. Then I could act like I normally did again.

"Well, she doesn't seem like the friendliest person ever," Jaret stated.

Alison rolled her eyes and walked into the room, taking her jacket off as she plunked herself down on the bottom mattress of the bed on the left side of the doorframe. Jaret, Quivlie, and I followed her lead and went into the room.

"I call top bunk," Jaret said, grinning as he quickly scrambled onto the top bunk of the bed on the right. I smiled as I went into the room, careful to ensure that nobody was there who would report me.

"Android, you're on the top of this one, you're light enough," Alison said, gesturing upwards and towards the top bunk of the bed that she was on. I gave a nod and stepped up the ladder, sitting cross-legged on the mattress.

Quivlie sat on the bottom bunk of the other bed, and Jaret started to unwind his cloth again. He whimpered a little in pain as the cloth peeled off his cut, and I quickly saw that a few of the stitches had come undone again.

"Miss Alison, Jaret's leg is bleeding again," I called to her, watching Jaret wince in pain as he moved his leg. She groaned in exasperation but crawled out from under my bed and went to the side of his.

"Okay, you know what, come on! I'm finding somebody who can actually do this right, and you're coming with me, now," she ordered firmly, starting towards the door. Jaret clambered down from his bunk.

"But, Miss Alison, you heard what Tala said before. If you go wandering around the factory, she's sure to find you, and then we'll be made to leave," I said worriedly.

Alison glowered at me. "Do you want his leg to get infected?" I lowered my head. "I didn't think so. Come on," she growled, as she and Jaret walked into the hall. I could see that he was hesitating, but he didn't want to get Alison angry at him. Over the past four days, I had realized that she had very little patience, and was quick to get angry at people over small reasons. She had only smiled a few rare times throughout the journey, and the moments where she seemed genuinely happy were generally short-lived.

I took the charger out of the pile of stuff that we had brought in, and I plugged it into the wall while Quivlie picked a book off the desk at the end of the room. After checking the time - six forty-three - I set the timer for twenty minutes and I glanced down at Quivlie.

"If you need me before the timer goes off, you can unplug me. I am just aiming to be charged enough so that I can make it through dinner and a short time afterwards without deactivating halfway through," I said to her.

She looked up at me and smiled. "Alright. I only will if I really need you though."

I nodded, and she smiled again as she opened up the book to the front page. I plugged the end of the portable charger into the socket on my lower leg, and I immediately felt myself deactivate, my vision going black.

jaret

She grabbed my arm and virtually started dragging me down the hall, towards the opposite end of the hall that we had come into the factory, the same direction that Tala had told us that the banquet hall was in.

"Honestly, your leg is going to get infected if you don't have it actually fixed. It's not like the stitches are going to stay in forever, it's just a temporary fucking solution," she grumbled as she continued to pull me down the hall.

Hm. I was finding it odd that she actually cared enough to try to get me to get something done about fixing it.

"If you're so angry at me, then why are you trying so hard to make sure that my leg heals?" I asked her, vocalizing my thoughts. She turned her head towards me briefly and scowled, a few of the shorter pieces of her hair coming undone from her ponytail again.

"Because you'll be even more useless if you can't walk because you have a flesh-eating disease or some other bullshit," she answered.

Well, I'd learned that the less she wanted to admit something, the more she swore. Same for when she got angry, which was understandable. Something in my mind clicked: the only real reason she had for making sure that my leg got better was because she caused it to be injured. She felt guilty for shooting me, and she wanted it to get better so that she could feel better about it. I smiled. Funny to think that she would care, because she tried so hard to pretend that she didn't.

I heard footsteps coming down the hall towards us, and Alison abruptly stopped walking when she virtually ran into some guy carrying two boxes of something that looked to be quite heavy.

"Sorry," he said, trying to step around us so that he could continue walking. Alison stepped in front of him and lifted the box off of the other one so that he could see us.

"Where do you need these?" she asked, gesturing for me to take the other one. I smiled at him in a reassuring way and took the other box from his hands. He looked flustered as he smoothed his greying hair out of his face. I was right; it was heavy.

"Oh, thank you very much, dear," he said to Alison, smiling as he nodded to me in thanks.

Alison smiled back at him. "Not a problem at all."

"I was taking them to the residential unit for one of our new employees. I assume that you must be the visitors that Tala had told me about? Alison and Jared?" he asked, his brow furrowing slightly as the three of us started to walk back towards the residential unit, me trying to put as little weight on my bad leg as possible.

"Jaret with a 't,' but yes, we are them," Alison replied.

He gave a slow nod. "Apologies for the mispronunciation. So, where were you two off to just now?"

Alison glanced towards me briefly. "We were hoping to find somebody who could help direct us to the medical facilities, Jaret cut his leg on the way here," she explained, purposefully leaving out the part where she shot me as to not give the man any suspicion as to why we were there.

He glanced down at my leg. "Ah, yes, I see. Well, after we have these in his room, I will be able to show you the way to the medical facilities, my shift is nearly over anyways."

"Thank you very much, sir," Alison said. She was, surprisingly, actually pretty good at getting people to do what she wanted. The look that she gave me beforehand told me she wanted me to remain silent, so that was why I wasn't contributing to the conversation.

A few moments later, we had put the boxes into one of the bunkers in the residential unit and had started on our way to find the place with the people who could actually fix my leg right.

chapter thirteen

tala

As soon as the four of them got here, I knew that something was off. Different. When I had let them in, I knew that the human girl had lied to me about the fact that there were two humans. The boy, Jaret, was a Cainan as well, and I was sure that he could tell that I was, too. That wasn't too problematic, however, I could understand their hesitance at telling me, but that also made them untrustworthy.

When I was leaving their room, I could tell that none of them had noticed the security camera that was outside in the hall, nor the audio recorders that the company had planted when the factory was first built. Just as precautions, so that we would be able to find out if any of the workers were stealing anything from the plant. None of the employees, except for the higher-ranking members of the workforce and the people in charge of reviewing any audio and video footage, knew that they were there.

I walked back into the control room and seated myself at my place at the long, U-shaped table that the rest of the monitoring people were sitting at.

"Tala, I need you to listen to this, alright?" one of the employees, Rawden, called to me. I sighed and stood, walking around the table and standing beside my colleague.

"What is it?" I asked.

He handed me the headset he had been listening to the audio with, and I put it on. He pressed a series of buttons on the keyboard, and a second later, the familiar soft buzz of the recorder came through, followed shortly by voices talking, the sound of an Android's voice clearly speaking first.

"If you need me before the timer goes off, you can unplug me. I am just aiming to be charged enough so that I can make it through dinner and a short time afterwards without deactivating halfway through."

I furrowed my brow and gestured for Rawden to replay the audio. I had heard right the first time, and in the time before the Android had spoken, none of the others in the room had spoken to it. And if the Android was 'just aiming' for anything, that would be against its programming. Any normal Android would have only done that if it was instructed to charge itself, and it wouldn't have any independent thought as to what it should be doing, or how long it should have been doing it for, or for what purpose it should have been doing it for; it would just be doing it. I glanced to my colleague.

"Yeah. Independent Android, or what do you think?" he asked.

I frowned slightly in doubt, but by the time he had replayed the audio for the third time, I was certain. I gave a short nod, and he smiled in satisfaction.

"Mister Faolan will be very happy to hear that," he stated.

I gave him a warning look. "'Hofferson.' Remember, he doesn't want to be connected with his life before Walkton," I scolded.

He nodded sheepishly, a blush rising to his cheeks. "Yeah, sorry," he said. A look of confusion passed over his face as he turned to me. "Wait. What are the visitors' names again?" he questioned suspiciously, as if he had just realized or remembered something.

I shrugged my shoulders. "Uh, the human girl's Alison Hawthorne, the Drurida is Quinn Deshnerim or something like that, and the Cainan is Jaret-" I cut myself off as I remembered what he had said. "Jaret Faolan."

I felt a spear of shock shoot through my chest.

"Mister Hofferson had a younger brother, didn't he? Before he came to Walkton?" I asked, while the pieces of the puzzle started to come together in my mind. "He said that he died in the desert, but what if he didn't? Charles only changed his last name to 'Hofferson' because it was his adoptive parents' surname, so if he had a brother, his last name would still be 'Faolan.'"

Rawden's eyes widened with recognition.

"The kid said that they all wanted to get to Walkton. What if he is looking for his brother?" I said.

Another thought slammed itself into my mind. "The girl said her last name is 'Hawthorne.' Charles was going to get married to a Hawthorne, although it can't be the same girl, she died," I continued; the puzzle was almost complete.

"Amelia, was it?" Rawden offered.

It all clicked into place at that time. I nodded. "They could be sisters, or cousins, or something - they look like they would have been around the same age," I stated.

The two of us sat for a moment in shocked silence.

"I have to tell him," I said finally, turning and racing towards the desk where the phone sat. I dialed Mr. Hofferson's phone number and waited. The phone picked up a second later.

"Charles Hofferson," he said as he answered the phone.

"Tala Yawker, Manager of Hofferson Vehicle Manufacturing and Repairs. We've found three things that may be of interest to you, sir," I said.

"And what may that be?" he asked, his voice raising slightly in anticipation.

I smiled to myself. "We think we found your brother. Jaret Faolan, if I'm not mistaken."

There was a pause.

"How?"

"He and three others showed up here, asking if they could stay for the night, sir. They were making their way to Walkton, but they say that they got lost in a sandstorm."

There was another pause before he spoke again. "He is of little importance to me for the time being," he stated, although I could hear the strain of anger in his voice. "What else did you have to share with me?"

"Does the name 'Alison Hawthorne' mean anything to you, sir?"

"That was... she was Amelia's twin sister, but she died at the same time as her sister and parents did," he answered, the pain of loss evident in his voice.

"She was one of the others who showed up on our doorstep. Mewling like lost kittens, if you ask me."

"What was the third thing?" he asked, his sadness and disappointment clearly noticeable.

"We found an Independent Android," I stated proudly.

There was another short silence.

"Have it taken to the research centre immediately. I don't care how you get it there, I don't care how much money it takes, I don't care if you have to kill the others to get the Android there. My people will be ready by tomorrow morning. Have it there by tomorrow afternoon, or risk all of your people losing their jobs - you included. Do I make myself clear to you, Yawker?" he demanded.

I felt the blood drain from my face. "Yes, sir. Crystal clear," I replied obediently.

The line went dead a second later.

charles

I hung up the phone and walked back into the kitchen, a smirk of triumph present on my features.

"Who called the phone?" a small voice questioned me.

I turned around and saw that Christopher had come down the stairs, and he walked towards the kitchen. I knelt down and he came over to me, wrapping his arms around my neck as he hugged me. I returned the hug.

"It was somebody who works for me. She said that they found another Android, so now I can get my research done," I explained to my four-year-old son.

He nodded and his smile grew wide. "Does that mean you'll be home more?"

I smiled. "Yeah, it does."

His face lit up with excitement and he ran back up the stairs. I could hear him talking animatedly to his twin brother, and I knew that Lily, their younger sister at three years old, would soon hear the news from him too. I started back up the stairs, and I immediately heard three little pairs of footsteps racing towards me.

"Daddy's coming home more?" Lily squealed, her eyes wide as she bounced happily in front of me. I grinned and nodded. "Yay!" she exclaimed, clinging to my leg when she hugged it. I laughed and lifted her into my arms.

"Alright, that's enough excitement for now. It's getting late. You ready for bed, or do you want to play with your brothers for half an hour?" I asked her.

She frowned as she tried to decide. I could see that she was tired, but I also knew that she would want to finish the puzzle that the three of them were making.

"Puzzle," she said definitely.

"Alright," I replied, setting her down.

The three of them raced back to the playroom and I could hear their giggles and mild arguments as they tried to figure out where the pieces went. I sighed deeply. *Finally.* It had been almost a year since we had found and captured the other Android. When they had taken the recognition chip out of it, it had barely worked for a few days afterwards, a seemingly permanent blank look on its face while it sat slumped in the corner. That had gone away after a few days.

I glanced into the playroom and saw that the nanny was watching the kids.

"Merida, I would like to speak to you for a moment," I said firmly as she looked up to me.

She stood, her eyes wide and her face pale as she came out into the hall. "What may I be of assistance with, sir?"

"Don't flatter me with your pleasantries," I said, my teeth involuntarily clenching.

She lowered her head slightly in shame.

"It has been brought to my attention that we have found another Independent Android, and we are in the process of having it brought to the research centre. For the time being, I must be more focused on work, and therefore will not be returning home until later in the evening for approximately a week, presumably around eleven o'clock."

Her eyebrows knit together in disbelief. "But, sir, the children already miss you so much when you're gone during the day, I don't think that-"

"What you think is irrelevant right now, Merida. Unless you would like to find yourself unemployed, I would suggest not arguing with me," I replied, and she gave a soft nod. "Good. I'm glad we have that straightened out."

I started back downstairs. The girl was intolerable sometimes, although I couldn't go around firing people for irritating me, or else I would have no employees any longer.

The machine was almost complete. We just needed one more recognition chip from an Independent Android, and then it would be complete.

The abominations that called themselves shapeshifters would be gone forever. They couldn't hurt anybody anymore. I couldn't save my friends, I couldn't save my mother, I couldn't save Amelia; but let it be assured that I would be able to save my children. If it was the last thing I did, I would make sure that the freaks that called themselves Cainans, Felids, Avians, Reptilians, and Dracids, none of them would hurt anybody ever again. They wouldn't wreak havoc amongst the humans as they lied about their true forms. They wouldn't hurt anyone anymore, they would never kill again.

You can't kill if you're dead.

chapter fourteen

alison

After the guy had led Jaret and I down the many maze-like hallways, we had eventually gotten to the medical facilities, but I was forced to go back to my room while they stitched up Jaret's leg. I begrudgingly agreed, and found my way back to our room.

Quivlie was reading a book as she laid on the bed, and the Android was leaned against the wall on her bed, her face blank. Even though I couldn't see the charger from my position, I assumed that she was charging. Quivlie looked up at me as I walked into the room, raising her eyebrow in question.

"They made me leave," I said, sitting down on my bunk.

"We should probably leave for dinner soon, once Dot reactivates. She said that she was only charging for a little while so that she would not deactivate during dinner," she explained.

I nodded, and as if on cue, the quiet noise of the charger falling onto the bed came from above me, the springs in the bed squeaking with the movement of Dot starting to move over to the ladder.

"Where is Jaret?" I heard her ask as she started to descend.

"He's in the medical facility. They made me leave, he said he'll meet us in the banquet hall when they're done stitching up his leg," I answered.

Quivlie made note of which page of the book she was on and she stood as well. The three of us started down the hallway again, to the right as Tala had instructed. Four doors on the right side of the hall later, we walked into the banquet hall, which looked a lot more like a school cafeteria than anything. Folding tables were situated around the large open room, mismatched chairs at each table, and a long line of trays of food along the longest side of the room. I glanced over at Dot in confusion. She had regained her stoic position and posture, but as she glanced around the room, it was a sure sign that she was nervous.

"What time is it?" I asked her.

"The time is seven thirty-four, Miss Alison," she replied robotically.

Only about twenty other people were in the hall, despite there being seating for probably close to four hundred people, only three of them sitting at the same table. *Weird*. Out of the corner of my eye, I saw Tala come in through the doors behind us.

"I see you found the banquet hall," she stated, glancing to Dot. Quivlie and I nodded simultaneously.

"I thought it would be more..." I started, looking around the room at the employees, most if not all appearing to be human, "occupied."

Tala shrugged her shoulders. "Well, we don't need that many workers here at the moment. The machines are working fine, we don't have much else to do," she said, although I could hear the dishonesty in her voice. Either way, I nodded, and she led Quivlie, me, and the Android to the start of the table. She handed Quivlie and I each a plate, and she started putting food onto hers as she walked. Quivlie and I did the same, and she led us to a table near the back of the factory.

"You can eat here. I'll direct your other friend to you once he gets here, but I have to discuss something with the head of security, so if you'll excuse me..." she said, starting across the large room and seating herself across from a woman who was sitting alone at her table.

I glanced at the door as I heard footsteps approaching the banquet hall, and my eyes soon met Jaret's when he entered the room. He got his food, and then came and sat with the three of us.

"Okay, so we'll just eat dinner, go back to the room, and then leave in the morning," I stated.

Jaret and Quivlie both nodded, and Dot kept her rigid posture, saying or doing nothing.

After we were finished eating, we started to leave the hall to go back to the room. As we stepped out the door, I felt Tala grab my arm. I stopped walking and turned to her.

"Sorry, but I realized that your Android isn't working as well as it should," she started. I glanced back to Jaret, Quivlie, and Dot, who hadn't yet realized that I had stopped walking because I was at the back of the group.

"Yeah. She was pulled into a lake on our way here," I said, being careful as to my wording.

"We don't have the resources here to fix it, and there aren't any Android repair centres in Walkton, but there's one that isn't very far from here - about two hours, if you're driving," she said, brushing her hair out of her face. "I could provide directions and vehicles for you to get there," she added.

I raised my eyebrows. There had to be a catch to what she was saying. If there wasn't, however, there would be a much better chance of us not getting lost on the way there.

"That would be awesome, thank you," I replied, trying to ignore the sinking feeling of distrust in the pit of my stomach.

She smiled. "Not a problem. We'll be ready to have you transported there by tomorrow morning."

"Great, thanks!" I exclaimed, shaking her extended hand before hurrying to catch up with the others.

quivlie

"Really?" Jaret asked Alison as she sat down on her bed. She had just explained to us what Tala had said to her as we left the banquet hall. "And she doesn't want us to do anything for the directions?" his suspicion was evident in his question.

Alison shrugged. "Not as far as I can tell. She just said that she realized that the Android was broken, and that they couldn't fix her here, but she knew where we could get her fixed."

Jaret furrowed his brow. I looked to Dot.

"Do you want to go?" I asked her.

She squinted her eyes and frowned. "I am doubtful that these are her only true intentions, but I would be willing to risk that small chance to be able to guide you safely to Walkton."

"Alright. So we're choosing to trust her?" Alison said, hoping to confirm the plan.

Dot gave an affirmative nod. "Yes."

I glanced up at Jaret. He was biting his lip a little. I did not trust Tala maybe as much as I should, but I thought that Jaret was in the same boat. We were both thinking about how Tala had never said that she was a Cainan. It wasn't exactly a thing that most people felt like they had to hide from their own kind, and it was clear that if Jaret knew that she was a Cainan, then she must have known that he was one too.

However, she did trust us enough to only feel obliged to tell us not to wander instead of taking more severe precautions. It wasn't much, but it was enough for us to have a little bit of faith that she wouldn't be lying. She had no reason to help us, and supposedly no ulterior motives. But we should have known better than to trust her; you can't trust anybody if they want nothing for helping you. Nobody wants to help just for the sake of being nice. But that was what Tala was telling us: that we should trust a total stranger about something that could potentially set us off track by a number of days.

I would listen to what Dot said about this. If she was telling the truth, and the people there could fix her, then there would be less of a chance of us getting lost on the way to Walkton, therefore putting us in less danger. We would also be getting to Walkton faster if we did not get lost. That was, if she was telling the truth and they could actually fix Dot wherever she was planning on sending us to.

"Okay," Jaret said, "so, we'll leave tomorrow morning, we should be there sometime in the afternoon, depending on how fastly they can fix Dot, we'll be in Walkton in a few days - maybe a week, tops."

He looked to each of us in turn. Dot and Alison both nodded.

"Alright. I'm going to try to sleep. I'm tired as hell and we have to get up at a specific time tomorrow," Alison said, pulling the sheets partway down the bed.

She looked up to Dot's bunk and gestured at her pillow. Dot nodded and handed it to her.

"Thanks," Alison said, putting the extra pillow by the side of her bed before she crawled in, creating a kind of barrier between her and the edge.

I got into my bed and as did Jaret and Dot. I could tell that it was not very late, but we were all exhausted. I pulled the soft blankets over myself, and sank into the mattress, a few of the springs digging faintly into me. The slight discomfort, however, was greatly overshadowed by the fact that this was the first time that I had slept in a bed for nearly a week, and sleep quickly swept off the lights from his bed perched above Alison's bunk.

dot

"Alright, so flying would get you there the fastest, and you'll have an easier time not crashing into something seeing as that there isn't nearly as much in the air," Tala explained as she led the four of us towards the factory's parking garage. "Do any of you know how to fly anything?"

I barely remembered to pretend like I didn't know that I was being addressed, so I turned my head to shake it 'no,' but I immediately froze as I remembered, looking towards the left. I pretended to study one of the vehicles there before I turned my head back to her.

"No," Jaret said.

Alison shook her head.

"I do," Quivlie stated.

Tala nodded in satisfaction, but both Alison and Jaret's expressions were confused.

"You do?" Jaret questioned softly.

"Okay, good. What ship do you know how to pilot?" Tala asked, ignoring the fact that Jaret had spoken.

"The basic controls on most of them are the same, but I learned specifically how to fly with a '42 Hawk," she answered.

Tala nodded again as we continued walking. "Alright. Our controls aren't too different from that make, but they also aren't the fastest hovercrafts. We were working on something new for the past few years. They're basically dragon Androids," she explained nonchalantly.

I glanced to Quivlie in confusion, but I quickly realized that her, Jaret, and Alison were just as lost as I was.

"What do you mean by that?" Alison questioned.

A grin broke out over Tala's face. "I'll show you. We started testing them out last year, and so far there haven't been any accidents, so we think that they'll be ready to go out on the market soon," she said.

So, she was sending us out on a dragon-like Android-vehicle that had only been tested for a year? I was not so keen on the idea that my comrades' lives would be in jeopardy, but it would probably be safer than trying to drive across the rocky terrain and then crashing, although I was skeptical that this was going to work.

We stopped walking as we neared a door, which Tala quickly opened and then stepped through, gesturing for the four of us to follow her. The room was large and open, the wall at the back made up of doors that would all simultaneously slide upwards and open to the roof of the building.

In the middle sat a row of four large cages, each one inhabited by a creature, its body and wings covered with shimmering metal plates, the lights beaming off of the reflective surfaces as Tala turned on the bank of brightly shining white lights overhead. Three of the four animals turned their heads to us, the fourth remaining with its head laying on its two front pays. A soft growling noise echoed through the room as one of them opened its mouth, calling to us in greeting.

Tala grinned and grabbed a set of keys off of a hook on the wall, walking towards the cages. Jaret's mouth was agape in shock, and Alison's eyes grew wide as she set her sights on the creatures. While Quivlie's skin morphed slightly brighter in curiosity, her facial expression remained blank. I tried my hardest not to let any emotion seep onto my features, but I knew that I probably looked strained.

Tala approached the cage of the creature who had not lifted its head as we came in, and she knocked the keys on the bars as she walked past them, the metallic clang ricocheting around the room. It lifted its head and looked in displeasure at Tala, a certain fire in its eyes that couldn't be matched by any living creature that I had seen before.

"Good. Get up, Ohen, you're taking them," she ordered.

The dragon rose to its feet as it stretched, its metallic wings spreading through the cage.

"Um... these things are safe?" Alison questioned skeptically as Tala went to the cage door and put the key in, turning it.

"Perfectly. The only thing that might happen is that he might tend to fly a little faster than you'd like him to, but if you tell him to go slower, he usually will. If he can hear you, that is," she replied, pulling the door open and stepping back.

She gestured for the four of us to move to the side, and we obeyed, stepping quickly away from the cage. Ohen stepped out of the door, his paws each ended with a large, dagger-like claw.

"Ohen, go wait," she said, pointing to the back wall. Ohen lowered his head slightly in submission and stalked to the back of the room, his tail swishing back and forth.

"What's with the claws and spikes?" Jaret asked, gesturing towards the dragon, where the edges of his face were framed with more spikes, the sharp ends jutting out from his head.

"Oh, that. It's in case any wyverns, phoenixes, dragons - anything along those lines, really - tries to steal his 'prey,'" she answered, using her fingers to make quotations when she said 'prey.'

Great, more things to worry about.

"He can use that to protect you."

"Alright, then," Alison said.

Tala grinned and started over to where the large beast was waiting for us. The four of us followed.

"So, you ready?" she asked.

"Ready as I'll be if I'm not able to have sixty years to actually be ready," Alison replied.

jaret

"Okay, so you just have to tell it where you need to go. Take control of the reins to direct it, this button here-" Tala pointed at a small button near the reins on the dragon, "-makes it go faster. Just pull back on the reins and it'll go slower. Got it?"

Alison and I both nodded.

"What do we do if something tries to attack us?" Quivlie asked, unintentionally tilting her head to the side.

"It'll take care of it. Just stay strapped in, and you shouldn't get thrown off," Tala answered.

"Alright," Quivlie replied.

I looked over to Dot, who was still trying to mask their expressions with blankness.

"Okay, so you got all your stuff?" Tala questioned.

We glanced around and I nodded. We didn't bring much in the first place, but what we did bring, we had - aside from the bikes. Somebody had offered to buy them from us, and we had no use for them anymore, so we'd agreed.

"Alright. So just address it before you tell it to do something, otherwise it won't comprehend that you're talking to it," Tala reminded us.

Quivlie nodded, seeing as that she would be the one flying him.

"Okay, then, I'll help you guys get loaded up, and then you can be on your way to get it fixed," she said, gesturing to Dot.

She led us up a ladder-like series of metal bars on one side of the dragon, and she directed the four of us on top of him. He tossed his head slightly as he felt our weight on top of him and he spread his metal wings, readying himself to fly.

"Not yet, Ohen!" Tala called to him.

He lowered his wings. Alison had grabbed onto one of the chairs that were set into the metal dragon's back to avoid falling, and Quivlie was using her tail to brace herself against a ridge along his spine.

"This thing is one hundred percent safe?" Alison asked skeptically.

Tala nodded enthusiastically. "Yep! Alright, so the robot can go here," she started, pointing to the seat closest to the back of the dragon's body. I could see Dot start to go to the seat, but quickly realized that they hadn't been directly addressed.

"Dot, go to your seat," Alison said, remembering that Dot couldn't do it unless they were specifically directed to. Dot obediently went and sat down, fastening the seatbelt around their chest to create an *X* with the leather material.

"You can sit there," Tala said, making eye contact with me and pointing at the seat in front of Dot. I nodded and went to strap myself into the seat. "You there, and you there," she said to Alison and Quivlie, gesturing for Alison to sit in front of me and then Quivlie in front of her, in the pilot's seat. They both nodded and got into their respective seats.

Tala went forward to show Quivlie how exactly to fly the dragon, and Alison turned around to look at Dot and I.

"You good?" she asked.

I nodded, and out of the corner of my eye, I saw Dot shake her head very slightly - a motion that Alison missed. Alison nodded and turned back to the front.

"Okay, when you're in flight, gliding, if you want to, you're able to turn the seats so that they're facing in kind of a square. The pilot just needs to set the dragon on autopilot, and then press a certain button on its head; right here," Tala pointed to a button by the bottom of the dragon's head. "So, yeah. That's mostly what you need to know. Press it again to go back to normal," she started to climb back down the ladder, but then paused and added, "Oh, and to land, just tell it to land. It'll do it."

"Alright," Quivlie said.

Tala went to the front of the dragon.

"You ready?" she called to us.

Quivlie glanced to Alison and I and then nodded after I gave her the thumbs-up.

"Okay, Ohen, take them to-" the next words out of Tala's mouth were unintelligible to my ears, but the dragon seemed to understand her, as he immediately spread his wings and pushed himself into the air.

chapter fifteen

alison

Ohen pushed himself into the air as soon as Tala told him to go, and my fists tightened on the seatbelt as my knuckles went white and the blood rushed away from the tight grip that I held. I pressed my eyes shut as I felt my hair whip against my face, and my heart leapt in my chest.

A second later, the only thing that I could feel was the soft wind blowing past us and the occasional flap of the metallic wings as Ohen propelled us through the sky. I opened my eyes. The blue sky surrounding us, the fluffy white clouds floating overhead, the sun just starting to rise above the horizon; we were actually flying.

I turned my head around to see that Jaret was looking around excitedly, not a trace of fear on his features. Dot, on the other hand... Her eyes were clenched shut, and her hands were holding the seatbelt almost in a death-grip. Quivlie's hair blew over her shoulders as she held the reins, glancing at the open map that was sitting on her lap, directing the dragon a bit more to the right.

"You okay, Dot?" I heard Jaret call back to the Android.

I glanced back and saw that she was shaking her head furiously. "What if we fall off?"

"We won't, it'll be fine. Tala said that Ohen won't let us fall!" he replied, his voice almost getting lost in the wind.

"But what if we do?" Dot asked.

"You don't have to be scared, it's okay," he answered.

She shook her head. "I am not scared, it's just-" she cut herself off before she could finish her sentence.

The robot was scared of heights.

Alright, then.

I sighed and slumped back against the chair, letting my head rest on it. I looked around us, over the dragon's wing that I was sitting beside.

On the ground below, the colour of the sand barely ever changed tint, only slightly in the shadows of hills.

Ohen must have started descending, because the dragon started tipping forward at a minuscule angle, but it still causing my back to come away from my seat as I involuntarily leaned forwards.

I heard a small noise of fear from the Android and I rolled my eyes as a second later, the dragon extended his wings and we started to glide over the sand.

quivlie

As Ohen dipped lower in the air, I tugged the reins back slightly and he straightened the path.

"Hey, we going to try out the seating thing?" Alison called up to me.

"Alright," I called back, finding the small button labelled AUTOPILOT. Ohen's wings straightened and we continued in a near-direct path forward. I glanced down and found the button that Tala said would put the seats into the square. I pressed it and my seat immediately lurched backwards and started rotating to the right. My seat clicked into place as Dot, Alison, and Jaret's chairs all made up the rest of the square.

A worried expressed veiled Dot's face as she nervously glanced to the side, over the edge of the dragon. She quickly turned back so that she was facing Alison, who was across from her.

"Okay. So when we get there, you're getting fixed and stuff," Jaret started, gesturing to Dot. "And then the three of us are waiting until you're good to go again, and then we'll all go to Walkton. Right?"

Alison and I nodded, and a second later, Dot gave a minuscule nod of her head in agreement.

"What part of Walkton does your family live in?" Jaret asked, turning his head to me.

"We live above our shop, just less than halfway to the courtyard on Main Street in Section C," I responded.

Jaret nodded, but I could see that he did not know where I meant. "Where is that?"

"After you go through the gates and the security office, Main Street is the first street in the city. It is, like the name implies, the main road in Walkton. It goes from the front gate to city hall and the courtyard, which are a few minutes from the middle of the city," I explained.

I glanced to Alison. By the look in her eyes, I could tell that she was not paying very much attention to our conversation. Because her sister had lived in Walkton, she probably already knew the setup of the city, learning whenever she visited her.

"What's the courtyard for, exactly?" Jaret asked.

Alison glanced briefly to him, but a second later continued looking over the wing of the dragon.

"Any festivals that are held, that is where they usually set it up. Also, if there is an announcement to be made, the City Council gathers people into the courtyard to make the announcement from the stage. Basically, if there is anything that the Council wants us all to see, they do it in the courtyard," I answered.

After a few more moments of talking, a small screen on the arm of my seat turned on, a sentence forming on the white surface.

> Approaching destination; please prepare for landing.

dot

The four chairs lurched back into position and I quickly shut my eyes again. It would be very bad if we fell.

Very, very bad.

"Are we almost there yet, Miss Quivlie?" I called to the front of the dragon, my eyes still shut tight.

"Another few minutes and we should be there," she said in response, Ohen increasing the speed of our flight slightly. I opened my eyes and peered over the wing of the dragon. Sand and rocks blanketed the ground below us, the vivid blue sky brushing against it in the distance. As I dared to look with even more concentration, panic washed over me again as I realized just how high off the ground we were. I immediately shut my eyes. A distant screeching sound echoed through the sky and my fear worsened.

"What was that?" Jaret called, hoping that one of us had the answer.

I didn't know, and there was no way for me to check.

"Nothing good. Probably a wyvern," Alison replied. "Whatever you do, don't get out of your seat. It wants us out of its territory, the worst it'll do is..." she trailed off. "Well, the worst it will do is kill all of us, so," she finished, her voice nearly getting lost in the wind.

Another loud screech rang through the air, much closer this time, another one following close behind it. There were two, at least.

"Um, okay. So what do we do?" Jaret called, his shoulders tensing.

"The gun and bow are in the storage compartment at the back of the dragon, but if we don't get them in the next minute, we will be totally defenseless to help ourselves against the wyverns," Alison replied sharply.

My eyes flashed open. I was the closest to the weapons. If I could somehow get them to Jaret and Alison without falling off of or being blown off of the dragon, we would be able to keep the wyverns off of us for long enough to get to the facility.

I had to do this; for them. If it weren't for me, they would have already been to Walkton and not on our way to go somewhere where they may or may not be able to fix me.

"I can get them," I called, putting my hand on the seatbelt clip to unlatch it.

"No, do not get out of your seat, you will get blown off!" Quivlie called back to me, turning her head to look around the headrest of the chair. I quickly slipped the straps off of my shoulders and ducked out of the seat. As soon as I was out, the wind plowed against me, nearly knocking me off of my feet, but I grabbed the back of my chair to make sure that I wouldn't fall.

"Are you crazy, what the hell are you doing?" Alison exclaimed, her voice laced with anger.

I ignored her and crouched lower to the ground. Ohen slowed his speed - Quivlie must have instructed it to. Yet another loud call burst through the air as the wyverns got closer, and I quickly grabbed onto one of the spikes along the dragon's back.

The wind pushed me backwards and I tried to scramble forwards, closer to the gun and bow.

"They're right there - if you don't want to fall off, hurry up and get back to your seat!" Alison shouted to me.

The weapons were so close, but I couldn't quite yet reach them. I pulled myself forward and reached for them, my fingers brushing against the bow. I strained my reach as far as I could, and my fingers locked around the bow. I quickly pulled it into my grip, the quiver closely dragging behind it, and reached for the gun. My knee was getting precariously close to the edge of the dragon's tail.

I shut my eyes in fear and made one last frantic grasp for the gun as the dragon lashed his tail slightly, nearly causing me to tumble off. My hand closed around the metal body of the gun and I quickly backed away from the edge of the dragon's tail, scrambling to get the gun to Jaret and return Alison's bow to its rightful owner.

A pair of large wyverns came soaring into view, their wings outstretched as they glided towards us. I hurried forwards, bracing myself against the spikes on the dragon.

"Hurry up!" Alison exclaimed as I virtually tossed the gun onto Jaret's lap. I saw him scrambling to pick it up, and I pushed Alison's bow and quiver into her outstretched hands.

I clambered to get back into my seat at the same moment that Ohen's head snapped to the side, staring straight at the wyverns. The smaller of the two gave a loud shriek and dove towards us, and I threw myself into the vacant seat, hurrying to do up the straps.

Ohen gave a loud bellow towards the wyverns and suddenly twisted himself to the side, nearly pushing the four of us behind his back as he turned to face them. The four of us were now almost perfectly vertical in the air as the dragon dove towards the creatures. One of Alison's arrows whizzed through the air, hurling towards the larger and closer of the two animals. It gave a shriek of pain and annoyance as the arrow pierced into its large, leathery wing.

"You realize that didn't do anything, right?" Jaret called to her, his voice laced with panic as the dragon swiped his large paw towards the closer wyvern, nearly catching a wing with his claws.

"Shut up and either shoot or give me your gun!" she yelled as the other wyvern swooped towards us, veering away at the last second before it barreled into the side of the dragon.

Jaret scrambled to pass the gun to Alison, but it slid from both of their hands as the dragon contorted its body around to ward off the other wyvern, which was now determined to knock the dragon, and us, out of the sky by attacking his wings.

Alison reached onto the back of the dragon close to under her seat, but the gun slid out of her grasp due to the dragon's sudden movement. She made a noise of exasperation, and I quickly unstrapped myself from the seat, hurrying to grab the gun before Ohen moved again too much. However, I was too slow, and the dragon twisted himself again, trying to protect us from the creatures. I slipped off of my feet, catching one of the spikes in an effort to prevent myself from falling back and off the dragon.

As soon as Ohen grew stiller, I scrambled forwards, towards his front and grabbed the gun from where it had been lodged between two of the spikes. I threw it to Alison, and despite not exactly expecting the move, she caught it with ease.

She quickly loaded the gun and a *boom* echoed through the air as the bullet fired towards one of the wyverns, its wing getting pelleted by the shot. It gave a loud cry of outrage, but when it tried to beat its wing once more to grain altitude, it realized that it was more hurt than it had thought it was, and in turn started to glide towards the ground to nurse its injury.

The second wyvern gave a call of anger and dove towards us once again, but Alison managed to fire off one more shot as it ascended upon us. It hit the larger creature right by its shoulder, but it was barely deterred as it shrieked again, slashing its claws towards Ohen's wing. As the sharp claws met the steel, the sound of scraping metal surrounded us, piercing through the air. The dragon tried to spin out of the way, but as he did so, I fell and slid closer to the edge of the creature.

With one last grasp, I tried to latch onto one of the spikes on the edge of Ohen's back, or the corner of his wing - anything that would prevent me from falling - but it was too late; I was falling towards the ground, the air whipping around me, the shrieks of battle echoing above as I plummeted to the sand below.

jaret

Mouths agape in shock, we could do nothing but watch as Dot plummeted down towards the ground below us. With a sudden lurch, Ohen bellowed to the remaining wyvern, and almost simultaneously, the two gargantuan creatures dove towards the ground. The wind blasted into my face and made it nearly impossible to see as we went rocketing downwards.

I felt my hands involuntarily start to clutch the seatbelt straps and I shut my eyes, terrified at how fast we were moving at such a steep angle. I forced myself to open my eyes and the wyvern gave a loud shriek, its thin wings wrapped around its body as it spiralled downwards. Ohen's wings were nearly perpendicular to his body, not moving at all as he dove towards the quickly-approaching sand.

My breath caught in my throat as we suddenly lurched upwards, a metallic clanging noise coming from below us, followed right after by a cry of surprise from the Android, who was now held in the dragon's claws. I breathed out a stuttering sigh of relief, and the dragon leveled out his flight.

The wyvern, screeching about its loss of prey, spread its wings and started to glide away from us, back in the direction of where it came. Ohen's wings straightened and we started to glide again, and the three of us still on the dragon's back sank into our seats in relief.

"Are you okay?" I shouted to Dot, who was still clutched in the dragon's claws.

"I am unharmed, although, when Ohen caught me, he dented my arm. It is not anything that could not be easily fixed, however," they called back up to us, inspecting a large dent in their upper left arm. I let out another relieved breath while the dragon continued to soar through the sky.

"I can see the facility!" Quivlie called back to us a few moments later.

Alison and I both immediately straightened up in our seats.

Took us long enough to get here.

As soon as Ohen slightly lowered his head, the large building came into view. Made of red bricks with tall metal chimneys reaching into the sky, the building was surrounded with a couple hundred people, who looked to be guards.

A bank of bright red lights lit up in the corner of one area, and a small swarm of guards moved towards it, making a sort of runway for the dragon to land. He immediately veered to the right to aim more for the landing area, and as we approached, he dipped lower into the air.

The ground quickly approaching, he turned his wings back and we slowed, the descent coming much less sharply. As soon as we were just about a metre off of the ground, there was a thudding sound combined with softly-clanging metal as Ohen gently dropped Dot onto the pavement. The dragon, now basically hovering above the ground, softly landed and became nearly still as he waited for us to dismount. By now, the swarm of guards hustled towards us, offering to help us off of the dragon.

"What's your name, pilot?" one of the guards called up to Quivlie.

She turned her head to the guard as the three of us unbuckled and started to clamber off of the creature.

"Quivlie Deshnerim. We came here from Hofferson Vehicle Manufacturing and Repairs - Tala Yawker said that you would be able to repair our Android," Quivlie responded.

The guard nodded and came to the side of the dragon, helping Alison to the ground as she hopped down. I stood and shakily climbed down the stepladder, feeling the guard's hand on my arm as he helped me to the ground.

Finally feeling solid ground under my feet again, I followed the guard, Quivlie, Alison, and Dot as he led the four of us towards the building.

chapter sixteen

alison

The four of us were led into the building, the intimidating-looking metallic walls looming in the hallways. I could hear one of the guards talking to the Drurida.

"How long do you figure that the process of repair would take?" he asked him.

The guard glanced to one of the others accompanying us and then back to Quivlie. "We can't say for certain without assessing the damage beforehand. Once we start fixing the problem, we'll be able to get back to you with that information."

"What would the repair entail of? How much of the Android would stay the same? Would it still remember everything that happened until this point?" Quivlie questioned.

"The Android would barely be any different afterward. We figure that the main part of the problem is the internal computer, so we would just need to repair that, and then it should be ready to go. None of the memories or what it's learned from past experiences would change or be erased. It would be just as good as new, but with all of its acquired knowledge remaining," he answered, turning down another hall and gesturing for us to follow him.

Jaret and Dot were a few steps behind me, and I heard the heavier of the two sets of footsteps speed up as Jaret hurried to my side.

"What do you want?" I asked, my brow furrowing in irritation. I was trying to pay attention to what the guard and the Drurida were talking about, not to what he wanted to know.

"What if they figure out that Dot's an Independent Android? They would be destroyed," he said, a sense of urgency in his voice.

I rolled my eyes. "It'll be fine, quit worrying. They aren't messing with her memories or anything, just the part of her that got screwed up when she was saving you, the computer-y part," I said in response.

He gave a small nod and fell back into step with the Android. Seriously, the kid had to quit overanalyzing everything, he was just going to get us into bigger trouble than we were already in.

A few moments later, the small party of security accompanying us came to a stop.

"Okay, so we have a nicer residential unit than the manufacturing plant does, so Kyle could get you three set up in there. The sooner we get working on fixing the Android, the sooner you four can get to Walkton," the guard explained, his eyes darting between each of our faces.

I was more than ready to be able to relax and sleep for the night.

"Alright. That'll be great," I smiled, trying my best to seem like a pleasant person. He grinned back at me and gestured to another member of the security team, presumably Kyle. Kyle gave a wave in my direction, and I nodded back.

"Okay," Jaret said softly, following my lead.

Dot remained expressionless, her facial features blank as she stared at the wall in front of her.

"We'll keep you updated on the repair process," the guard said, nodding to Kyle, who continued down the hall, gesturing for us to follow him.

The three of us started after Kyle, a few more of the guards, the ones who were carrying our stuff, following after us. The other guards and Dot continued down the hall, towards the part of the factory that I assumed was where they would be doing the repair.

"We have four vacant rooms at the moment, so you three will each have your own room for the next few nights. On the inside of the main doors to each of the room is a map for the layout of the factory, just in case of an emergency. You can also use it to find the banquet hall," Kyle told us as we started up a small flight of stairs.

"Alright, thank you very much," Quivlie replied.

Kyle nodded once in response and flashed a quick glance in her direction before turning down yet another hallway. A large, and very tall, circular room greeted us at the end of the hallway, multiple flights of stairs leading upwards and spiraling around the room, balcony-like platforms in front of each of the many doors around the room. The small group of us started up the stairs, and only stopped ascending when we were on the most elevated level of the room.

"The last four rooms on this level are vacant, you three can figure out who gets which room, it doesn't really matter all that much to us. If you have any questions, there are directions to the information desk on the map, feel free to visit any time," he explained.

This seemed oddly like a hotel - not that I was complaining. A comfortable bed, a cup of coffee and a book and I was happy. Soon enough, the three of us each claimed a room and were bringing our very few possessions into them. I laid my bow on the couch that was in the room and shut the door. It was close to the first time that I'd been actually alone in more than a week.

I immediately kicked off my shoes and laid down in the large, plush bed, enveloped in sleep within a minute of shutting my eyes.

quivlie

I sat down in the too small chair and shut my eyes, sinking into the chair. I glanced around the room. The bed was pushed against one wall, the chair that I was currently sitting in against the other wall beside a small coffee table.

The room was much nicer than those at the manufacturing plant, the design almost mirroring those of the more gaudy business hotels that could be found in Section B of Walkton. Despite living in Section C of Walkton, the smallest of the three ring shaped sections of the city, I had only been in Section B once except for when we were entering or leaving the city. Haishin and I had to go to a craftsmen convention in the section, and we stayed at one of the business hotels.

I turned my head to the clock on the beside table and watched the second hand tick to the side. The soft noises seemed to echo through the room.

It was less natural for Druridi to be alone. When living in the communities, we were rarely ever alone, mainly for safety reasons, but also cultural. It was rare that you would find a Drurida on their own unless they were hunting, although even that was a rare occasion. We tended to hunt in pairs or groups of three, as a way of keeping a fairly low profile. Three could still be relatively quiet. It was also simultaneously strategic in the sense that we could carry more of what we hunted or gathered back to the community.

My heart rate increasing slightly and my skin flushed darker as I realized how isolated I was. I stood and walked to the door, pushing it open and stepping onto the metal walkway, the whirs and clangs of the machines in the factory buzzing down the halls. I turned to my left and counted four doors down before I knocked on Jaret's door. A second later, the door swung open and a beaming Jaret stood behind the door.

"You wanna come in?" he asked, grinning as he stepped away from the door and gestured for me to come inside.

I smiled back at him. "Thank you," I replied, stepping through the doorway.

"Do you want to watch a movie? I was going to try to figure out how you work a TV," he proposed, gesturing to a large television sitting across from the couch in his room.

My skin lightened in curiosity. "I have only seen one a few times at my friends' houses when I was younger. My parents wanted to stay slightly more traditional to the Drurida lifestyle, so we never had one," I responded, moving towards the box-shaped object.

"I never had one either. When my parents, Charlie, and I were living in the village, we didn't have very good electricity, and whatever we did have was usually reserved for heating our houses and lighting them," he replied, following me into the room.

I recognized the small rectangular box that was sitting on the table, many small buttons with barely visible labels scattered over one surface, as a 'TV remote.' Seeing me looking at it, Jaret picked it up in his hand and looked it over before handing it to me, shrugging his shoulders. I scowled in confusion as I glanced over the many buttons. A triangle, circle and a square were all aligned at the bottom of the remote. The rest of the symbols were mostly intelligible, but I couldn't make sense of those three shapes.

What did they have to do with anything?

Apparently, Jaret was thinking the same thing.

"What does that do?" he asked, pushing his finger down on a ring with a short line going out of the top of it. I shrugged my shoulders.

We both jumped in alarm as a soft sound came from the television. I turned my head towards it and a small light that had been red blinked green. A second later, the black screen slowly faded to grey before an image flashed onto the screen, a children's TV show full of bright colours and a talking cat, its high pitched squeaky voice thundering through the room. My ears involuntarily turned backwards as the loud sounds of the cat teaching colours to the audience in Terish. I immediately began frantically scanning the length of the TV remote, desperate to find some way to eliminate the sound. I pushed a button at random, and the neon orange cat disappeared, replaced by a trio of humans trekking through the forest. As an alligator lunged towards them, we quickly realized that the sound hadn't been quieted when one of the humans let out a yell of surprise.

    I jabbed at another random button on the remote and a small grey box came up on the screen, the show continuing to play behind it. I experimentally pressed the same button once again, and the box disappeared. I shoved the remote towards Jaret, desperate for him to try something to lower the volume of the television. He picked another seemingly random button and once again, the show that was playing switched, this time to a commercial very loudly advertising a new automobile that was now being sold in Walkton.

    The next sound that we heard was the shutting of a door from outside Jaret's room, and then angry footsteps coming towards the door. There was a momentary pause before we heard the loud knocking on his door. We shared a glance and a second later, Jaret went to go let whoever it was in. I heard the door open.

    "What the hell are you doing in here?" Alison exclaimed angrily.

    Jaret started to explain. "We were trying to figure out how to work the TV, but we-"

"Just give me the fucking remote!" she cried.

I peered around the corner and saw her storming towards me in the living room, glaring down at the remote. She pointed the remote at the TV and pressed a button, the volume of the TV immediately plummeting.

She grabbed Jaret's wrist and nearly shoved the remote in his face. "This button here-" she pointed to a button on the remote, "-makes it quieter. This one-" she pointed at another one. "-makes it louder. This one and this one change the channel," she gestured to another pair of buttons. "Now, don't make it any louder than it is now, got it?" she frowned.

Jaret and I both nodded slightly.

"Good. Now be quiet," she said, turning on her heel and walking back out the door, kicking it shut with her foot as she walked into the hallway.

dot

As they led me through the hallways of the factory, a feeling of uneasiness burrowed into me.

The humans around me were conversing amongst themselves, unaware that I was completely aware and comprehensive of what they were saying.

"So, what are you, Cara and the kids doing this weekend? Anna and Jack keep on asking about seeing Vicky and Ty," one of the guards asked another, bumping his arm against the slightly taller guard's.

The other guard shrugged. "Probably not much. I think that Cara wanted to take the kids to Section A to go visit her parents on Saturday, but I don't think we're doing anything on Sunday. The eight of us could go out for lunch or go for a picnic in B if you wanted to," he replied.

The other guard nodded. "Yeah. I'll talk to Sean, that'll probably work fine," he answered.

Normal people with normal families.

It was getting easier to see the people working for the government as actual people and less of Androids. Lately, more of the less creative jobs were being taken over by Androids, giving the other species time to work on different things. Bakers, carpenters, architects, construction workers, farmers, manufacturing; most of these jobs were being given to Androids instead of other species because we could do them more precisely and accurately. Besides, it wasn't like they were interesting jobs that they wanted us to do. They were the more tedious jobs, the ones that nobody with better things to be doing would love to do all day every day.

As we ventured further down the hallways, a few more guards came to accompany us to wherever we were going. That was when the small feeling of uneasiness grew. Now, there were nine such guards walking me down the hall.

As soon as the tenth and eleventh guards showed up, I realized something.

They *knew*.

I immediately whirled around, turning back towards where we had came from, and pushed through the few guards behind me, running as fast as I could away from them and down the hallway.

I tried to remember which direction we had come from, but the static buzz cut through my thoughts as I heard the humans start to run after me, calling on their radios for backup. Seeing as that I both could not remember where we had come from, and that I could not access a map of the building, I picked a direction at random, sprinting down the hallway.

I knew that it was the wrong way as soon as I heard the first cry for help coming faintly from ahead of me. I should have escaped while I still could. I had a head start on the guards, they had been safely out of range. I should have run. But I didn't. I continued down the hall to see from where emitted the plea for assistance. I pushed open a door, the plaque on the door reading ABSOLUTELY NO ENTRANCE PERMITTED, and froze in shock as I looked into the large room that was ahead of me.

Large and open, the room was. Along each of the walls, boxes upon boxes of container-like rooms sat, stretching from the floors all the way to the ceilings. Behind each of the glass walls: living creatures. Mostly the humanoid species, some more animalistic, the vast majority barely moving, seeming to be almost in a comatose state.

As my wide eyes darted around the room, they met those of another Android. A Farmhand Android Version F23, the small sheet of paper beside his door reading *Nemvar Taliat* beside the space for the name of the resident of the glass room. Something, however, wasn't there. As I unintentionally did a skeletal scan of the Android, I found that his recognition chip had been removed. He wouldn't recognize that I was another

Android unless he had learned so before the chip was removed. He tilted his head to the side, and not a second later, I heard the echoing footsteps of the guards running towards me.

I broke my gaze away from the Android's and I frantically looked around the room for any possible escape, but to no avail as another group of guards came running through a different door across the large room. I suddenly felt something stab into the back of my left shoulder, and within the second, I felt myself slump to the ground as I powered down.

jaret

Beep. Beep. Beep. The alarm clock that sat beside my bed blared in my ear, the same loud buzzing having blared in my ear for the three previous days. I slapped the *off* button on the alarm and buried my head under the blankets.

We had been here at the factory for three days already, and they still weren't any closer to fixing Dot; at least, not as far as we were aware of. They said that they were making progress with the repairs, but that they didn't know when they would be able to completely finish repairing the damages.

Three sharp knocks came at my door, and I rolled out of bed, hurrying to open the door before Alison tried to break it down. Apparently I wasn't moving fast enough, because another three knocks came on my door accompanied by the doorknob rattling, indicating that Alison was seeing if I had, by chance, left my door unlocked. I hadn't. As I reached for the door to unlock it, I misjudged where I had left my boots the night before and I stumbled over them and to the floor.

"Are you alright?" Quivlie called, her voice slightly muffled by the door.

I scrambled to my feet and unlocked the door, Alison pushing into my room less than a second later.

"Yeah, I'm fine, thanks. It wouldn't kill you to be patient for two minutes," I replied, turning to Alison.

She shrugged her shoulders. "You don't know that for sure. Tala called me this morning to wake you and Quivlie up. She wants us to meet her in the cafeteria today."

"Tala's coming here? Why? Did she tell you what she wanted to talk about or why we're meeting her there?" I questioned, a stream of thoughts flooding into my mind.

Alison furrowed her eyebrows in annoyance. "I don't know anything more than what I just told you, so chill."

Quivlie stepped into my room from in the hallway. "Parker's coming up the stairs to walk us there," she stated, pointing towards the set of stairs closest to us. I nodded.

"Alright, just let me change into decent clothes," I said, grabbing a change of clothes off of my dresser and ducking into the bathroom.

▼

"Tala Yawker," the Cainan said, standing as she introduced herself to Parker a moment later.

He shook her extended hand, a look of suspicion eminent on his features. "Frank Parker."

Tala smiled and sat back down at one of the many tables in the Cafeteria, gesturing for the three of us to follow suit, which we did.

"So, what's the deal? Why'd you want to meet us here?" Alison asked.

Tala glanced around the room before returning her gaze to the three of us, seeing that we were relatively isolated. "Before I sent you here, I knew that it was an Independent Android. We had auditory security recorders throughout the factory," she stated.

I felt the blood drain from my face, but somehow both Alison and Quivlie remained to keep straight faces, except for Quivlie's skin dulling slightly.

"Why didn't you destroy it, then?" Alison questioned. "You obviously know that they're illegal. You can't not know that."

Tala bit her lip and sighed. "I had orders from my superiors to report an Independent Android to them, and not to the authorities. I didn't know why until recently," she started, her hand shaking as it sat on the table.

"Why do they want them?" I asked her, prompting her to continue talking before she shut down completely.

"You know Charles Hofferson?"

Charlie's full name was Charles, after his mom's dad.

"He owns the manufacturing plant, and this factory, and a lot of the different factories and businesses around here. He came to Walkton seven years ago," Tala said, looking directly towards me.

I froze, my eyes open wide in disbelief.

"His name was Charles Faolan, but he changed his last name to that of his adoptive parents," Tala continued.

Both Alison and Quivlie turned their heads towards me. My heart nearly stopped.

"He's my brother," I stated, despite the feeling that she already knew that fact.

She nodded a second later, confirming my suspicion. "Yeah, we figured out that much. He's also the superior who told us to not report the Androids to the authorities and to tell him about it first. Anyways, he's making a device that uses the advanced recognition chips found in Independent Androids. All we know is that the device will be able to distinguish the difference between humans and shapeshifters in their human forms. That's why I tried to get you to come here, so that they could harvest the recognition chip from the Android."

I was still too shocked to properly comprehend what she was saying. My brother was alive. He was alive, and more than okay. That's what mattered. He was okay.

"So you lied to us and tricked us into coming here so that your boss could steal something from our friend?" Quivlie countered, more of a statement than a question.

Tala's face fell slightly. "Yes. I'm sorry, I know that you won't be able to trust me after this, but you need to listen to me. You need to get the Android, as soon as possible, and get out of here. Don't let him get his hands on the Android, he wants-" she was cut off as a small group of guards came into the cafeteria, heading directly towards the four of us.

"Tala Yawker, you are being asked to leave the premises immediately," Harper said, coming up behind her and placing his hand on her shoulder.

She gave a small nod and pushed her chair back as she stood. She turned and I instantly saw the symbol that she was making with her hands behind her back. Her pinky and ring finger on her right hand drawing a small circle on her back, the shifter hunting signal for 'shift.' Her back straightened and I knew that she was about to shift.

Barely in time, I leapt to my feet as Tala shifted, the large reddish dog crouched in her place.

chapter seventeen

alison

The Cainan girl suddenly shifted and Jaret quickly stood up, his skin starting to ripple into fur as he began to shift. Both Quivlie and I shot to our feet as the small cluster of guards scattered away from the two Cainans, grabbing our knives to ready ourselves for the inevitable conflict as the guards drew their taser guns. Both of the animalistic versions of Tala and Jaret stood their ground from the guards, partially shielding Quivlie and I from them.

"Shift back and we won't have to hurt you!" Harper exclaimed loudly, his voice cracking as he shouted.

Jaret turned his head back to look at Quivlie and I, a pleading expression in his large brown eyes. I gave a small nod of understanding. The four of us were going to get Dot out of there and get our asses to Walkton.

Tala gave a low growl of apprehension and the guards raised their tasers towards the shifter. In one sudden movement, Tala leapt towards the guards, bowling them over and landing harmlessly on the ground beside them. She gave a bark to Jaret, and he ran towards one of the halls.

Quivlie and I immediately ran after him, both of them a few strides ahead of me, Jaret further ahead of both of us. Somehow, he figured our vaguely where we were going, because he lead us down a hall towards a single door, the words ABSOLUTELY NO ENTRANCE PERMITTED on the door.

He halted at the door, unable to open the door because of his lack of opposable thumbs, and Quivlie ran towards the door, flinging it open. It was just big enough for Jaret to fit through, and he and Quivlie ducked through the door, me following a step behind them a second later.

My heart skipped a beat as I saw the rows upon rows of glass cages stacked around the room, nearly all of them inhabited by some humanoid creature or another. One of them, directly across from the door, was filled with water and a mermaid bobbed in the water as it pressed its hands against the glass, watching us, its lips pulled back is it bared its teeth.

"There she is," Quivlie said, starting to the right as she spotted the Android with whom we had come.

My eyes lingered on the mermaid as the three of us started towards where Quivlie saw Dot. I tore my eyes away from the creature and saw the Android. She was slumped against the wall of the room she was in, a dark red panel replacing one of the grey panels that was previously on the side of her temple.

As we started quickly towards her, a loud alarm started blaring through the factory.

Took them long enough to call reinforcements.

Dot's head jerked up as she saw us coming, and the blank look on her face changed to one of excitement. For the first time, I realized that there was another Android in the room with her. This one was sitting in the far corner of the room, its knees drawn to its chest as it rocked slightly back and forth.

She pointed to a control panel that was stationed in the middle of the large room, and then pointed up. I glanced above the glass wall and saw the serial number above it; *WY-261*. I immediately started off in a run towards the control panel, Quivlie staying behind with Dot and the other Android and Jaret loping after me.

Less than a second after I reached the panel, two different sets of doors opened on either side of the room, two swarms of guards flooding into the room towards us. Quivlie immediately ran to Jaret and my side. I scanned the buttons on the panel as the guards stopped advancing, their taser guns raised ready to shoot. The three of us froze.

"This is your only warning!" one of the guards said, his voice projecting through the nearly empty room. "Get the dog to shift back, and we won't hurt you."

Jaret shot a glance back to us, and I immediately knew that he couldn't. If he did, the guards would be able to shoot all three of us and we would all be down. However, the tasers weren't equipped to being able to shoot through an animal's fur, including Cainans. As long as he didn't shift back, and we had enough time to escape before they had the chance to access different weapons, we would be able to get out.

There was a sudden loud call of pain from a number of the guards closest to one of the doors, almost all of the guards immediately turned just in time to see Tala barrel through the door, knocking guards off of their feet as she barged into the room. Chaos immediately erupted as the guards quickly tried to get Tala away from the guards she had knocked over, and Jaret instantly ran towards them to help her.

I turned my focus back to the panel and Quivlie came right beside me, facing the line of guards who were now advancing towards us. Throwing a guard away from his side, Jaret leapt in front of the guard as she raised the taser to shoot at me.

I pressed a button labelled *open* and in the top right corner of the panel, a small screen flashed on, a small *open* sign in the corner of the screen.

Quivlie suddenly hurled her knife towards one of the guards barely a second before the taser gun that had been pointed towards me fired harmlessly into the air.

In panic, I quickly pressed the series of buttons that I figured would unlock Dot's room; WZ-262. I pressed the *open* button once more for good measure, and both Jaret and Tala ran towards Quivlie and I to protect us from the guards who were continuing to advance upon us.

The sound of glass sliding caused me to glance back to Dot's room, but in alarm I saw that not that panel was sliding open, but the one beside it. WY-261 was Dot's room. I had just opened the one that would release a large swarm of large bee-like creatures. The buzzing of their wings as they flew out of the room was nearly deafening, but even more so were the cries of fear from the guards.

Shit.

quivlie

"Do not run," I called to the others. "If you move too fast, that is when they will attack."

The three of them immediately froze, although none of the guards heeded my warning, or they surely would have been better off, as the swarm of archeowasps flew towards them with alarming speed.

The vast majority of the guards all started to run for the exits of the room, away from the mouse-sized insects, but little did they understand that their movement would make the wasps see them as prey, each of the stings from the creatures leaving the guards paralyzed.

"If I move slowly, can I unlock the right thing this time?"Alison asked slowly, careful as to not move too much as she asked me the question.

"Don't move too fast," I responded.

She slowly put her hand to unlock Dot's room, and a second after, the glass slid downwards, opening the room.

Dot slowly walked to the back of the room, extending her hand to help the other Android to its feet. The Android looked upwards and took her hand, standing. The two of them started at a slow walk towards the rest of us, and the six of us started moving towards one of the large sets of doors, Jaret and Tala being careful to move slower because they were larger and more noticeable.

I finally made it to the door and I pushed it open, stepping out into the hallway and holding it open for the rest of them. As they started out of the room, we all nearly collapsed with relief as we realized that none of us had been stung. Both Jaret and Tala started at a dead sprint down the hall, and the four of us remaining stood still in confusion.

"They most likely went back to the cafeteria to gather their clothes before they shifted back," Dot stated, glancing around the hallway.

"Alright. We should go to meet them close to there. We can't stop moving for too long, we'll be too easy to find," Alison added.

Dot nodded and the four of us started hurrying down the hall, Dot staying back a few feet so that she could run with the other Android.

Alison skid to a halt as she rounded the corner. As I nearly stumbled into her, I saw that there were multiple guards gathered around the cafeteria doors. A yelp of alarm came from the cafeteria, and a second later, I felt a hand on my shoulder. I jumped slightly as I turned my head to see Jaret standing beside me, a mildly pained expression on his face.

"She told me to get you guys and get out of here fast, she's distracting them for us," he said softly.

I nodded.

"Come on, then, we have to go!" Alison exclaimed, starting at a sprint down the hall.

With one last glance down the hall and into the cafeteria, I started running down the hall after the rest of the group. Dot and the other Android led the five of us as we ran, possibly using internal maps of the facility to navigate our way out of the building as the alarm continued to blare through the halls.

dot

Most of the guards had run to the main part of the building once they realized that we were escaping, so there were very few spots that we had to completely avoid in the factory as we made our way to the garage. I took a quick glance back towards the others and saw that Jaret was falling behind by a few steps, limping slightly on his right leg.

Was his leg healing properly?

I didn't have time to evaluate the wound, because less than a second later, I heard a door in the distance slide open and the murmurs of people talking echoing through the hall.

We were so close to the garage, yet the only convenient path was directly through where the new group of guards was. We didn't have a choice. Confrontation was necessary at this point.

I felt a hand grab my wrist and I nearly fell backwards as I was virtually jerked to a stop.

"What the hell are you doing? Trying to get us fucking killed?" Alison exclaimed angrily, keeping her voice quiet.

"The only way to the garage is down that hall. If we get to the garage, then we can steal a vehicle and get to Walkton much faster than if we had to travel on foot," I responded.

Her frown fell and she nodded slightly, dropping my hand. "Alright. Let's go, then," she replied, continuing to walk briskly down the hall, the rest of us following behind her.

As the guards came into view, they saw us and immediately reached for their guns. Almost simultaneously,

Nemvar and I pushed our way to the front of the group, protecting the others from harm.

Alison reached for the knife in her pocket and sent it hurling towards one of the guards, striking him in the upper stomach as he stumbled against the wall. Two of the other guards instantly started to help him, but soon realized their mistake as Jaret raised the taser gun that he had stole from one of the guards he disarmed and fired two shots towards the pair. One of them slumped to the ground convulsing, but the other two guards shot towards us, trying frantically to ward us off. Both shots hit me in the arm, but it did very little damage, the protective coating on my metal plating quickly working to absorb the shock.

As soon as the two shots were fired, the five of us started at a brisk run towards the two guards who remained standing, Quivlie easily outpacing the rest of us because of her longer legs.

The guard closest to her frantically tried to duck out of her way as she ran towards them, but he miscalculated his movement and she was able to shove him towards the wall, his head colliding with the concrete. The other guard having reloaded his gun, tried to shoot at the Drurida, but as the shot was fired, Jaret barreled into him, the gun flying out of his hand as they both went tumbling to the floor, the guard practically landing on top of Jaret.

I heaved the guard off of Jaret and he went sliding across the linoleum flooring as I grabbed Jaret's hand and helped him to his feet. He was shaking, but the grin on his face was unmistakably huge.

"Come on!" Alison exclaimed, having run ahead of us, gesturing for the four of us to follow her down the hallway.

With one quick glance back to the guards, I did a scan and found that none of them suffered life-threatening injuries - the guard whom Alison stabbed in the stomach only having his side cut by the blade, none of his major organs having been injured.

Okay, that works.

"Dot, come on!" Jaret called as they rounded the corner.

I started at a run after them, and as I went around the corner, I saw the doors to the garage at the end of the hallway. Quivlie held it open for us and Nemvar immediately started towards the back of the garage.

"We can use one of the vans, they have more seating than the other vehicles," he stated, taking a pair of keys off of a hook on the wall and pressing the *unlock* button, one of the vans in the back of the room clicking as it was unlocked.

The five of us quickly piled into the van, Alison in the driver's seat, Quivlie in the passenger seat, and Jaret, Nemvar and I on the bench seat in the back. Alison turned the key in the ignition and the van sputtered to life.

She quickly pressed her foot down on the gas and the van started forward as she steered towards the exit to the garage, finding and pressing a small button labeled *garage door* as we approached the exit. The door slid upwards and the van flew forwards as she nailed the gas.

jaret

As Alison peeled the van away from the facility, she took a sharp turn to the right and I slid against Dot, who in turn was pushed against the other Android, who was pushed against the door of the van.

"Dude, watch your crazy driving!" I exclaimed, moving back to the left side of the seat as she started driving straight again.

"Sorry," I said, turning to the two Androids.

Dot shrugged their shoulders and the other Android offered a small smile and a nod.

"Wait, so who are you and why were you there?" Alison asked, turning her head to face the second Android.

They jerked their head upwards to face Alison. "Nemvar Taliat. Two years ago I was working with Zaupa in the fields, and Crackers was running around, and somebody told them that I was there, so they came and got me, and then they took the thingy out of my head and now I don't know what anything is really unless somebody explains it to me, and yeah..." they replied.

Alison glanced back to me in the rearview mirror, frowning.

"Dot, care to explain what he means?" Quivlie asked.

Dot smiled. "Of course. He, his partner and their dog were working outside on their farm, and somebody alerted the authorities that Zaupa Taliat was hiding an Independent Android on her farm. The people at the facility took him to the research centre and removed his recognition chip as they did mine. Had I not known beforehand, I wouldn't be able to recognize what specie any of you, or I, were. I only recognize whatever I knew before they removed the chip, but if you asked me to establish who of a group of people whom I didn't know beforehand was a shifter, I wouldn't be able to tell. Neither would Nemvar," they replied.

I nodded in understanding.

"So neither of you would recognize what this is?" Alison asked, gesturing to the radio in the car.

Dot frowned slightly and looked closer at the radio. They shook their head, and Nemvar followed suit shortly after.

"Because I didn't specifically know what it was before they removed the chip, I wouldn't be able to tell now," Dot answered.

Alison nodded. "Alright. It's a radio, by the way, it plays music," she answered.

Again, Dot frowned slightly in confusion. "What is music?"

Both Nemvar and I turned towards her, parallel looks of confusion on our faces.

"You've never heard music before?" Quivlie asked, turning her head to look at the Android.

Dot blushed slightly and shook their head. "Should I have?" they asked, a nervous edge in their voice.

"It's not like it's a necessity to living, but it's really awesome," I answered.

"Wait, Quivlie, see if you can find a cassette or CD or something like that," Alison directed, the car speeding up.

Quivlie nodded and opened the glove box, peering inside. Her skin brightened and a second later she sat up again, a stack of CDs in her hand. She shuffled through them.

"Elvis Presley, My Chemical Romance, B. B. King, Simon and Garfunkel, Panic! At The Disco," Quivlie said, reading the artists off of the CDs as she flipped through them.

"Which My Chemical Romance album is it?" Alison asked.

I assumed she instantly recognized the band, because her face lit up as soon as Quivlie read the band.

"Um... 'Danger Days.'" Quivlie responded, showing Alison the CD.

Alison's face immediately lit up even more than it had before. "Figure out how to put it in, please," she exclaimed, nearly bouncing in her seat.

I didn't really know the band too well, but I had heard a few of their songs; just the more popular ones that had occasionally came on the radio that we had had with my adoptive parents in Walkton. Quivlie laughed and her skin brightened.

I sighed slightly in happiness and leaned against the back of the seat. After the last week of trying to stay alive, it was nice to be able to not worry about anything other than what album we were going to play. We were almost in Walkton.

I can find Charlie. He's alive, and he's okay.

That's all that I really knew, and I didn't know why he needed Dot or Nemvar's recognition chips, but it didn't really matter. I knew that my brother was alive, and that was more than I had known in the past seven years.

We continued driving through the desert as Gerard Way's voice filled the car, a look of amazement and thrill on Dot's face as he sang, the words to 'Save Yourself, I'll Hold Them Back' blasting through the speakers of the van.

chapter eighteen

alison

I had grown up listening to this band, and it had remained one of my favourites throughout the years. I glanced back in the rearview mirror and saw that Dot's mouth was still agape in amazement as one of their softer songs, 'Summertime,' was playing.

Jaret had fallen asleep sometime in the past hour, and Nemvar was looking through the window, every few minutes asking Quivlie and I about what something was.

"What's that thing that's over there that's big and grey?" he asked, gently tapping Quivlie on the shoulder.

Quivlie turned back to face him and looked towards where he was pointing. As I focused on the horizon, I saw the 'big and grey' thing come more into focus as we got closer.

"The wall around Section A in Walkton. We're almost there," Quivlie answered, her back instantly straightening as she saw her home town.

'DESTROYA' started playing, but it was much quieter seeing as that I had turned the volume down at Jaret's request so that he could sleep. I put my hand on the volume knob and turned it far to the right, the volume growing significantly louder just as Gerard Way screamed the last "destroya" in the verse.

Jaret jumped as he was awoken by the shout, his eyes darting around the van. He sighed as he realized that I had just cranked the music.

"We're almost there!" I called to him, raising my voice so that he could hear me above the music.

He frowned slightly. "What?"

Apparently I hadn't yelled loud enough before. "We're almost in Walkton!" I yelled back to him.

He shrugged his shoulders an shook his head. He still didn't hear me.

"I said, 'we're almost-'" I started to shout.

Quivlie turned down the music in the midst of me yelling at Jaret. That was probably a better plan than trying to yell.

"I said, 'we're almost there.'" I replied, my voice at a regular speaking volume.

His eyes widened in excitement and he sat up straighter as he looked through the windshield, straining forwards to see the wall.

"Why does it have a wall?" Jaret questioned, covering his mouth as he yawned a second later.

"Each of the three sections of Walkton has a wall around it." Quivlie started. "This one, Section A, is so that none of the creatures that live in the desert can get into the city as easily. It's also so that they can regulate who comes into and who leaves the city, just for safety precautions. The other two, the ones around B and C, are so that in case somebody does get into Section A that they decide they do not want there, the higher concentrations of people can be shut into the other two Sections for protection. They're mostly for safety precautions," she explained.

About half an hour later, we got to the front gates of the outermost section of the city. I drove the van to the line at the entrance gates, behind a carriage with a Terin family inside as they tried to enter the city.

"Do you guys have any ID stuff? I don't need stuff from you two," I said the last part to Dot and Nemvar, "but I need something from you and you, they'll probably ask to see it," I added, turning to Quivlie and pointing to Jaret.

"Yeah, just one moment," Quivlie responded, arching her back to put distance between her and the seat as she reached in her back pocket.

I grabbed my wallet out of my pocket and found my Scavenger license. Most of the time, if you were to try to sell something to the other Traders in a town, you would have to show your license so they knew that you were selling them stuff legally and that you weren't just trying to trick them with fake products. She handed me a card with the words HANDEONA WEAPONRY printed at the top, her picture and information below it.

"Thank you. Got anything, Jaret?" I asked as the Terin's carriage pulled through the gates as they got admitted into the city. He nodded and handed me a Hunting license. "Thanks."

One of the people at the gate waved for me to pull the van forward. I stepped out of the car, the three licenses in my hand.

"What's the reason for your entrance to the city?" she asked me.

I smiled at her, trying to appear to be a sociable person. "We're moving here. Separately, we just came together as a matter of convenience," I answered her, trying to be mostly honest.

She extended her hand for the licenses. I handed them to her and she looked at each one, looking to me, Jaret and Quivlie as she did so.

"Whose Androids are they?" she asked.

"Mine," I replied instantly.

She wouldn't have believed me if I told her that they were Quivlie's, and Jaret looked too young for her to believe that they were his. She nodded and handed the licenses back to me, taking one last longer look at Jaret before furrowing her brow slightly and waving for me to get back in the car.

"Alright, you can go," she said, "enjoy your stay in the city."

I smiled at her and she offered a mildly forced smile in return. Even though it wasn't very sincere, she still had a pretty smile.

"Thanks. Have a good day, Marie," I responded, glancing to her name tag.

She gave a more genuine smile and I turned and walked back to the van, pulling my ponytail tighter as I approached the vehicle. I opened the door and slid into the seat, starting the car again and pulling through the now opened gate. As soon as we got into the city, Dot scooted up on the seat more.

"Whose Androids are we pretending to be?" she questioned.

I gestured towards myself. "Mine," I answered, slowing the van as the streets became more crowded.

"Alright. Nemvar, just try not to let them realize that you have independent thoughts, and then as soon as we get somewhere, we can try to hitch a ride back towards your farm, okay?" she said to the other Android.

Nemvar nodded as he continued looking curiously around the factories that were in this section of the city.

"We can find Zaupa and Crackers and then get you and them somewhere safe where they can't find you. I can try to talk to the Law Enforcement Officer and try and get our existence legalized," Dot added.

Nemvar smiled widely. "When I was in the factory, Zaupa had came to buy a Farmhand Android to help her around the farm and things and she realized that I could think for me before the people who worked there did, so she bought me and we went home, and then a little while later she wanted to get a dog, so we went to our friends' farm because her dog had puppies, and one little puppy really liked us, so we gave him a cracker, and he really liked the cracker, so we got that puppy and we named him Crackers because he likes crackers a lot," he said, continuing to watch the factories outside the window.

"We would sit outside in the fields and chase away the crows before they ate all our food. He liked to try to catch them, but he never caught them. One time, the crow tried to attack him because he started to chase one of the crow's friends, so I threw a rock at the crow to try to scare it away, but it accidentally hit the crow and then it flew away, but I felt bad for the crow because I didn't mean to hurt it," he added, stopping talking abruptly.

I nodded slowly and looked into the back seat. He was smiling and swaying back and forth slightly.

Yeah, pretty sure this one's crazier than the one that we had been locked in the earthquake room with.

quivlie

About twenty minutes later, we got to the second of the three gates. Again, we had no trouble getting through, Alison continuing to talk to the gatekeepers. As we got closer to C, I started to recognize more of where we were. I saw the business hotel that Haishin and I had stayed at a few times, and one of the parks that we sometimes went to with Paulto.

My skin brightened and I smiled as I thought about the fact that I would see my son and mate soon. I really hoped that they were okay, and that they were not too worried about me.

I leaned against the back of the seat and shut my eyes, sighing.

I jerked awake as the music in the car started blasting loudly again, my skin brightening dramatically in alarm. I scowled at Alison, whose hand was on the volume dial on the radio. My skin dulled and she grinned widely at me, turning down the music to a suitable volume.

"Why do you like doing this to people?" I groaned, rubbing the sleep out of my eyes.

"We're almost at the third gate. When we get there, you'll have to help us figure out where we're going," she said, ignoring my question.

I nodded and sat up straighter, stretching my arms in front of me.

"First, it would make sense to find somewhere to drop Jaret off. That way, he'll have longer to start looking for his brother. It would make sense from there to go to the residential area so that you could start looking for an apartment or somewhere to live. After that, we could drive to my shop, drop me off there, and then Dot and Nemvar could take the van and start going back to Nemvar's farm to get Zaupa and Crackers," I responded.

"Alright, that's fine," Alison replied. "Are we going to have any way to keep in touch or anything, or is this goodbye?"

A panicked expression immediately became apparent on Jaret's features. "We aren't planning on that?" he asked. "We're not going to keep in touch? But why not? I like you guys, you're, like, my only friends!" he exclaimed, his nervousness becoming apparent in his voice.

"We never said that we weren't going to, I was just asking if we were planning on it, and from your answer, I'd say yeah, we are," Alison answered defensively.

Jaret smiled. "Oh, okay, that's good."

"Yes, it is. Whenever you want, you can come and visit Haishin, Paulto and I. I can point out our shop when we pass it," I told him.

His face lit up. "Awesome, thanks!"

"That applies to you too, Alison. You two as well, and once you come back with Zaupa and Crackers, they can come and visit too," I said, turning to face Dot and Nemvar. Dot smiled, and Nemvar started bouncing in his seat, nodding enthusiastically.

"There's the next gate," Alison pointed out.

The main road led directly to it, and there was a lineup of three different vehicles ahead of us. Alison got into the line and turned the music down again, taking the IDs from her pocket again. Ahead of us, the gatekeepers were having each human individual exit the vehicle and were holding their hands to some sort of device that I did not recognize, not bothering to do the same with the Xeran who was sitting in the car with them. I heard a car pull into the line behind us.

"What's that that they're doing to their hands?" Jaret asked, looking towards me.

I frowned and shook my head. "I do not know. It was not here before I left."

He gave a nod.

dot

Jaret and Alison went to talk to the gatekeepers, and Quivlie, Nemvar and I stayed seated in the car. I watched the gatekeeper take Alison's left hand and put it against the machine. A second later, the gatekeeper looked at the machine and then nodded, saying something to her that I couldn't hear. She handed him the three of their IDs, and the gatekeeper handed them back to her a second later.

The two of them should have been back in a moment, after they put Jaret's hand on the machine to do whatever they were doing with it. Speaking of which, the gatekeeper took Jaret's hand and put it on the machine. He frowned a second later when he looked at it, motioning for Jaret to stay.

The gatekeeper picked up his radio and a minute later, a pair of guards came down to the gate. After a second of discussion, they lead Jaret into one of the two buildings on either side of the gate. The gatekeeper walked Alison back to the van and she got in as they opened the gate, waving her through. She drove through the gate but didn't stop as I had thought she would.

"Where did they take Jaret?" I asked her.

She shook her head and shrugged. "They said that they would take him to see his brother if he wanted to, and he said yeah. He asked if he could say 'bye' to you guys, but they said that he'd have time to do that later today. They told us that everybody in the city was supposed to come down to the town centre at five o'clock this evening, sharp. Public meeting."

I frowned slightly. Something about this didn't seem right.

As Alison drove the van down the busy street, I caught a glimpse of the guards that had led Jaret into the building. When I looked closer, I also spotted Jaret within the group of ten or so people who they were with, the guards and gatekeepers leading them to a bus-like vehicle. I raised my hand to wave to Jaret, and his eyes briefly met mine.

Although the visual contact was very brief, it was enough for me to realize that something was very wrong. His eyes, and those of many of the people who he was with, were filled with fear and concern. As I looked closer, I saw something that made panic instantly stab through me. Each of the people's hands were tied with a length of rope behind their backs.

jaret

The twelve other people and I were all packed into the crowded bus, the rope digging into my wrists. We drove for what felt like forever, but in reality was probably only a few minutes, the windows completely blacked out so that we couldn't see outside.

Taking me to my brother wasn't the only reason that I was there. It was also because I was a shifter. All of us that were in the bus were.

The back door of the bus was opened and I was pulled out of the back of the vehicle, landing on the ground in a heap, the breath knocked out of me as my eyes adjusted to the sunlight.

I was pulled to my feet and the guards started to drag me down a walkway towards a large mansion, the gardens ornate and the trimmings on the house pure white. I almost tripped over my feet as they shoved me towards the marble staircase, barely catching myself before my head smacked against the rock.

"Hofferson's more than ready to see you, Faolan," the guard spat, pulling me up the last few stairs.

One of the guards knocked on the door, and a second later, it creaked open, a small boy standing on the other side of the door. Soft footsteps quickly came towards the door, and a woman, probably about twenty years old, picked up the boy, pushing the door open slightly more.

"You can come in. He's waiting for you in his office. Follow me," she said.

The two guards dragged me towards the house.

I tripped as I tried to step over the doorframe, my shoulder slamming against the marble flooring in the hall. One of the guards lifted me onto my feet and they started to continue to drag me towards the stairs.

I took another quick glance at the boy. He looked almost exactly like a younger version of Charlie, only with black hair instead of brown. The lady put him down on his feet and he watched me as the guards brought me up the stairs.

"Jack, go back to the playroom with Lily and Christopher, okay? I'll be there in a few minutes," she said.

The boy nodded and ran off down the hall, the lady coming up the stairs after us. We walked down a hallway, the plush red carpet sinking under my dirt-covered running shoes, towards a set of doors. She rapped her knuckles on the door.

"Mister Hofferson, he's here," she said, the door creaking open slightly.

"Yes, bring him in, thank you Merida," a familiar voice from inside the room answered.

My heart skipped a beat in my chest as they led me through the door, where my brother was sitting at the table across from the doorway.

"Hey, Jaret. Long time no see," Charlie said.

chapter nineteen

alison

"What do you mean?" I asked Dot.

She scowled. "I mean exactly what I said. He and a group of other people were being taken somewhere, against their will. I could tell that they didn't want to be there."

I rolled my eyes. "You're overreacting, alright? He's going to be fine, jeez."

Her frown grew larger. "I am not overreacting. Something is going to happen to him."

"He's fine. There's nothing we can do to help him anyways, alright?" I said. "We'll see him tonight, and you'll see, he'll be fine," I added.

She sighed and hung her head, giving a small nod of understanding.

"So, where we going?" I asked the others in the car.

"My shop is close to here. You could meet Haishin, Paulto and Ella before you have to go," Quivlie said, a hopeful edge to her voice.

She really wanted to see her family, I could tell.

"Yeah, sure. Tell me when to turn where," I answered.

Her skin brightened dramatically, although she turned her head to look out the window to try to prevent me from seeing the large smile that was forming on her face.

Three minutes later, I was pulling into a parking lot so that the four of us could walk to her shop. As soon as I parked the van, she was practically bouncing in excitement, and as we walked through the crowded streets, Dot and Nemvar holding onto each other and Dot's hand on my arm so that we didn't get separated.

As she saw the sign to their shop in the distance, she pointed it out to the three of us. Handeona Weaponry Repairs and Trade. While we were in the car, she explained that her parents' last name was Handeona, and as humans usually do, she took her mate's last name when they got married, but they kept the shop's name the same as to not confuse people.

The little bell on the door chimed as she pushed the door open. A small, elderly human lady who was sitting at a desk in the store looked up as we came in. Her eyes grew wide and a grin broke out on Quivlie's face as she ran forward to greet her.

"Quivlie, my dear! We were so worried about you, child!" the woman exclaimed, tears springing to her eyes as she embraced the Drurida.

"I missed you, Ella," Quivlie said.

The size difference between the two was almost comical. The woman looked to be barely five feet tall, and the Drurida was about six feet, four inches tall.

"Are Paulto and Haishin home?" she asked the small lady.

Ella nodded and grinned a toothless smile, pressing a small button on the side of her desk. A set of footsteps started down the flight of stairs that was partially visible near the back of the room. A second later, a Drurida man, presumably Haishin, carrying a small child, probably Paulto, came down the stairs. As the child saw Quivlie, his skin brightened drastically and a huge grin formed on his face.

"Mommy!" he all but shrieked.

Quivlie immediately ran to the two of them, and Haishin saw his mate. She wrapped her arms around the two of them, Haishin's unoccupied arm wrapping around her and both of her son's arms coming around her to hug her to the best of his ability.

"We were so worried about you, Quivlie," Haishin said, burying his face in her hair.

"I'm sorry. I don't remember anything that happened, only after I escaped where some people were holding me. How long was I gone for?" she answered him.

"Almost a month. We missed you," he responded, kissing her forehead. She stepped away from them and Haishin put their son in her arms. She hugged him and Haishin wrapped his arms around the two of them.

`quivlie`

The six of us sat upstairs in our living room, Haishin, Paulto and I on one couch, Alison in the armchair, and Dot and Nemvar sitting on one of the other couches. Paulto was sitting on my lap and Haishin's arm was around my shoulders.

"Would any of you like something to eat? It must have been a long day," Haishin offered, standing.

Alison shook her head. "I'm fine. Thank you, though."

Haishin smiled slightly before turning to me. "Should I make some tea for us all?" he asked, glancing behind the couch and towards the kitchen.

I smiled. "That would be nice, thank you," I responded.

Haishin nodded and walked around the smallest of the three couches in the room, moving towards the cupboard to get the teakettle. A moment later, the tea water was boiling on the stove and Haishin had came to sit back down beside me.

"So, what happened?" he questioned after a moment of the six of us sitting in near silence.

I bit my lip.

"I was in a building, I don't know why and I do not remember anything that happened before that. I escaped and got to Traiton, where I met Alison, Dot and Jaret in the earthquake room. We got halfway here, but Dot got pulled into a lake and she could not direct us here," I said, shortening the story for the time being. "Alison found out that Jaret was a Cainan, so she shot his leg, but they made up and we kept walking," I said, saying the last sentence in Druridish so that Alison could not understand what I had said.

She looked at me in confusion for a moment, but I offered no explanation and continued talking. "We got to a manufacturing plant, but they told us that if we went to this other facility, they would be able to fix Dot. They did, but they took the recognition chips from out of both her and Nemvar. We do not know why, we only know that it is because they are Independent Androids," I said, and Haishin nodded, "we escaped and got here, but when we tried to get into C, the guards took Jaret away to see his brother."

"Do we know who his brother is?" he asked.

"Charles Hofferson," I replied.

Haishin's skin immediately dulled dramatically. "He is not safe. That is why Hofferson is holding the gathering tonight. That is why you were checked on your way in, because he is filtering the city for any of the shapeshifters. That is where we assume Demitri is, he was supposed to go this morning and he has not came back. Shaelene and Sachi went, too, they have not been back. They told me last night that they did not know why they were going there, or what was going to happen," he said, putting his arm back around my shoulders.

Shaelene and Sachi were two of our most frequent customers; Shaelene was an Avian, Sachi was a Dracid, and Demitri was a Felid.

"See?" Dot said definitively, turning her head to face Alison. "He's in trouble. They all are. We cannot only sit by and let Charles go through with whatever he is planning."

Alison's face had gone pale, and all she could do was offer a weak nod in response.

"How can he just hold a gathering like this? Isn't it only the mayor that can do that?" Alison questioned in confusion.

"If someone has enough money, even the mayor will relent," Haishin sighed.

dot

"What can we do? We don't know where they are, we don't know what's going to happen, we don't know how to help them. What can we do to help?" Alison asked, an edge of sarcasm in her voice.

Haishin shook his head slightly and a second later, the whistling of the teakettle echoed through the room.

"We have to go to the public meeting tonight," Haishin said, standing to go make the tea. "If we can go, then we can try to help in any way we can. We can only hope that we will not be too late," he added, taking four mugs from the cupboard and putting them on the counter for the four of them for tea.

"What about Paulto? If push comes to shove, he will not be safe if he is there," Quivlie stated, holding her son closer to her.

The young Drurida glanced up at his mother.

"Ella could stay here with him. She and him can stay safe in the cellar. When the guards are filtering us through, we can say that he is sick and she is staying back to care for him," Haishin responded.

Quivlie nodded and gently pressed a kiss to the top of her son's head. He looked over at his father.

"What's happening later?" Paulto asked innocently, turning to face Quivlie.

She looked downwards at him. "You and Ella are going to stay here at home while me, dad, and our friends are going to go to the public meeting again."

Haishin came back to the table, two mugs of tea in his hands which he handed to Alison and Quivlie. Quivlie smiled.

"Thank you," Alison said, setting her mug down on the coffee table beside the couch on which she was sitting. He nodded once and went back to the counter, bringing back his and Paulto's mugs and then returning to the kitchen to bring back cream and sugar. He poured a large quantity of cream into

Paulto's mug to cool the tea and handed it to his son, who almost immediately started to drink it. Quivlie lifted her son off of her lap and set him on the couch beside her so that she could put some cream and sugar in her tea.

"How would we stay safe? We don't have any very good advantages over the guards, or weapons, or anything, do we?" Nemvar asked.

Haishin and Quivlie both immediately looked to him, their skins brightening almost instantaneously in amusement.

"We own a weapon repair shop. We have lots," Haishin responded, laughter in his voice.

jaret

"You're... you're alive," I said in disbelief, nearly choking on my words as I talked.

I knew that Tala had told me before, but it hadn't really hit me until I saw him sitting at his desk for the first time in seven years. He smirked.

"As are you, although I didn't expect anything less from you," he replied.

I nodded and looked around the room in confusion. "How did you get here? Like, here, as in 'how did you get this mansion and who's that kid who came to the door?'" I asked.

He frowned, his smirk disappearing within a second. He was always like this; very abruptly changing emotions.

"When I got here, a wealthy couple took me in, and when they passed away a few years ago, they left their house and fortune to me. 'That kid' is one of mine, either Jack or

Christopher because Lily's asleep," he responded, being surprisingly gracious with his answers.

My jaw became slack with shock. "You have kids? With who, how old are they?"

His frown deepened. "I brought you here, I'm the one who should be asking the questions."

I felt my brow furrow in confusion. "Wait, why *did* you bring me here? Why am I being treated like a convict?"

He shook his head and stood, walking around his desk and walking over to me, running his hand over his mouth and short brown beard.

"Because that's what you are. Come on, it'll be easier to show you than tell you," Charlie said, grabbing my shoulder and pulling me after him as he stepped into the hallway. I stumbled after him down the hall as he lead me to another room. He took a key and unlocked the door before stepping through, pulling me through after him.

Meanwhile, I was getting even more confused as to what he had said.

I'm a prisoner to him? But I'm his brother, I haven't seen him in the past seven years. I can't have possibly done anything to have him mad at me that is valid for him still being angry.

"Sit," he said as we walked into the room, pushing me towards a white plastic chair in the middle of the room.

I tripped towards the chair and barely caught my balance as I staggered forward.

I sat and looked around the room. Many different cabinets and such furnishings decorated the room; it was one of which that my brother pulled a helmet-like machine out of before coming to my side.

"Stay still," he said, raising the device towards and above my head.

I complied and didn't move my head, and a second later, I greatly regretted that decision as everything in my vision went black.

"What are you doing?" I asked, struggling to free my hands so that I could get the helmet off. Despite my effort, the screen that was in front of me seemed to completely envelop my vision as everything around me went black.

chapter twenty

jaret

A small light grew closer on the screen, and within a few seconds, I realized what the picture on the screen was.

Our village; the one where Charlie and I had grown up. I saw a group of younger shifters playing in the sand, in their animalistic forms, and I immediately recognized them as myself and the friends that I had grown up with, including Kailena, the girl who had later conducted the attack against the village. Charlie sat on the steps of one of the nearby buildings. I remembered that dad had made him come with me when I went to play with my friends to watch over us.

The image faded into another. One of the elder shifters, Yazaraii, had been teaching us to control our shifting. Again, Charlie sat away from the group of the younger shifters, his brown hair hanging partially over his eyes as he watched us.

Again, the scene changed. It was the night that the village had been destroyed, fire and smoke billowing out of the houses and screams of help echoing through the night sky as the rogue shifters burnt the houses. I saw Charlie and I, two of the three survivors of the attack, running away from the buildings and into the desert. I felt my throat tighten as I saw my mom's necklace dangling from my small hand.

I didn't recognize the next scene. I hadn't been there. Charlie, dehydrated and covered with dirt, was stumbling towards Walkton, the high wall visible in the distance. A carriage driving past and slowed as it saw him, stopping a few metres away. A couple got out of the carriage, rushing towards him and helping him into the vehicle.

The next scene was at a place that I recognized to be the mansion that we were currently in. Charlie looked a few months older that he did before, and as he walked, the scene followed him through the streets of Walkton, towards one of the doctor's offices, his hand hanging limply in his other. We walked into the hospital and I followed his gaze as a girl walked around the corner, wearing a nurse's uniform. If I hadn't known that Alison had lived in Walkton, I swear it could have been her with darker hair.

"What happened to your arm?" she asked, walking towards him.

He took a moment before he answered her, staring with a dumbstruck look at her face.

"Oh, I, uh, I tripped down the stairs," he answered, a blush rising to his cheeks.

She smiled and nodded, taking his non-broken arm and leading him into one of the other rooms. "What's your name?" she asked, grabbing a clipboard and pencil from the desk.

"Charles. You can just call me Charlie. though, everybody else does," he replied, sitting in the chair as she had instructed him to.

"Okay. It's good to meet you, Charlie. Well, not good that you broke your arm, but you know what I mean. I'm Amelia," she said, smiling.

He smiled back at her and it faded into the next scene.

It looked to be a few years later. Amelia and Charlie were at the hospital again; but this time, it was Amelia who was the patient. In her arms, there lay a sleeping baby, and in Charlie's laid another.

"What will their names be?" the doctor asked.

Amelia and Charlie shared a glance.

"Jack and Christopher," Amelia replied, smiling.

Charlie gave a small nod and glanced down at the baby in his arms.

Another scene, and the four of them were at the park, having a picnic. The boys seemed to be about a year old, and were both sitting up on the blanket.

The scene shifted once again, and this time, the four of them were back at the mansion, but Amelia was holding another baby swaddled in a small, light-pink blanket.

The next scene, it was just Charlie and Amelia at a restaurant. I could see that Charlie was a little nervous.

"Amelia," he started, coming around the side of the table. The scene shifted once again, briefly morphing into the image of the two of them walking down the street, holding hands, their engagement rings on the ring fingers of both of their left hands.

Amelia and a few other people were in a carriage drawn by two ox, the caravan moving across the desert. As I saw into the carriage, I saw with surprise Amelia sitting with three other people, her parents and Alison. I remembered that Alison had said that she had a twin sister named Amelia who, along with her parents, had died a few years prior to our meeting.

The carriage bumped along the sandy ground, one of the wheels getting caught on a rock as the sun started to set. The caravan lurched to a halt and the four of them got out of the carriage, inspecting the damage to the wheel.

As they started to try to mend the wheel, there were a pair of low cautionary growls from the darkness. The scene morphed into another just as the snarling faces of two Cainans appeared through the darkness.

Charlie, Christopher and Jack were sitting on a bench in a church, Alison sitting across the building on another bench, somebody mourning the loss of Amelia and her parents as Charlie's young daughter laid sleeping in his arms.

As the helmet was lifted off my head, I was transported back to reality; back to sitting in my brother's house, nothing more than a prisoner to him even though he meant the world to me when we were growing up.

alison

"Alright, follow me," Quivlie said, standing and picking up Paulto as she did so.

The rest of us stood and followed after her as she went towards the stairs. Down the stairs and through the back part of the shop, and we were in the secondary part of the store, where I assumed was where they kept the weapons that they were fixing or going to be fixing soon.

Soon enough, each of us, excluding Paulto, of course, were armed with new weaponry. I was eager to try out my new bow, but I couldn't exactly do that in the store, I would have to wait until we were in the practice range.

"Ella, could you watch Paulto while we go into the practice range?" Haishin asked.

Ella turned her head to face him and she nodded, smiling toothlessly.

"And would it be possible for you to take care of him tonight as well?" he added, smiling hopefully.

Ella's eyes crinkled further as she grinned.

"Of course I will, dear. You and Quivlie are going out for dinner later?" she guessed.

He grinned and shook his head, his skin lightening dramatically.

"Not tonight. We have to go to the town meeting. You have to stay here, it isn't going to be safe for you or Paulto to be there. We can tell the guards that he is sick and that you are staying back at home to look after him," he responded.

She nodded abruptly, the smile on her face falling. "What's happening? Why isn't it safe?" she questioned, turning to face him more seriously.

"We're suspecting that Hofferson is planning something against the shifters. He ordered for Demitri, Sachi and Shaelene to meet him somewhere last night, and they have not came back. One more person came back with Quivlie; a Cainan named Jaret. He's Hofferson's younger brother. He was taken to see Charles with a group of other people who we assume are shifters," Haishin explained.

Ella frowned in confusion. "Wait, so he's a shifter too?"

I knew that he wasn't; I remember Jaret explaining to me that they were half brothers.

"He's half-Cainan, half-human. Jaret's whole-Cainan," I said, responding for Haishin.

Ella turned to face me, not having realized that I was there, a look of slight confusion on her face.

"They have the same dad, and he was a Cainan, but they had different moms. Charles' mom was human, Jaret's was a Cainan too," I added.

Ella nodded, understanding.

"Alright. Either way, yes, I can watch after Paulto tonight," Ella stated.

Haishin smiled. "Thank you very much Ella."

"It's not a problem, my dear," she responded, standing and extending her hand for the youngest Drurida to take. "Come on, Paulto, we can go and start making lunch, alright?"

He took Ella's hand as she lead him back towards the stairs.

quivlie

I started walking towards the practice range at the very back of the shop, Dot, Nemvar, Alison and Haishin following behind me. I glanced towards the clock on the wall. 3:42 PM. It was a bit late for Ella and Paulto to have started making lunch. It was more of an early dinner.

I pushed open the heavy door to the practice range at the end of the hall and flicked the light switch as the few banks of lights flickered to life, illuminating the previously darkened hallway.

"Alright. Dot, you can go here," Haishin instructed, gesturing to one of the rooms on the right side of the hallway, the side in which was specialized for training with melee weaponry.

I went to the door and pushed it open, gesturing for the Android to follow. The mannequin was stuck onto the post in the middle of the room, its arms and legs hanging onto the cloth torso by mere threads of fabric and as Dot followed me into the spacious room, she gave the mannequin a glance of confusion.

"Okay, stand about here," I said, using my foot to trace a large square into the straw on the ground.

She nodded and stepped into the newly formed box.

"I will yell to you right before I press start. Yell back to me if you need me to stop it," I added, stepping out the room.

Dot looked back at me in confusion as I shut the door. I went to the control panel outside the room and set the controls to 'advanced' and 'fast,' selecting the type of sword she was using from the weapon inventory. I knew that she would be able to handle the faster-than-usual erratic movements of the mannequin.

"Okay, I am starting it! Do not be worried about breaking the mannequin, it won't break! Just try not to get hit by the mannequin!" I called to her.

"Alright!" was her muffled response, confusion clear in her voice. I pressed the start button and I heard the muffled clunking of the post starting to move. I glanced in through the small window on the door and saw that Dot was stepping away from the mannequin slowly. The cloth doll's arm raised quickly as it started to spin towards her. An expression of pure uncertainty on her face, the Android swung her sword towards the mannequin's arm in an attempt to block the arm from hitting her in the face.

"What am I supposed to be doing, Quivlie?" she called to me.

"You are training to protect yourself and injure your enemies!" I yelled back to her. "Not that you really need it!" I added after a second.

"What kind of enemy spins towards you and tries to grab you with the arm that it's spinning?" she called back in bewilderment.

"None that I know of, we just want you to be prepared for anything weird!" I said back to her, raising my voice above the metallic whirs of the post moving rapidly around the room.

She raised her sword again as the doll flung closer to her, both of its arms and legs lurching towards her as it flew forwards. She swung the sword with more speed and accuracy than I had ever seen, and the post veered backwards to bring the mannequin out of her reach. There was a sudden loud tearing sound as the sword caught on the shoulder of the fabric doll, the cloth ripping apart as the mannequin fell to the ground. The post ground to a stop and Dot turned towards me, an expression of concern on her face.

"I'm sorry, I did not intend to break the mannequin! It was an accident!" she called, coming towards the door. I grinned and opened the door.

"You do not need to apologize, we have many more mannequins. That is what is supposed to happen. Good job. Let us go and see how the others are doing," I said, holding the door open for her. She nodded slowly in understanding and walked out of the practice room.

dot

Quivlie and I walked down the hall towards the rooms where the others were practicing. Haishin stood by a control panel outside of one of the rooms, the muffled sounds of a gun firing coming from the other side of the thick glass that he was facing.

As I peered inside, I saw that Nemvar was aiming a gun towards a row of mannequins that were lined up on the opposite side of the room. The two of us had spent nearly three days with each other in that room, alone except for each other's company. He was getting a lot less anxious then he was when I was put into the containment room with him.

After they had removed the recognition chip, they repaired the paneling they destroyed when they tried to open up the side of my head to get the chip. That was why the bright red panel was there instead of the one that was there previously, the silvery grey one. He had one there too, from when they had taken the recognition chip out of him, in the same placement as mine.

We spent those three days doing practically nothing except for telling stories to each other and me listening to him talk about Zaupa and Crackers. When Zaupa Taliat had gone to buy a farmhand Android, she was the first to realize that Nemvar had independent thoughts, so, in an attempt to save him, she bought him as fast as she could and took him home to her farm. The factory workers never did realize that he was to be destroyed.

The two of them were living there for a few years, and they started to develop romantic feelings for one another, so they decided to get a dog that could help Nemvar ward off the crows that would constantly threaten to eat their crop. They adopted one of Zaupa's friend's puppies and named him Crackers, over the fact that he loved and would do seemingly anything to find and devour them.

About a year after, somebody had broken into their farmhouse at night. Crackers' barking woke them up, and they ran downstairs to see what was wrong. By the time they got downstairs, Crackers had managed to grab the thief and had bitten his leg, making it impossible for the robber to escape from the large dog. Zaupa called the authorities, and they arrested him, but the burglar had told them that she was hiding an Independent Android at her farm. Because hiding any creature that is prohibited by the law is seen as a bigger felony than burglary, the authorities found Nemvar and brought him to the research facility.

He was tested on multiple times since then, after they had removed his recognition chip, and he had never completely recovered. He had regained most of his memory, though, and that was what he was happiest about. Being able to remember Zaupa and Crackers.

After a quick round of gunshots, the head of the mannequin fell backwards, hanging on by mere threads as the bullets pierced through the fabric, that specific kind of ammunition scorching the cloth and turning into near ash.

Nemvar turned to face the window, grinning widely and bouncing up and down slightly in excitement. As his eyes met mine, I smiled in congratulations as Haishin pressed the button that opened the door. Nemvar raced out of the room.

"Did you see, I was doing good, Zaupa would have been proud of me, if I would have had a gun like this when Crackers was fighting with the wolves, I wouldn't have actually shot them, but I could have scared them away and he wouldn't have been hurt, and Zaupa wouldn't have had to take him to Walkton to the vet to get him better, and he would have been happier, and then we could have afforded to get a real scarecrow to help Crackers and I scare away the crows from eating our corn," Nemvar said hurriedly, grinning widely.

His grin suddenly fell as he registered what he had said. "I want to go back home soon, Dot," he said. I nodded in understanding, resting my hand on his shoulder.

"I know you do. We can bring you home shortly after today, most likely. Maybe tomorrow we can start driving you back home," I stated.

His frown lessened slightly in relief as he realized that he could return to his family soon.

chapter twenty-one

jaret

"Now do you see?" Charlie said, tossing the helmet onto one of the nearby tables. I flinched as the metallic ringing echoed through the room.

"Your kind destroyed my family. If it weren't for them, Dad and Emily wouldn't have been killed. Neither would Laura, or Paul, or Nathaniel, or any of them," his words dripped with malice. "If it weren't for them, Amelia wouldn't have been killed," he added, his voice cracking.

He coughed, clearing his throat. "If it weren't for your kind, my kids would still have their mother."

I shook my head slowly. "That's such a huge generalization, Charlie. Not all of us are bad. Dad was one of them, and so was my mom. They were good people, you've gotta know that. It was only a few of them that weren't so good. They're the ones who aren't good, not all of us," I said, a pleading edge in my voice.

He shook his head. "That's where you're wrong. It may not be all of you, but you all definitely have the potential. One thing doesn't go your way, one person disagrees with you, you have the capacity to rip them to shreds," he responded disparagingly, disgust laced into his tone.

"But the majority of us would never do that. We don't all want to hurt you."

He frowned and started slowly pacing. "Too many of you did. Too many of you will. You're unpredictable."

I shook my head slightly in disbelief. "I'm sorry about your fiancée. I really am, but you can't judge the actions of a whole group of people based on a few incidences," I said, struggling against the restraints holding my wrists together.

"A few?!" he cried in outrage, whirling to face me, fire in his eyes. "A few incidences? More like countless people being murdered in cold blood! All of the people in the village! That was at the very least two hundred people!" he shouted, his face turning beet red.

I paled. This wasn't the Charlie that I remembered growing up with. The quiet, shy brother who walked me to the schoolhouse every day. Who stayed up with me until five in the morning because I had a nightmare and was too scared to go back to sleep. Who did everything in his power to make sure I was treated just like the other kids, even though he, not being able to shift, was not.

"Them in addition to Amelia, her sister, and both of her parents!" he yelled.

My heart jumped in my chest as I realized that I was scared. This wasn't my brother. This was some tortured, broken and miserable clone of him. Not the one who I had grown up with.

"Those were the only two things that happened any time close to now. Charlie, you've gotta believe me. You know that Dad wasn't like that, you know that Mom wasn't like that, you know that I'm not like that," I pleaded. "If dad was like that, would your mom have loved him?" I said pointedly.

His eyes flashed as soon as I finished the sentence.

"He wasn't like that," Charlie said, his voice quieting to a normal volume. "There are the few exceptions, him being one of them."

"What about my mom? She didn't do anything wrong," I said, knowing fully well that I was overstepping the line.

Charlie turned his head to face me again. "She was the one who broke my family apart. If it weren't for her, Dad and my mom would still be together," he said, frustration clear in his voice.

He was referencing the fact that when Dad and Megan were still together, he met my mom and shortly after had divorced Megan to be with my mom.

"What does that have to do with anything? That was still Dad's decision, it wasn't her fault!" I exclaimed.

He threw up his hands in exasperation. "Why does it matter?" he shouted, the volume of his voice exceeding what it had been previously. I flinched as he yelled again. "The shifters are too unpredictable. We didn't know that Kailena and the others were going to do that. Amelia didn't think that she had to be cautious of the shifters because they're so fucking harmless," he spat, his words scalding my skin as he spoke.

"You're unpredictable," he said in defeat, his shoulders slumping. "That's why you're dangerous. That's why the rest of us would be better off without your kind. Better off without the freaks," he finished, filled with conviction, sending fear pulsing through my veins.

merida

I could hear Mr. Hofferson yelling from downstairs. Lily looked up at me, an expression of concerned confusion on her face.

"Why is Daddy mad?" she asked.

I gave a small smile to try to comfort her. "He's just talking to somebody that he's mad at. He isn't mad at any of you though, okay, Lily?" I responded.

She nodded and turned back to the puzzle that the four of us were building.

"Jack, that doesn't go there though," Christopher said to his brother, his bottom lip sticking out in a halfhearted pout as Jack tried to force a piece of the puzzle into where he'd thought was the right spot. I gently shook my head and glanced to the door. I heard one of the doors upstairs slam open.

"Peterson, Ross, get up here!" I heard Mr. Hofferson shout from up the stairs, presumably from his office. I sighed, and Kyle and Marcus started going up the stairs, hurrying to get to our boss before he got mad at them for not coming quickly enough. Jack tugged gently on the sleeve of my dress.

"Merry, why is he mad at that man?" he questioned.

I bit my lip. "He's your dad's brother. Your dad wants the rest of the shapeshifters to leave so that we're safe, but his brother, your uncle, doesn't want the shapeshifters to have to leave," I explained, trying not to get too in depth to avoid having Mr. Hofferson getting angry at me for telling them too much information.

"Why does Daddy want us to leave?" Jack asked in confusion.

My heart skipped a beat in my chest. Mr. Hofferson didn't know. "Not you, Jack, he doesn't want you to leave. He just wants the bad ones to leave," I answered, hoping that my answer wouldn't just whet the appetite of the boy's curiosity. It seemed to have been an adequate answer, as he turned his attention back to the puzzle.

I sighed softly. The poor boy. Not even five years old and already having his own father wishing death upon him and the rest of his kind. Although the shifting gene wasn't expressed by Mr. Hofferson, it was passed unknowingly onto one of his children.

I'd been working for the Hoffersons, looking after the children and cleaning around the house since Jack and Christopher were born. I didn't need to do as much because Amelia was here to help out, but whenever both she and Charles were at work, I would be in charge of taking care of the twins. I had been the one to first find out that Jack could shift. He didn't have very much control of it due to his age and lack of mentoring on the subject, so I was always careful to make sure that he remained as calm as possible. Neither his father or mother had realized before I told his mother. Amelia was much more understanding than Charles. When I had told her, she asked for me not to tell Charles, for fear that it would alienate her son from his father.

"Take him to the stables," I heard Mr. Hofferson yell from upstairs, followed shortly by the sound of another shout and a loud thud as someones knees slammed into the floor. I stood and lifted Lily into my arms.

"Come on, boys, let's go get something to eat," I said, extending my unoccupied hand to Jack. The two of them both stood, Jack clinging onto my hand as I started to the kitchen to avoid them seeing Mr. Hofferson's brother as Kyle and Marcus took him past the playroom and outside to the vacant stables with the other shifters.

alison

A small set of footsteps came padding down the hall towards the practice range. Paulto stuck his head through the door.

"Ella told me to tell you that we got done making food," he said, looking up to me expectantly. I smiled and bent down closer to his level.

"Alright, we'll be there in a minute or two, okay? Thank you for telling me," I responded.

He smiled and his skin lightened before he scurried back through the door and towards the kitchen. I walked back towards where the others were.

"Paulto says lunch is ready," I said to Haishin, gesturing towards the door.

"Okay, thank you, Alison." Quivlie stepped out of one of the practice rooms. "Lunch is ready," he relayed to her.

"Come on, guys!" I called to Dot and Nemvar. The two of them started walking towards us down the hall, and we followed Haishin as he started back towards the main part of the shop. The bank of lights flickered off as we all stepped out of the hall and Quivlie flipped the light switch.

"Alright, we made soup and sandwiches, and I just put a pie in the oven for after," Ella told us, brushing her hair out of her face.

"You really didn't have to go through all that trouble, Ella, thank you very much," Haishin said, grinning as he glanced at the spread of food on the table.

The elderly woman smiled and nodded her head, pulling one of the chairs out for Haishin and another beside it for Quivlie. Haishin lifted Paulto into the chair beside Quivlie's, and the three of them and Ella sat, Quivlie gesturing for the three of us to follow suit. I smiled at Ella and sat in the chair beside hers and across from Quivlie. Dot sat beside me, and Nemvar beside her.

I nearly jumped as the unexpected chimes of a grandfather clock rang though the room, indicating that it was four-fifteen. Just enough time to eat and then leave to get to the town centre in time for five.

"We wanted to, though, making food for other people is always worth the work," Ella smiled and gestured around the table for us to serve ourselves.

Paulto turned his head towards me, meeting my gaze from across the table. "Can you get me food?"

"Yeah, sure. What do you want to eat?" I asked.

Haishin looked to me and grinned. "I can help him, Alison, it isn't a problem," he said.

I shrugged. "Alright."

I glanced to Ella and Quivlie, both of whom were waiting for Haishin to put Paulto's food on his plate. The Drurida girl looked lovingly towards her mate. When Haishin put Paulto's plate in front of his son, Quivlie and Ella both started to get their food. I frowned in confusion as I saw that Haishin wasn't putting any food on his own plate. His gaze met mine and he smiled slightly.

"It's a Drurida dinner custom. Children are served first, then women, then men," he explained, gesturing for me to get food too.

"Well, thank you," I said as I ladled some soup into my bowl. After I set my bowl and plate on the table again, he got his food. However, none of them began eating, so I didn't either. I waited for an awkwardly long moment where the four of them sat and stared blankly at their food before they began eating. In confusion, I picked up my spoon and started eating.

"Four forty-five, please begin making your way to the town centre."

I jumped as a loud voice blared from outside. Quivlie glanced towards Haishin with concern clear in her eyes. He smiled reassuringly at her and stood, taking his plate towards the sink.

"Alright, we will have to leave soon. Paulto, you and Ella are going to stay here, okay?" he said to his son.

Paulto smiled at his dad. "Okay. I can help Ella make more food for when you are home. We can make cookies?" he questioned, turning towards Ella.

"Yes, of course we can, dear," she responded.

His skin brightened drastically and he grinned and started bouncing enthusiastically in his seat. The six of us started to put the leftover food away in plastic containers and then into the fridge.

"Okay, Paulto, we will be back soon, we will not be gone long," Quivlie said, kneeling down to face her son.

He hugged her tightly. "Okay, Mum," he answered. Quivlie smoothed his hair down with her hand as she stood. She went to say goodbye to Ella and Haishin took her place saying goodbye to Paulto. I saw him as he lifted his son into his arms.

"I'll be back soon, alright?" he said. "You and Ella can make cookies, and when we get back, we can all eat them together."

"We're gonna make lots of cookies," he said proudly, looking towards Ella who smiled and nodded. Paulto leaned his head against Haishin's shoulder as he hugged him. Haishin handed his son to Ella and she lifted him into her arms.

"Are you going to wave bye to them? They'll be back soon," Ella said, pointing towards is with her unoccupied hand. Paulto waved frantically as the five of us started down the stairs.

quivlie

As soon as we left the shop, we were swept into the mass of people who were moving towards the town centre. I kept the grip that I had on Haishin's hand firm as I did not want to lose track of him in the crowd. Dot was holding onto my other arm, and her hand and Nemvar's were clasped together. Nemvar held onto Alison's arm as she trailed behind the rest of us.

I glanced to my side to see the couple who owned the bakery beside our shop, Leah and Nelson. Leah's eyes met mine a second later and they widened in surprise. Soon enough, her and her husband were lost in the sea of bodies.

Luckily, the town centre was relatively close to our shop, just a few streets away, so we did not have to walk too far. Soon enough, the space opened up and the city hall laid ahead of us, the large courtyard nearly vacant except for the people who were flooding into the large circular area. Haishin led us towards one of the lines that was filtering people through and into the courtyard.

The stench of garbage and pollution washed through the city, just as I had remembered it to smell in Section C. In the outermost parts of the Section, in Section A and in parts of Section B, however, the aroma was replaced with that of the clean open farmlands that were found in certain parts of the city.

Haishin's hand started to sweat as the increasing number of people filtered towards the centre and into the lines, although he squeezed my hand reassuringly before he let it go in order to merge into one of the the single-file lines. It would be okay. We would both be able to get home and see Paulto and Ella again, and the shifters would be safe. The four of us lined up behind him and waited as we were filtered through.

"Remember, Paulto is staying with Ella at home because he is sick. I'm not going to tell people that we're with Alison, Dot and Nemvar, that will only make it more complicated," Haishin said, turning towards me again. I turned back to see that Alison was talking to Dot and Nemvar. I rotated my ears towards them so that I could better hear what she was saying.

"So when they ask, you're both mine, I got you both a few months ago," she was saying. "You, I bought new; you. I bought secondhand, you don't remember who owned you before, got it?" she explained, looking first from Dot and then to Nemvar.

They both nodded.

"Okay," Dot replied.

"Of course, Miss Alison," Nemvar said obediently. The lines continued to move forwards, and soon enough Haishin was being ushered into the booth at the front of the line. My heart skipped a beat as he pointed back towards me, and the human man that he was talking to glanced back.

I turned towards Alison to tell her the plan. I pretended to kneel down and pick something off the ground. I stood up and thrust my empty hand towards her. She frowned in slight confusion and extended her hand, palm up. I opened my hand and pressed it into hers.

"For all intents and purposes, you do not know Haishin or I, the only thing you know is that you dropped a few pieces and I just handed them back to you," I said, before turning back towards the front of the line.

"Next!" the guard called as Haishin walked to the other side of the booth and waited. I walked forwards. "Name?"

"Quivlie Deshnerim," I said.

"Who's he to you?" he questioned, gesturing towards Haishin, who was waiting a few metres away from the booth.

"My mate, Haishin Deshnerim," I answered.

He typed our names into the machine that was sitting beside him in the booth. "Where's your son?" he asked, looking up from the computer-like device.

"Paulto is sick, our secretary is at home taking care of him," I said.

"Who's your secretary?"

"Eleanor Bettman."

He extended his hand. "ID of any sort?"

I reached my hand into my pocket, grabbing my shopkeeper's license and handing it to him. He glanced at it before nodding.

"Alright, you can go," he dismissed me. I walked to Haishin on the other side of the booth. He took my hand in his and drew me towards him, planting a kiss on my forehead. I smiled.

"I love you," I stated, my skin brightening. His skin brightened instantaneously and he grinned.

"I love you too, Quivlie," he replied, squeezing my hand gently.

A second later, Alison, Dot and Nemvar walked through the booth and into the courtyard, casually walking by us to continue the charade that we were unacquainted. Haishin and I started making our way towards the front of the crowd, closer to the stage and podium so that we could better see what was happening.

A strong gust of wind passed through the town centre, and both Haishin and I nearly froze. The scent of sweat, shifters, blood and fear wafted by us, not that anybody else around us picked up on it. I turned towards him, a worried expression on my face. He shook his head and we continued pushing our way through the crowd towards the front.

As soon as the stage came into view, my stomach churned violently and my vision started to blur slightly. My body nearly went limp with shock as I saw what was on the stage. Line after line of shifters, hands cuffed together in a chain; Charles Hofferson standing off to the side of the stage with a few of his guards; Jaret, Tala and a younger boy all being held by a few of the guards near the side of the stage, large guns pointed at each of their heads.

dot

"Next!" the guard called as soon as Quivlie passed through the booth and went to her mate. Alison walked forwards, Nemvar and I both walking mechanically behind her. "Name?" he asked.

"Alison Hawthorne," she responded.

I kept my gaze focused on staring blankly towards the crowd of people. Nemvar, however, was staring intently at a dog that somebody was walking through the crowd.

"Are these your Androids?" he asked, gesturing towards Nemvar and I. Alison nodded her head once in affirmation. "When did you purchase them?" he prompted.

"The housecare Android, I bought new a few months ago, the construction one I bought then too, but it was already being used for a few years. They didn't want it anymore."

The guard nodded. "Alright. What was your intended purpose for them?"

I could see out of my peripheral vision that Alison was fighting back a scowl, but she forced it away with a smirk. "Housecare to keep my house clean and stuff. Construction because I'm a trader. When I go gathering or hunting, I take it with me to carry my stuff because I'm not strong enough to carry an elk if I kill one," she explained.

The guard nodded once. "Have any ID?"

She held up her index finger to signal for him to wait for a second as she reached into her coat pocket. A second later, she handed him her trader's license. He glanced at it and then handed it back to her.

"One more thing, then you can go," he said. She nodded as he pulled a small bag out of the drawer in the booth. "Give me your hand," he ordered. She placed her hand face up on the table and he pinned her wrist to the table, pressing a small purple flower to the inside of her wrist. After a second of watching her wrist for a reaction, he waved us through.

"What was that?" Nemvar questioned as soon as we were safely out of earshot of any guards.

"Wolfsbane flower," she replied, her lips tight. I frowned. They were definitely doing something to find the shifters. Wolfsbane would burn a shifter's skin on contact, no matter what animal it shifted into. They were being very indifferent as to if they hurt any of the shifters or not. They were the only race that it had any effect on, so it was definitely them that they were trying to find.

The three of us walked past Haishin and Quivlie, pretending to not know them and we started towards the front of the crowd. Alison slowed her pace as the stage came into view and she stopped a second later.

"What is it, what is-" I stopped talking in the midst of my sentence. A small crowd of shifters were on the stage, a line of guards holding their shackles to prevent them from escaping. As I looked across the stage, she immediately saw Jaret and Tala being held near Charles Hofferson, a small boy standing next to them. Jaret lifted his head and his eyes met mine, a trickle of blood streaming down his temple as a cut on his forehead reopened. His eyes widened slightly with recognition as he saw me again, but his expression quickly turned to an expression of fear as he saw the guards starting to shut down the booths, blocking all escape from the town centre.

chapter twenty-two

charles

"Good evening, citizens of Walkton," I said, stepping forwards to the microphone in the middle of the stage. The entire city's eyes were on me. They were all going to witness the beginning of the new world; a world of peace.

"Why are you doing this?" my brother's voice was barely audible over the noise of the crowd clamouring.

"That's a good place to start off. Why am I doing this?" I started. I smiled. "I'm doing this to protect you," I stated, facing the audience. Calls of confusion came from the sea of people.

I heard one call from the audience very clearly: "From what?"

"The freaks known as shifters, that's what I'm protecting you from. It's unnatural to be that way. A person shouldn't have the choice to change between being two different creatures," I answered. "Not only is it unnatural, it's dangerous. I've witnessed how dangerous they can be on multiple occasions. The first time, I was a child. A small group of rogue shifters killed my entire village; more than two hundred people. The only people who survived were me, my freak brother and one other," I explained.

There were many calls of confusion from the crowd. "Sir, an explanation might be necessary," one of my guards mumbled to me.

"Half-brother, that is," I added. "The second was two days before I married the love of my life. The mother of my children. She went to retrieve her family for our wedding, but their carriage was attacked on the way back to Walkton. Shifters killed her, both of her parents and her sister. It's the shifter's fault that none of my children remember their mother."

"They didn't kill all of us," a voice from the audience exclaimed, close. I frowned and looked towards the voice. My heart stopped in my chest as I saw who the voice belonged to. Long hair, bright eyes; for a second, it looked as if Amelia was standing in front of me again.

"Get her," I said abruptly. Almost immediately, a small group of guards were dragging her towards the stage, one of them wrestling a crossbow off of her shoulder. She resisted slightly against them, but to very little avail as she was outnumbered four to one. The guards forced her onto her knees by Jaret and the others.

"Is this how you solve all of your problems? Violence and torture?" she spat.

I felt my face flush in rage. "You were with my brother. You helped him get here."

She scoffed. "And so what if I was?"

I glanced at the bow that my guard had taken from her. I smirked. "You were the one who shot him," I said simply. Her face turned red and she scowled. "Don't think I can't tell. It's obvious that it was a hunter's arrow that shot him, within the past few days. Yawker here explained that you were with him for the past few days, probably the only hunter near him for the past week that you were in the desert."

"What does that prove?" she questioned defiantly. I could definitely see that she and Amelia were related.

"It proves that you know that I'm right about the shifters being dangerous. Do you understand, people? She was willing to help him to Walkton, but as soon as she found out that he was a shifter, she realized how dangerous they were and she shot him. Her entire family, killed by the creatures, and then she realized that she had befriended one who was lying about his identity. If she hadn't known that I'm right, she wouldn't have shot him," I exclaimed, almost laughing at how well this was proving my point.

"That's not true," Jaret started. I looked at the guard closest to him and nodded once shortly. He pressed a small plant to the back of the freak's arm. Jaret immediately started to writhe in pain, involuntarily crying out.

"It pains me to have to do this. This is for the good of the people of Walkton. For the people of the world."

There were shouts of encouragement from the crowd, causing me to grin. I was finally getting through to them.

"I'm doing this for you. Eventually, there will be another incident. It isn't a matter of 'if,' it's a matter of 'when,' and 'how bad.' There will be more deaths caused by these freaks of nature. Sometimes, you have to make sacrifices to better the world."

dot

I grabbed Nemvar's wrist and started to lead him through the crowd. The bright colours of the crowd blurred my vision and made it hard for me to stay oriented, but I managed to get halfway to the stage before I lost Nemvar's arm. I turned my head, looking at him.

"Nemvar, we have to help, we have to do something," I pleaded, reaching for his hand again.

"But not that. It won't help if we try to distract him, but it will work if we get the other ones free, and then they can help us help them, and then everything will be okay. Zaupa always says that it's better to do things as a team and do them right than to try to do things on your own and do them wrong. Teamwork is better than independence sometimes, and I know that this is one of those times that she meant," he explained.

"You're right. What should we do?" I asked.

"I don't know that part, I just know that right now, teamwork is the answer, but I don't know what teamwork, or how teamwork is going to work this time. One time, we were-" I grabbed his wrist and continued to push towards the stage, cutting off his story.

I knew how we could help.

We pushed past the front row of people, and I saw where the side of the stage was, the side that would lead to behind the shifters. I also saw that it was being blocked by multiple guards.

"They didn't kill all of us."

With that single line from Alison, my plan was set into motion. A few seconds later, the guards who were blocking off that side of the stage ran to grab Alison before she could do anything else. As soon as they were gone, I darted behind the stage, leading Nemvar behind me. I heard Charles continue speaking on the stage. We would have to do something, soon. I saw that there were only three guards who were standing behind the stage, all of them too transfixed with what Charles was saying to notice Nemvar and I.

chapter twenty-three

jaret

I felt the wolfsbane searing into my skin as it was unexpectedly pushed against my arm, and I let out in involuntary whimper of pain, the sound eerily close to the whine of a dog. I let out a sigh of relief as the guard removed the herb from my arm. I could hear a few noises of concern from some of the other shifters at the other side of the stage.

"We've given them many opportunities to leave before. We've given them chances to go, to leave us to live in peace and go forge their own path," Charles stated, raising two fingers.

My breath caught in my throat as the scorching pain of the wolfsbane burned through my upper arm again. I heard Charlie talking, but the pain was muffling his words. I gasped loudly for breath as the wolfsbane left my arm, leaving the skin stinging and numb.

"Stop it!" I heard a cry from my left. I turned my head and saw a young shifter with tears in her eyes. The crowd grew silent in terrified anticipation. Charles fixed his gaze towards the girl. "Stop hurting him," she said softly, "he didn't do anything wrong."

One of the guards behind her grabbed the girl by the arm, pulling her towards Charlie. A few of the shifters in the group made feeble attempts to prevent the guard from dragging her away, but to little avail as our hands were still tied behind our backs and our ankles were shackled together.

"What did you say?" he asked, nearly snarling at the child.

Her face contorted with fear, but soon she wore a mask of bravery and defiance. "I said he didn't do anything wrong. And you lied. You didn't tell us to leave before. If you did, my mom and my dad and my brother and me would have moved away."

"But that's the problem now, isn't it? They would have just moved to another town, a smaller, more defenseless town where its citizens would be less able to protect themselves. That's why we're here today," Charles stated, turning towards the crowd of people. I could hear distinct murmurs of confusion from them in response. "To rid the world of the evil that it cannot protect itself against."

He turned to the guards and nodded once, raising his hand to his side. The guards all immediately raised their guns, training them onto us. There were few calls of alarm from the shifters and a small uproar of either anger or excitement from the crowd. As I looked forwards, I saw one of the guns trained directly on me; another directly on Tala; another on Jack and another on the girl. Charles motioned for the four of us to be brought forwards, and the guards quickly and roughly dragged us towards him.

"If I were to only be doing this for myself, why would my son be here? Why wouldn't he be at home with his brother and sister, safe? Because he, too, will become a danger to you all one day. Maybe not right now, but soon."

Once again, the tears started streaming down Jack's cheeks, his face reddening.

"You are a monster!" a familiar, and unexpectedly outraged call came from the nearly dead silent crowd. Everybody on the stage turned to try and see who it had been who shouted, but no obvious culprit was seen.

"Me, the one trying to protect you, or them, the ones who are trying to hurt you?" Charles asked rhetorically.

"You might be trying to protect us, but this is not how you do it. You do not kill dozens of people who may or may not be a threat to potentially one person in their lifetime," the person called back. This time, it was clear to see who had said it.

Quivlie.

alison

When Quivlie spoke in the crowd, Jaret's eyes met mine and they widened in concern.

"They will hurt somebody. Not potentially, eventually. You're the Drurida that was travelling with my brother and sister-in-law, aren't you?" he questioned.

Quivlie adjusted her posture, her skin lightening as she stood taller. "I am. Your brother would never hurt anybody without having good reason to, and if your son is raised properly, like Jaret was, then neither will he."

Charles shook his head. "He will. It's in their instincts to protect themselves against others, at all costs. How they were raised doesn't matter. What does matter is instinct, and theirs is more animalistic than ours. They won't hesitate to hurt one of us if it meant saving one of them."

"That's exactly what you're doing. Hurting one of them to save one of us. Except it's not one of them, it's dozens. And it's not one of us, it's potentially one out of the twenty-thousand people who live in Walkton," I spat in anger. "That's such a low percent of the population that's at risk for such a huge percent that you're willing to kill."

"But if you eliminate the risk, you eliminate the potential of death. With them, you can't tell if it'll just be one. Or if it will be two, or ten, or seventy," he responded. "That's why they have to die."

Tala turned to face him, her face bloodied and swollen from the force that they inevitably used to get her here. "We could say the same about you. You're willing to kill not only elders and children, willing to rip families apart for the sake of a nonexistent risk, but you're willing to kill your own son," she said weakly. "If we were to eliminate you, we would be eliminating the risks of such a large number of us dying. You don't even know that your machine barely works. There are more than a thousand of us in Walkton alone, but there clearly aren't more than a hundred of us here," Tala stated.

A sickening smile split itself over my brother-in-law's face. "This is only today's cull. We still have more than a week's worth of shifters to eliminate being contained elsewhere," he answered, and Tala's face paled. "One thousand two hundred and sixty-four."

There were mutters of confusion and concern from the crowd. That was more than five percent of the population of the city that was about to be executed. I had to do something, now.

After the seeming eternity of the past few moment's events, the next few were a blur. I straightened and shoved the guy behind me away from me. The guard stumbled back in shock as the rest of the guards immediately rushed to grab me.

Chaos erupted on the stage as Tala stood, having untied the rope around her ankles. She ran and shoved one of the guards away from me, and I instantly jumped to grab my bow back from the guard who had taken it from me moments before. My fingers clenched around the familiar wood, and as I raised the loaded bow to aim directly towards Charles, the entire population of the town centre became silent.

"Well done ladies," Charles said, putting his hands together in a slow, exaggerated clap. I frowned slightly in confusion and quickly glanced around the stage. Most of the guards had their guns trained directly on me and Tala, only a few on the other shifters. Quivlie and Haishin were slowly making their way to the front of the crowd and towards the side of the stage, towards the stairs. They were barely noticeable in the sea of people watching us in fear.

Tala, noticing that none of the guards were making a move to stop me, moved towards Charles. As she walked in front of me, I could see that her wrists were raw and bleeding from where the wolfsbane had seared into her skin and the rope had started peeling away her flesh.

"When you hired me, and you told me to report any Independent Androids to you, I asked why. You said that if you had two, then you could make the world a better place. A world without diversity isn't a world worth living in. People are different for a reason, and not always a malicious one," she stated, stopping about two feet in front of Charles.

Click.

BANG!

I jumped as the noise of the bullet being fired shot through the air, nearly deafening me as Tala dropped to the ground, blood seeping out of the bullet wound in her chest. Bile rose in my throat as I instinctively shot the arrow, dropping to my knees. The world around me grew numb as I heard the muffled sounds of Charles shouting. I saw him stumble back, the arrow protruding from his shoulder as he dropped the handgun onto the stage.

`quivlie`

As soon as Tala fell, Haishin grabbed my hand and pulled me to him.

"I love you, Quivlie," he whispered, pressing a kiss onto my forehead. He stepped away from me and immediately ran to grab Alison's arm.

Before he could do anything to help her, another gunshot rang through the town centre. I felt everything inside me shatter as he collapsed onto the ground. All I could see at that moment in time was the blood staining his shirt as it seeped out of the newly carved hole in his torso. Everything inside me went numb. Everything except for the heartbreak spearing itself through my chest.

Cries of surprise snapped me back to reality, only for long enough to see the small pack of shifters on the stage starting to disable the guards. I ran towards Haishin, dropping to my knees beside him.

I barely felt the sting in my knees as I rolled him onto his back to face me. I gasped and tears immediately started falling down my cheeks as I held his head in my lap. His eyes blinked open as he smiled weakly at me, a trickle of blood streamed down his temple as people raced around us, frantic to either get away from the stage or help the people on it.

"It was enough of a distraction for the shifters to be able to catch them off-guard. I'm sorry, Quivlie. I had to do something, I couldn't just let them die," he said weakly, coughing.

I shook my head and ran my hand through his hair. "We could have figured out some other way to distract them, Haishin, you did not have to do this," I croaked.

He smiled, his skin brightening. "It was faster. Don't be sad, Quivlie. You need to stay happy. If not for yourself, for me. For Paulto," he said, wheezing slightly as a trickle of blood streaming down his lip. "I love you," he said with a shaky breath.

"I love you too," I said, another tear snaking itself down my cheek. His eyes closed, a small smile still present on his lips. His chest rose and fell in an unsteady breath for the last time.

dot

"You might be trying to protect us, but this is not how you do it. You cannot kill dozens of people who may or may not be a threat to possibly one person in their lifetime," Quivlie stated.

The three guards who were standing behind the stage were completely distracted by the conversation happening between their boss and multiple concerned citizens of Walkton.

"Maybe she's right, you know?" one of the guards mumbled to another.

The second scowled and shook his head. "No, she isn't. They're freaks. Never belonged here," he shot back in agitation.

The younger guard lowered his head ashamedly to the ground. I tapped Nemvar on the arm and pointed to the guard furthest from us. He darted towards the guard, grabbing his wrists and pinning him to the ground, sweeping him off his feet in one swift movement. The other two guards gave cries of surprise, but before they could do anything to help him, I quickly ran and grabbed the older of the two guards, the one whose view of the shifters was the same as Charles', and smoothly brought her to the ground, knocking her head against the dirt.

When I looked back to the younger guard, I saw in indifference that his gun was aimed directly towards me.

"Do you want to do the right thing and help us save them, or tell someone of more importance and have them all die?" I asked, keeping my point concise.

He lowered his gun hesitantly, putting his gun back in its holster. Nemvar and I quickly went to the edge of the stage, where the shifters were facing away from us, towards the crowd of people.

"The three of us are trying to help you, do not move quickly and do not be alarmed," I said softly to one of the shifters who was closest to the edge. "Do not let the wolfsbane touch their skin, it will burn them." I said to the others.

They both nodded in understanding. Nemvar, the guard and I all quickly started to untie the shifters hands, careful not to brush their skin with the wolfsbane that would sear their already raw and bloodied arms.

I heard Tala speaking from the other side of the stage, her familiar voice being projected by the microphone that stood a few feet away from her. I hurried through untying more of the shifters. The back row of people had started discretely untying the hands of the people in front of them.

"A world without diversity isn't a world worth living in. People are different for a reason, and not always a malicious one," Tala said.

A loud gunshot blast through the centre of the town, and with a start, I saw Tala drop to the ground. Alison cried out in despair and she shot the arrow that was loaded in her bow, the sharp point sinking into Charles' shoulder, mere inches away from the spot that would have granted him instant death. He stumbled backwards, and seconds later, *BANG*! There was another gunshot. Almost immediately, some of the shifters who we had freed shifted into their animalistic forms. That was the point where all chaos had officially erupted.

chapter twenty-four

jaret

I ducked my head instinctively as the second gunshot rang through the air. My eyes found Quivlie in the crowd again, dropping to her knees on the ground beside the Drurida man who had just fell. Charlie regained his composure, standing as he pulled the arrow from his shoulder. A Felid leapt towards Charles, grabbing his arm in her mouth and dragging him towards the ground. One of the guards shot at the Felid and she dropped Charles' arm, hissing in pain as the bullet grazed her side.

Testing the ropes on my wrists, I tried to pull my hands apart, but I slumped in defeat as the scorching pain of the wolfsbane shot through my wrists. I felt nimble hands behind me working to untie me. With a quick glance over my shoulder, I saw Dot skillfully unraveling the rope from around me. The rope dropped to the stage below me, and they helped me to my feet. I instantly ran to Jack and helped one of the guards finish untying the ropes around his wrists. I lifted him into my arms as he sobbed against my shoulder, and I ran towards the back of the stage, dodging around the people around me. A teenage girl ran towards me and stopped just before running into me.

"Do you need help? I know where I can take him until it's safe," she offered.

I nodded and handed Jack to her. As she lifted him into her arms, he wrapped his arms around her tightly and she immediately took off running in the opposite direction, away from the stage and the chaos. I turned back towards the stage and sprinted towards where I knew Alison would be. I saw her by one of the sides of the stage, away from most people but still with a good range for her bow. She was picking off the guards and whoever was trying to fight against the shifters.

Charlie.

My eyes briefly met Alison's before we both looked frantically around the stage. With a start, I saw a small group of guards running towards the town hall, creating a human shield around my brother. Both she and I instantly ran towards the building, slipping through the doors moments after Charlie and the guards. Hearing a call of anger in the distance, she and I both shared a glance before racing down the hall, towards the noise.

For the first time in all the mayhem, I got a good look at my friend. Her face was smeared with dirt and blood. Don't ask me where the dirt came from, I wouldn't know. Her ponytail had all but untied itself and her hair tie was on the verge of falling out of her hair. Blue eyes teary and glazed, strands of her hair dangling every which way in her face, she looked oddly calm. The Alison I knew would be visibly pissed off right now, not calm.

Somehow, calm Alison was a lot scarier than angry Alison.

alison

Numb. Everything was numb. Tala was gone. It was my fault. I couldn't save her. If I hadn't done that, then she would still be alive. She would still be alive. Now I couldn't do anything to help her. She was gone.

"Alison," Jaret said, snapping me out of my thoughts. I turned my head towards him, glaring. He looked almost relieved at my facial expression. "Up there," he said, pointing up a flight of stairs.

I nodded once and we softly started up the stairs. The door behind us creaked open, and my heart jumped in my chest as I whirled around, instinctively raising my bow. Quivlie and Dot stepped through the open doors, a familiarly numb expression on the Drurida's features, her skin more remarkably dull than I had ever remembered it being.

They were both gone. Tala, and now Haishin. All of them were gone. Amelia, mom, dad, Tala, Haishin. They were all gone. And they were never coming back. It was my fault. I could never do anything to help them. I never knew how. Amelia, mom and dad, I wasn't able to protect them, or myself. Tala died because of something that I did. If I'd never done that, she never would have died. Haishin was trying to help me. He was trying to save me, and he got shot. He has a family. A son. Now his son doesn't have a father. And it's my fault.

I started walking with the three of them as we started up the stairs, towards where we assumed Charles was. The four of us walked, together as we had for the past few weeks.

Blood smeared across our faces as we walked towards impending doom. We didn't have a plan. If we did, it wasn't a very good one, seeing as that not everybody knew the plan.

Numb for the most part, fearful and angry for the rest, we walked towards the same enemy that we had unknowingly been walking towards since the day of the earthquake.

quivlie

The four of us started walking quietly up the stairs, careful not to allow our feet to make any noise against the marble floor.

I could feel the heaviness bearing down on me from inside, but I pushed it away. For them. I could not let them to die and not do anything to help them. If I was not able to save Haishin, then I will try my hardest to help them.

Jaret ducked through a door, motioning for the three of us to wait for him, so we stopped walking. A moment later, he stepped out of the door again, in his Canid form in place of his human. The four of us continued down the hall.

His ears perked up and he froze. Jaret turned his head and started down a different hallway than the one we were walking down. Alison shot a glance of confusion towards Dot, but she shrugged. None of us knew where he was leading us.

A sudden loud series of gunshots rang through the empty building, the booming noise echoing through the vacant halls. Jaret immediately broke into a sprint, running towards the noise, and the three of us ran after him after a moment of confusion. Alison pushed open a heavy looking door as Jaret pawed frantically at the wood. The five guards that Charles had come in with were all laying in awkward positions on the ground, blood seeping from bullet-wounds in their bodies, primarily their chests and heads; the gun that shot them clutched in Charles' right hand. A sickening grin split itself over his lips as the four of us entered.

"It took you long enough," he said. Jaret growled, the rumbling coming from deep within his chest. "Why don't you shift back, freak?" he spat towards his younger brother, tossing one of the guards' capes towards him. The Cainan snarled at the suggestion. He knew he would be more vulnerable in his human form.

"What the hell is your problem? How can you possibly believe that your own people, your own family, would pose such a huge threat to the rest of us?" Alison asked angrily, stepping forward.

Charles immediately raised his gun and pointed it directly at Alison. "They're not my people. They're not my family," he answered coolly. "I believe it because it's true," he said, taking a step away from Alison, putting more distance between them. I saw Dot frown slightly out of the corner of my eye. I turned to face her.

"It was not the fault of the shapeshifters, but of the merpeople who were possessing them," she said.

The room grew silent.

"What do you mean?" Alison asked slowly, turning towards the Android.

"I mean that when the village was attacked by the rogue shifters as you call them, it wasn't the fault of the shifters. One of them got possessed by a mermaid, and the mermaid used the shifter to lure the others towards the lake, where the other merpeople would drag the shifters in and possess them, using them to both possess more shifters and then ultimately attack the village," she explained.

The four of us stared blankly at her in shock.

"And how would you know this?" Charles asked, his voice wavering. Jaret's eyes were open wide in an expression of confusion and devastation.

"Nemvar told me when we were in your research facility," she stated. Her eyes grew wide and she froze as she realized what she had just said.

"My research facility. You're one of the Independent Androids, that's where the metal plate on the back of your head came from," he said, stepping towards Dot, his eyes flashing. "You're not supposed to be here. Your kind is dangerous to ours," he said, gesturing vaguely around the room.

She frowned in confusion and she stepped backwards. "My kind has done less harm in the entirety of our existence than you have in the past twenty-four hours."

Charles shook his head. "But you have the potential. Don't you realize? You have the potential to kill every one of us right here, right now. And the only reason you don't is because you're too good, because you care?" he spat, raising his gun towards Dot. A flash of movement outside of the window behind him caught my eye. Nemvar. He had climbed up the side of the building and was now watching us from the window.

dot

"Charles raised the gun towards me. "Robots don't have the capacity to care."

"Which is why I did everything I could to protect your brother, Alison and Quivlie. That's why after your brother was dragged into the pond, I jumped in to save him, knowing fully that I would be risking my life. That's why I helped them escape from your facility. That's why I came here with them today to try and save Jaret and the other shifters from you. Because I didn't care about them," I said, the sarcasm in my voice a clear contrast to how it was usually. "If I didn't care, why would I have done any of that? Why wouldn't I have left them and went on my own, where it surely would be easier to hide than if I were with three others?"

His eyes narrowed and the sound of the bullet being fired barely registered in my mind before I stumbled backwards, feeling my body crumple to the ground as everything went black.

chapter twenty-five

jaret

Dot fell to the ground, their screen blank, and I gave a yelp of surprise as the window beside me shattered, broken glass falling to the carpeted floor as Nemvar catapulted himself through the window, tackling Charlie to the ground.

Quivlie spun around and raced to Dot's side, catching them before the back of their head smacked against the floor. Nemvar stood, dragging Charlie to his feet and shoving him towards the regal desk at the other end of the office.

"You took me away from my family. You took me away from Zaupa and Crackers, and it's your fault that I'm not there right now. I didn't hurt anybody, I barely tried to escape because I knew you would hurt them, but you did anyways, you hurt Zaupa and you hurt Crackers trying to get me to obey you when that was already what I was doing. You hurt them, and it's your fault that I can't see them anymore," he said softly.

Charles grinned as he pushed himself to his feet. "You would have hurt us. We were trying to prevent that from happening," he said, wiping a trail of blood that was streaming from the side of his mouth off of his chin.

Nemvar shook his head softly, lowering his face until his chin almost touched his chest. I didn't know what to do. I didn't know how I could protect the robot but not hurt my brother. After all he did to hurt us, I still didn't want to hurt him.

"The thought of hurting you wouldn't have even passed my mind if you hadn't hurt my family," he responded, his voice barely audible. I doubt that I would have heard it had I been in my human form.

"What was that, freak?" Charlie asked, confirming my suspicion that Nemvar was too quiet for the others to hear him.

"I said that I wouldn't want to hurt you if you hadn't hurt my family. I won't hurt you, because that would just be proving the point that you're trying to make. That we're dangerous," Nemvar said, louder this time.

Charles scoffed and rolled his eyes. He paused for a second before the sickly grin returned to his lips.

"But if I make it look like you did, then my point is proven," he stated.

The five of us froze in confusion.

I involuntarily cocked my head to the side.

With a sudden lurch, Charlie jumped to his feet and ran towards the largest window in the room. Both Nemvar and I immediately leapt forwards to grab him, but unfortunately, at the same time. He and I collided as we jumped to stop Charles, but instead, the three of us went crashing through the large window, down towards the cobblestone street below.

alison

As the three of them crashed through the window behind the desk, Quivlie and I stared in shock at the scene ahead of us. I ran to the window and looked downwards. Jaret was struggling to his feet, Nemvar had already recovered, and

Charles lay motionless on the ground on top of the shattered glass. People who were standing around came to investigate the scene.

What the hell is Charles' problem?

Quivlie's eyes met mine.

"Go. I will stay with her," she said. I stopped myself before I stepped through the door. The Android's screen flickered slightly and I breathed a sigh of relief.

I ran through the door and down the stairs, hurrying to get there before a mass of judgmental beings did, wanting to burn Jaret and Nemvar at the stake for "hurting" their "beloved leader" or whatever bullshit they would say. I shoved the heavy doors open and ran towards the side of the building that they jumped out of.

"What happened?" I heard somebody shout as they ran towards the shattered window. As I ran, my hair blew into my face, alerting me to the fact that my ponytail had come undone. I didn't have time to fix it now.

"He was going to jump and we tried to stop him," I heard Nemvar reply.

"Bullshit, why would he have jumped?" somebody else said. I realized how hard it would be to get Jaret and Nemvar out of this situation.

"Um, well..." Nemvar started to answer. I rounded the corner just as Jaret started to speak. He had shifted back into his human form.

"He wanted to prove his point that we were dangerous," he explained. "I'm his brother, I wouldn't have tried to hurt him," he continued, dropping to his knees beside his brother, rolling Charles onto his back, the movement emitting a sickening snap and crunch as presumably one of his bones shattered. Jaret cursed under his breath and put his face above Charles' mouth to see if he was breathing.

He sat back on his heels. "Where are the doctors in the area? We need to get him there fast. He's breathing, but not steadily," Jaret asked, panic in his voice as he looked around the small crowd gathering around them.

"We can't move him. Didn't you hear something break?" I said, irritation edging into my voice. "None of us know how to move him properly, and doing so will just hurt him more, so if you're that intent on keeping him safe, then you can't move him, you have to go get help and bring them back here."

Jaret's eyes met mine. "I can get a doctor," one of the people in the crowd said, immediately starting to run towards the buildings.

"How do we know that you aren't just saying this to save yourselves?" one of the people asked.

"They aren't, I was there. He went to jump because he knew that they would try to save him. He was trying to make it look like they pushed him, they were just trying to help," I piped up from my place in the crowd.

The person who had ran off moments before was running back towards us, bringing a middle aged woman towards us, a pair of nurses leading a large horse-like animal towing a hospital carriage behind it.

"Get out of the way, stop crowding him!" the doctor exclaimed, shooing us away from him. The small crowd of people parted for the nurses and the doctor, who got him onto a stretcher and into the back of the hospital carriage. Jaret, Nemvar and I stood, watching as the group of people dispersed from around us.

"You three are coming with us," one of the nurses ordered, gesturing to the three of us. Jaret gave a small nod, lowering his head to his chest. The centre of the town was now all but empty, multiple people laying on the ground, either unconscious or worse, guards and civilians alike. In the distance, I saw the stage, the setting sun casting the dark shadow of a single body into the non-existent crowd.

"I need to go get our friends. They deserve to know where we're going," I replied, starting back towards the building. One of the two nurses followed after me; making sure that I wasn't just ditching them, I assumed. I retraced my path down the marble stairs and hallways, heading to where the two of them were inevitably waiting. I pushed open the door to the office.

Quivlie and Dot were both still sitting on the floor, despite the fact that the Android was functioning again. "Jaret and Nemvar are okay. The want us to go with Charles to the hospital, they want to question us or something," I told them. The two of them both looked up upon hearing my voice, and they followed the nurse and I out of the room and to the hospital.

quivlie

The four of us were waiting in the hallway of the hospital, waiting for them to finish questioning Alison. She was the last one of us to be interrogated. Checking to ensure that we all had the same story.

I became anxious as I looked around the narrow hallway. I had never loved being indoors.

Paulto and Ella were probably wondering why we weren't back by now. I was doubtful that they knew that it would be just me coming home. As I thought about Haishin, the heavy weight of sadness returned to my chest.

"Jaret?" the nurse called into the hallway, looking through the door. His head snapped up and he looked hopefully at the nurse. "He's stable, but there's severe trauma to his central nervous system. He may not be able to walk again," she said softly. Jaret nodded and she went back into the room. He gave a sigh of relief and sat back in his chair. Suddenly, he abruptly sat upright again.

"Jack," he muttered. "I don't know where that girl took him."

I heard footsteps coming down the hall, and Alison and one of the city guards came towards us. The guard gestured for us to stand.

"You can go. Your stories check out," he grumbled, "however, you two," he said, gesturing to Dot and Nemvar, "have to come with me."

I frowned and my skin darkened. "They helped save numerous people, you can not say that they are still seen as dangerous. It was because of them that the shifters escaped," I said angrily, standing.

"I'm not on Mr. Hofferson's side with this, but that doesn't matter. The Androids are still illegal and seen as dangerous by the authority," he stated firmly. "Now, I wasn't ordered to destroy them, I was ordered to take them to the chief officer so he can decide from thereon what to do. If they can prove that they aren't dangerous, then they'll be legalized. If not, then they're destroyed," he explained. "Come with me."

"We will be fine. We can convince them that we aren't a threat," Dot said, turning to me. She and Nemvar followed the guard down the hall. Jaret, Alison and I stood, going down the hall and out of the hospital.

"What did he mean by he 'wasn't with Charlie?'" Jaret asked. "If he's one of the guards, then why would he have been helping him in the first place?"

"He was one of the guards, but one that the city hired. Charles' guards are his personal guards. The city guards were fighting with us, Charles' against us."

"So, what should we do now?" Alison asked. "You found your brother, you got back to your family, Dot's seeing about getting the Androids legalized. Not under the circumstances that we would have preferred, but we're all here. Just like we wanted to be from the start."

We pushed through the doors of the hospital, walking into the streets.

"Haishin and Tala deserve a proper burial. They died trying to protect the ones who could not protect themselves," I said, my voice shaking. The other two nodded in agreement, although I could see the hurt and sadness that was in both of their eyes. I know that they would both partially blame themselves for Tala and Haishin's deaths. Alison couldn't protect Tala, and neither could Jaret. But nobody could have at that point. It was her own reckless behaviour that put her in that situation.

"What are the customs for a Cainan burial ceremony?" I asked, turning to Jaret.

A weak smile was his initial response. "In the forest, buried under some kind of fruit tree by a river alongside their favourite weapon."

"I know a place by the Drurida community if that would be suitable," I offered, and Jaret nodded.

"Why a fruit tree by a river?" Alison questioned, turning towards him, a look of confusion on her face.

"Because that's usually where there's a larger quantity of game animals grazing. It's said that it helps you become part of the forest again, because your body will give the tree nutrients and will help the tree grow more fruit. Whichever animal first eats a piece of fruit from the tree after you helped it grow, that's the next animal you'll come back as," he explained. Alison nodded slowly in confusion. She did not understand why the forest was such an important part of the cultures of a lot of the other races.

dot

Nemvar and I were led through the streets of Walkton, our hands handcuffed behind our backs, where it was clear how much damage the past few hours had caused.

An abundance of people were trying to help others who were hurt were sitting through the streets; others were arguing about which side of the argument about the shifters was right. The majority seemed to be on the shifters' side.

The two of us were led through the town centre, towards city hall. Many people were scattered around the courtyard, helping hurt people to medical facilities and trying to revive unconscious people. Many of them would never wake up. A few moments later, Nemvar and I stood in front of the head law enforcement officer.

"So, why shouldn't you be destroyed? If you give me a good enough reason to legalize Independent Androids, then I will," she said matter-of-factly, leaning back in her chair. I glanced nervously to Nemvar.

"Neither of us have ever intentionally hurt anybody without a good reason. The only person who I've ever hurt was a mermaid who was trying to possess my friend, and two guards who were trying to kill hundreds of people," I said. "If it weren't for us, none of the shifters would have been able to escape. Nobody else would have tried to save them, so if it weren't for us, they would all be dead by now."

The chief nodded, but the expression on her face remained blank.

"I just want to go home to see my partner and our dog, I don't want to hurt anybody or take over the world. I just want to go home and keep the crows away from our garden," Nemvar said softly.

chapter twenty-six

jaret

Quivlie stood at her mate's side, looking downwards as his blood dried onto the pavement below, creating a snaking pattern through the cracks in the dark gray rocks.

Some of the guards around the town centre were on clean-up duty, and were bringing the lifeless bodies to the morgue. Others were being taken by families to honour their cultures' traditions more accurately.

"How many are there?" I asked one of the city guards who was wheeling away a corpse on a stretcher.

"So far: twelve humans, three Terins, a Xeran, a Drurida, nineteen shifters," he replied.

My stomach turned. Thirty-six people, and more than half of which were shifters. Charlie still got what he wanted. Less shifters. I looked around the town centre as Alison went to the stage to get Tala's body.

With a breath of relief, I saw the girl starting towards me, a small pack of four children following her anxiously, Jack amongst them. As soon as he saw me, he recognized and ran towards me. I lifted him into my arms and wrapped him in a hug.

"I told you he would be okay," the girl said proudly.

"Thank you for keeping him safe for me," I replied. She gave a small smile and nod in response before turning and starting towards the residential area of town, the small chain of children following behind her like ducklings following their mother. Jack looked up at me.

"Where's Daddy?" he asked, his voice barely audible even in the near dead silence of the town centre. I swallowed the lump of regret that was forming in my throat.

"He isn't feeling very good right now, so he's going to be gone for a while. We can go home and see Lily and Christopher soon though, okay?" I explained.

When we were in the stables, he had told me about his two siblings and life at their home. After Amelia had died, Charles was rarely home, because he was always working. They always spent their time with Merida, their nanny. She became their new motherly figure; their main parental figure they had for most of their childhood. She was most likely still at the mansion with Lily and Christopher.

I turned back to look towards the others. Alison was helping Quivlie lift Haishin onto the cot beside Tala. We would have to register for their deaths at city hall, and their funerals would take place as soon as possible.

Jack looked to me in confusion. "Why are they sleeping?" he asked me innocently.

I shook my head slightly. "They aren't sleeping, Jack. Well, in a way, they are, but they aren't going to wake up again."

"Like Mommy?" he questioned after a moment of silence.

My breath caught in my throat. "Yeah, like Mommy."

alison

After we registered both Haishin and Tala's deaths, Jaret and I brought Jack back to the mansion. Merida had been reluctant to trust us, but she agreed to watching the children until we returned two days later for an explanation. After that, we went to and find Dot and Nemvar, and see how they were making out with the legalization of Independent Androids. Quivlie was going back to her house to talk to Ella and Paulto about Haishin's passing and to start the cremation.

"You shouldn't blame yourself. I know you well enough to know that you are blaming yourself. It isn't your fault. It's Charlie's. He was the one who killed her," Jaret said.

I frowned slightly. "I couldn't help her. I was the one who put her in danger."

"It isn't your fault, Alison. You didn't put her in danger. She put herself in danger by talking to him like that. It's her fault and Charles' fault she died. If he hadn't shot her, she would be alive. If she hadn't talked to him like that, he wouldn't have shot her. Nowhere in there could you have prevented it."

"If I had shot him first she wouldn't have died," I stated, not filtering what I was thinking.

"But then you would have killed someone," he answered.

"And saved the lives of thirty-six people," I spat. He froze in his steps. "Look, I'm sorry that your brother's the bad guy in the situation," I started, softening my voice. "I really am, and that doesn't at all make you the bad guy. I also don't think it makes me the bad guy when I say that maybe it would have been better if one person died and thirty-six people lived, but correct me if I'm wrong," I added, my voice involuntarily raising slightly in anger as I talked.

He shook his head and continued walking after me. "I'm not meaning to imply you're the bad guy, not at all."

I rolled my eyes and pushed open the doors to city hall. The door nearly shut on him as it fell closed behind me as I didn't bother to catch it.

"Then what are you implying?" I questioned, walking brisker as I headed towards the law enforcement officer's office.

"I'm trying to say that nobody had to die in the situation, and it's super shitty that people did die," he called.

A few of the people in the hall turned towards him, looks of displeasure on their faces at his choice of words.

"Sorry," he mumbled, rushing to catch up with me.

As soon as Charlie had left and the guards stopped fighting back against the civilians who were trying to help the shifters, the town had slowly started to go back to normal. Well, not normal, per say. Normal-er. Most of the civilians had returned home, but the people who worked in the hospitals, as well as many others, had returned to work, including the members of the city counsel.

I heard a small group of people walking towards us from down the hall, the metallic footsteps of an Android a clear contrast to the heavier human's footsteps. Dot and Nemvar were being brought somewhere, towards us.

"The news will be broadcast as soon as it's possible, probably in the morning at eight o'clock," a voice stated.

I frowned slightly in concern. This could go either way. Either the news that Independent Androids were now legalized, or the news that two had been found and would soon be destroyed. Jaret cast an uncertain glance towards me.

The group of five guards came around the corner, accompanying the two Androids, unrestrained. That was a good sign. Dot's face brightened as she saw Jaret and I. She smiled and gave a small nod as the seven of them went into another room, off the side of the hallway. I smiled lightly in relief. After all of the bad that had come out of the past few hours, something good had happened.

"So they'll be fine? Nemvar can go back to his family and not have to worry about the government trying to destroy him or whatever?" Jaret questioned, the ghost of a smile passing over his lips, as if he didn't want to allow himself to smile in case he had misunderstood.

"As far as I understand, yeah, they're going to announce it in the morning," I answered.

Not trying to restrain his smile any longer, Jaret was nearly bouncing in happiness.

`quivlie`

Clutching his death receipt in my hand, I started up the small flight of stairs to the shop. The shop that my parents had left us when they retired. The shop where we had spent our lives together, growing up and then after we were bonded. The shop where we had done everything together.

My chest heavy and aching, I pushed the wooden door open, the silver service bell ringing softly as it fell shut.

Two pairs of footsteps came shortly after, coming from upstairs and starting towards the stairs that were behind the counter of the shop, near the back of the room. Ella was helping Paulto clamber down the stairs as he thought he raced to meet both of his parents at the door. As Ella lifted her head to look towards the door, her expression turned to one of concern. Paulto jumped off of the last step and onto the floor, and, letting go of Ella's hands, he ran to me. He wrapped his arms around my legs in a hug, and I lifted him into my arms.

His eyes were bright and he looked behind me, out the window on the door to see if his dad was waiting outside. He leaned back slightly and looked at me, clearly perplexed.

"Where did Daddy go?" he demanded, his skin darkening slightly in confusion.

The ache in my chest intensified. I shook my head slightly, my eyes meeting Ella's behind him. She gave a feeble nod of understanding, tottering slowly to her chair, despair clear on her features.

"When's he coming back?" Paulto asked after another moment.

"No, he will not be coming back, Paulto," that was all I managed to say before my throat constricted, threatening me with tears.

"Why, though? Where is he?" he asked, his innocent eyes wide in bewilderment.

"He went to go help Mielikki in the forest," I replied softly. That was the thing that we always told Drurida children. It was easier than trying to explain why they would never see their parent or friend again. After a second of silence, I realized that because he had not grown up in a Drurida community, he may not know what I was trying to say to him.

"Like Daddy's daddy did?" he asked.

I nodded. His eyes immediately welled with tears. He had never met Haishin's father, but Haishin had probably told him the tales of what his father had done in his days before he passed away when Haishin was six. He laid his head on my shoulder.

"Why did he go to help her? We want him, you have to tell her to get him back," he said, his slightly demanding tone turning to pleading as he started to cry softly.

"It was his time to help her, Paulto, you have to try to understand that," Ella said, wiping at her eyes with her sleeve. She could see that I was struggling not to cry, trying to be strong for my son. "He cannot come back, I'm afraid; Mielikki needs him now. We had our time with him, and now it's her time."

Paulto gave a small nod, but his tears did not cease, and from that moment, mine started to fall for the first time since I was a child.

dot

After the two of us had talked to more people about what would be done tomorrow, Nemvar and I were allowed to leave. The two of us walked into the hall, Jaret and Alison instantly intercepting us. Jaret pulled both of us into a tight hug, bouncing slightly on his heels. A pair of guards who were in the room with us came into the hallway and walked over to Nemvar and I.

"Ms. Jensen told me that, for the time being, we should accompany you to ensure your safety," one of the guards said, looking at me over Jaret's shoulder. "I'm Ryan Wesley," he introduced himself, and then, "Rita Foster," he added, gesturing to the girl. I pulled away from Jaret and offered my hand to shake his first, and then hers. With a nervous glance towards Jaret and Alison, Ryan shook my hand and then Nemvar's, Rita offering a less concerned expression.

"As you most likely already know, my name is Dot and the other Android's name is Nemvar," I explained, smiling.

They both nodded, almost simultaneously. "Yes. Miss, may I ask where I will be accompanying you until tomorrow?" Ryan questioned.

I glanced back to Jaret and Alison. "Where will we be going?" I asked them.

Alison glanced to Jaret. From the look on his face, I instantly knew where he wanted to go.

"We'll be going to our friend's shop down the road," Alison stated; Rita nodded once. "I'm Alison, by the way. Dog-Boy over there's Jaret. You have a problem with him, you can leave," she said firmly.

Jaret's face immediately reddened and he lowered his head slightly. Ryan gave a small nod, but it was clear, even to me, that he had become slightly uncomfortable in Jaret's presence.

"What shop, may I ask?"

"Our friend's weapon-repair shop. I don't remember what it's called, but I remember where it is," Alison replied, starting towards the exit of the building. "You don't talk much, do you?" she asked Rita over her shoulder. With a quick scan of the two of them, I saw that that probably wasn't the most appropriate thing for Alison to ask.

"She can't talk," Ryan answered. Rita's expression remained blank, as she was clearly used to people talking about the fact that she couldn't talk.

"Why not?" Alison questioned, being rudely blunt like usual. Rita sighed slightly.

"I'm not certain that that's necessary for you to know," Ryan responded firmly. Alison shrugged, but Rita gave Ryan a soft smack on the arm, using a series of hand movements - sign language - to tell him just to tell her and stop being rude. "Fine. She's deaf, but it's not like that has a huge impact on her ability to effectively do her job," he said, earning a glare and another smack on the arm from his partner.

Jaret held the door for the rest of us as we exited the building; it was clear that he was still trying to gain Ryan's approval. Rita nodded her thanks at Jaret's gesture, and the six of us continued walking towards Quivlie's shop. The sign reading HANDEONA WEAPONRY REPAIRS AND TRADE was visible in the distance, swaying slightly as the soft breeze blew through the semi-crowded streets.

Most of the citizens of Walkton had started to continue their days, walking through the streets, readying themselves for the night that laid ahead. It was now clear who the shifting population of Walkton was. The ones who looked defeated and withdrawn; the ones being hustled indoors by concerned citizens; the ones whose eyes were dull, sad and full of fear, not unlike Jaret's.

chapter twenty-seven

jaret

Alison gently pushed open the door to Quivlie's shop, the small bell dinging as the door knocked it forward. I heard a shuffling set of footsteps coming down the stairs. A small elderly lady gave an audible sniff as she hobbled down the stairs, a clear indication that she had been crying.

"I'm terribly sorry, I thought I had turned the sign. I'll have to ask you to come back tomorrow, there's been-" she glanced upwards for the first time, seeing that it was us standing at the door. "Oh, it's you. I'm sorry about that. This is your friend that you were trying to help?" she asked, gesturing vaguely towards me.

"Yes. This is Jaret. Jaret; Ella," Alison introduced softly. Ella gave a soft smile and nodded her head towards me. I returned the gesture. "Ryan and Rita were sent to make sure that nobody tries to hurt the Androids until the announcement of their legalization is made tomorrow," she explained.

As if noticing them for the first time, Ella looked up at the two guards, eyeing them warily.

"Alright. Well, Quivlie and Paulto are upstairs, if you wanted to talk to them for a little while," Ella explained, waving for us to follow her as she started walking back towards the stairs. "It would be best if the two of you," Ella said, looking pointedly towards Ryan and Rita, "stayed here for a few moments."

"Of course, ma'am," Ryan replied. Rita nodded her head solemnly. The four of us followed Ella, the small room becoming crowded by the bodies. We followed Ella up a flight of wooden stairs that were barely visible from the door, presumably towards the living area above the shop that Quivlie had told me about.

"He didn't have to leave, though. Mielikki should have let him stay," a soft voice came from up the stairs.

"He did have to leave, Paulto. It was his time, Mielikki needed him," I heard Quivlie reply.

Ella gave a pitiful glance in our direction.

"But it isn't fair, Mom," the young Drurida whimpered.

"I know it isn't, Paulto. But Mielikki needed help, and if it was his time to help, we should not question Mielikki's decision," Quivlie answered her son.

"Quivlie, dear, your friends are back," Ella called as she teetered up the stairs, motioning for us to follow her into a different room. Quivlie looked up as we entered the room, her skin duller than I had ever seen it, her arms wrapped around the small boy sitting in her lap. She gave a minuscule smile as her eyes met mine, but as her skin didn't flush to a brighter tone, I know that it wasn't genuine.

"Jaret, you're safe. Thank Mielikki," she exclaimed, standing, lifting her child into her arms as she did so. I smiled weakly. Paulto leaned away from Quivlie to look at me.

"Who's he?" he asked, shoving a pointed finger towards me.

"Jaret is my friend. He helped me get home," Quivlie explained.

Paulto yawned.

"Here, Quivlie, I can put Paulto to bed if you wanted to talk to them," Ella stated, extending her arms to take the child from her.

"You should go to sleep, it's late. Goodnight Paulto," Quivlie said to her son, kissing the top of his head. Paulto frowned and shook his head.

"But I'm not tired," he replied.

Quivlie shook her head. "You have to go to bed now, we have to talk about something that you won't be interested in," she answered firmly. Paulto sighed and reluctantly nodded his head. Ella took him from Quivlie and walked out of the room.

"Where would you like to have the funeral?" Alison asked a moment after Ella and Paulto left the room. Quivlie's skin dulled immediately again.

"There is a place near Kai'id where we buried our warriors who died in battle. It would only take a few hours to get there if we rented a hovership," she answered. "Only the warrior's direct family and those who they were in battle with when they died are supposed to attend the funeral."

"Alright. So, that includes you, Dot, Alison, Nemvar, Paulto. Who else?" I questioned. I deliberately left me out, seeing as that I wasn't in battle with him. I had never met him, and he died trying to protect me.

"You, Dot, Nemvar, Alison, Paulto, Ella, his mother and I," she replied, saying 'you' pointedly. I gave a small nod. "I should go and tell his mother. She needs to know."

"Would you like us to accompany you, or would you prefer to go alone?" Dot questioned.

Quivlie smiled without real feeling. "I should go on my own. I can help you get ready for the night, and I can leave after that. I'll be back shortly after."

Alison gave a soft sigh. I looked towards her. Her features were a confusing mix between relief and despair.

"I can find somewhere for you to sleep," Quivlie stated, starting down the stairs towards the shop.

alison

It didn't take long for Quivlie to find somewhere that Jaret and I could sleep and somewhere for Dot and Nemvar to charge themselves. Jaret and I were on the couches in the family room, and the Androids were in the shop downstairs behind the counter, and Rita and Ryan were keeping guard in front of the shop.

"Do you need anything else?" Quivlie asked, handing me a thin blanket.

I shook my head. "This should be fine," I answered, placing the blanket on the longer of the two couches. Jaret was taller than me, but he decided to be 'chivalrous' or whatever bullshit, so I got the longer couch. He said that he could sleep sitting up if the couch wasn't long enough.

"Alright. Jaret?" she inquired.

Jaret shook his head. "No, I'm fine, thank you."

"Okay. I should be on my way in that case. I will see you later. In the morning if not tonight."

As Quivlie left the room, Jaret plopped down on his couch, kicking his shoes off before swinging his legs up.

"What do you think happens after you die?" Jaret asked.

I rolled my eyes, taking my jacket and shoes off and sitting cross-legged on the couch. "I don't think anything happens. You just die."

He pondered this for a moment. "Okay," he said, and paused for a moment. "You can turn off the light if you want to sleep." I stood and flicked the light switch, stumbling back to the couch. "Did you ever date anybody or anything?" he asked.

"Why does it matter?" I snapped.

"It doesn't really, I just don't know much about you," he said softly. There were a few moments of silence, the only sounds being me trying to regulate my breathing.

"Once, when I was younger," I said quietly. I heard Jaret move on the couch, readjusting his sitting position.

"Who?"

"You wouldn't know them, so it shouldn't matter, so quit being nosy," I replied, trying not to raise my voice too much.

"Sorry," was his only reply. For some reason, I felt obliged to keep it from him. I didn't really know why. I just didn't want him to have to know everything about me.

I laid down on the couch, fluffing the blanket over myself. The top of my ponytail jabbed into the back of my head, and I sat up with a remark of annoyance. I undid my hair, putting the hair tie on my wrist so that I wouldn't lose it. I yawned and laid back down.

"What's your favourite animal?" he continued his line of questioning.

"Cat," I answered tiredly.

"Favourite food?"

"Spaghetti."

"Favourite place?"

"Don't have one."

"Favourite... um... favourite letter?"

"*T*." I replied. I frowned as I heard myself say that. *Tala*. It was my fault. My fault that she was gone.

"What's your favourite... um... what's your favourite colour?" he asked. I barely heard him as the sinking feeling in my chest overwhelmed me.

"Just go to sleep, Jaret, leave me alone."

He mumbled an apology and was softly snoring a moment later. I only had to tell her not to get too close to him. I only had to say for her to stop. Then she would still be alive. I would have been able to save her.

quivlie

I started down the street, walking towards Haishin's mother's house. She lived just down the road from us, so the walk would only take me a few moments. As I tried to think of a way to tell her how her only child was gone, I felt my heart sinking. I stepped onto the walkway leading to her door. It took all the strength I had to walk to her door and knock.

"Just a moment, please!" her distinct voice rang out, speaking in Druridish as she usually did. I gave a small melancholy smile as I heard her voice. The door cracked open, and she made a small noise of surprise as she saw me.

"Quivlie!" she exclaimed loudly, drawing me into a tight hug as I saw her skin lighten in the dim light. After a moment, she pulled away from me and gazed intently at me. "What happened to you, where were you?" she questioned, leading me through the door and into her kitchen. She paused and glanced behind me in confusion. "Did you see what happened in the courtyard earlier? 'm not entirely sure what happened, I was near the back of the crowd."

I gave a small nod and my heart fell. "I was near the front with Haishin," I answered weakly.

Her skin dulled in confusion. "Where is he now? At home with Paulto?"

"He..." I started, my voice breaking. I cleared my throat with a cough. "He was trying to protect somebody and he got shot."

Her skin darkened drastically. "Where is he? He's fine though, isn't he?" her voice grew frail and soft.

I shook my head. "I tried to help him, Yenstim, but it was too late, there was too much blood," my shoulders sagged as I answered. She gave a small, barely visible nod and I saw her face fall. She wrapped her arms around me again, her shoulders shaking as she started to cry.

dot

The small bell on the door chimed at 3:27 AM. When I looked to see who it was, it was, unsurprisingly, Quivlie. Unsurprisingly because it was her shop and I was expecting her back soon, although surprisingly because of the late hour. I would have thought that she would have stayed at her mother-in-law's house for the remainder of the night.

She jumped slightly as I stood, not expecting me to be awake, I assumed. She gave a small smile as I walked towards her.

"Dot, why are you still awake?" she asked quietly.

"It is Nemvar's turn to charge now. I was charging before he was, but it was his turn one hour and forty-three minutes ago."

"I'm going to go up to bed. Do you need anything, before I go to sleep?" she asked.

I shook my head. "No, I do not. Thank you, though."

Quivlie gave another weak smile and started towards the stairs. "Goodnight, Dot," she said over her shoulder

"Technically, it's morning, but goodnight. Sleep well," I replied. As she disappeared up the stairs, I sat down beside Nemvar again, resting my head on the wall.

chapter twenty-eight

jaret

I knocked on the large front door, Alison and Dot standing behind me. Quivlie, Yenstim and Nemvar were getting things arranged for the funerals tomorrow. The three of us had come to talk to Merida about the kids and about what had happened, like I had told her that we would.

After a moment of waiting, the heavy looking door swung open, Merida holding who must have been Lily. She smiled weakly and waved the three of us inside.

"Good afternoon, come in, we can talk, I was just trying to put the children down for their afternoon nap," she offered.

"Of course, thank you very much, Merida," I replied. Alison, Dot and I walked through the doorway, following her down one of the many hallways visible in the main hall.

"If you will be so kind as to wait in the dining room, we can discuss what happened after I get them in their beds," she requested, gesturing to the door at the far end of the hall as she walked back towards the main entrance, more likely towards the stairs that were accessible from that area of the house. Alison led Dot and I down the hall, and we found our seats at the long table, easily able to seat up to thirty people, probably many more.

About fifteen minutes later, Merida returned, seating herself in the empty chair that would create a square between the four of us, beside Alison and across from Dot, diagonal from me.

"The police notified me that Charles will be arrested for first degree murder as soon as he is discharged from the hospital, and that the children will not be able to be left in my care, as I am too young to properly take care of them. They are supposed to go to the next of kin, and since neither his parents or Amelia's parents are able to care for them, the responsibility would go to their siblings," she explained, and my heart thudded in my chest. "It wasn't decided whose sibling the children would be left to in case of an emergency, so the officer told me that it would be up to you two to decide." I glanced to Alison, who looked just as bewildered and shocked as I felt. "Of course, you'll have time to discuss it if you'd like, but the children need to officially be claimed by one or both of you before Saturday, or they will have to be put into foster care."

That gave us three days to decide, four including today.

After talking to her for about another twenty minutes, the three of us started back towards Quivlie's shop. Alison and I slowed slightly so that Dot was walking ahead of us.

"So... what should we do?" she asked me in a quieter tone, although I know that that wouldn't prevent Dot from hearing our conversation.

"I really don't know. I don't want them to grow up without parents, but I know that I don't know how to take care of kids," I answered slowly, choosing my words carefully. "Are you going to take them?"

Alison shrugged. "I honestly don't know what we should do, Jaret."

alison

There weren't many people there. Only Quivlie, Paulto, Haishin's mother; Yenstim, Jaret, Dot, Nemvar and I were supposed to attend Haishin's part of the service, and we didn't know anyone else to invite to Tala's. Yenstim held the urn holding Haishin's ashes, Dot was carrying the bowl, Nemvar was carrying Paulto and Quivlie led us through the forest; one hand holding the seed that we would be planting, the other reaching in front of her, causing most of the foliage to move from the path that we were forging through the trees.

Eventually, we came to a clearing, a wide creek splitting the forest in two. I was carrying Tala's urn. She had no weapons of her own when she died, so we were burying her with one of the longswords from Quivlie's shop, which Jaret was now carrying towards her soon-to-be grave.

A pear tree stood beside the water, the fruit strewn across the ground at its base, some starting to rot, others looking as if it had just fallen.

"This is a beautiful spot, dear," Yenstim said softly to Quivlie. The younger Drurida gave a small, although clearly forced smile. After a few moments of listening to Quivlie and Yenstim's instructions, the ceremony was ready to begin. Jaret, Dot, Nemvar and I were sitting in a semi-circle facing the creek; Yenstim, Quivlie and Paulto sat in front of the creek, facing us, Haishin's ashes and the bowl sitting in front of Quivlie. The ceremony was supposed to be completely silent until the very end, which was only about twenty minutes after it started.

Quivlie stood, lifting the bowl as she rose. She turned and walked towards the stream dipping the bowl into the clear water, filling it about half way. She came back to her spot in the semi-circle, placing the bowl on the grass in front of her.

Yenstim took the top off of the grey, porcelain urn, taking a small handful of the ashes and letting it go into the water. Quivlie did the same after her, and then Paulto. Quivlie gestured towards Nemvar, who was sitting on the left of Paulto, and he handed the urn to the Android. Nemvar put his handful of ashes into the Mielikki's Water, followed by Dot and Jaret, and then the urn was passed to me.

It was my fault that we had to put his ashes into the water. My fault that I couldn't protect him. My heart sank into my stomach as I took the remainder of the ashes into my hand, dropping them into the clouded water.

Yenstim brought the bowl towards her, setting it on the ground in front of her knees. She put her hands into the water, swishing the water and the ashes together until it was purely grey, and you couldn't tell the ashes from the liquid. Quivlie stood, walking towards a spot a few feet away from the water, on the opposite side of the clearing as the pear tree. She knelt, taking a small spade that we brought and starting to dig a hole for the seed. In turn, the rest of us took our turns helping Yenstim to mix the Mielikki's Water.

After I had done my share of stirring the water, the rest of us stood and joined Quivlie at the freshly dug hole. She stooped to the ground and placed the seed in the hole, standing up again after it hit the soil in the bottom of the hollow. Yenstim bent beside the seed and poured half of the ashy water into the hole with it. Everybody took a turn putting a scoop of the dirt on top of the seed and puddle of water. The dirt that was being dropped onto the seed was turning to mud as soon as it hit the water that filled the bottom half of the hole.

When the last scoop of dirt was on top of the mud, Quivlie poured the remainder of the water on top of the damper dirt.

She knelt beside the grave, and placed her hand on the soil above where the seed was buried. After a moment, the dirt started to part as the tip of the sapling started to push itself through the soil. As the green sprout grew larger, two small branches started forming, small, round leaves beginning to grow on them. She stepped away from the sprout, and Yenstim stepped into her place, her hand resting on the base of the sapling. When her hand made contact with the green bark, the seedling started to grow again at a slightly rapider pace than before.

When the young tree was nearly three feet tall, Yenstim motioned for Paulto to take her place. The young Drurida went forward and put his hand on the trunk of the tree, and another few small branches started to sprout from the seedling. After another minute, Quivlie put her hand on his shoulder, and he stepped away from the tree.

"Mielikki, we hope that Haishin will be able to help you well in your forest, and that this ceremony of parting has helped him to meet you in the afterlife. We hope that we will be able to meet with him again in the afterlife, and that he will be with us to help and guide us until that time has come," Yenstim said, her head raised towards the sky.

"We ask for you to tell him that we love him very much, that everybody is thankful for his sacrifice and that we will continue to remember him until we may meet with him again," Quivlie added.

"Mielikki, please take care of my daddy until I can see him again," Paulto said, clinging to his mother's leg. It was only the Druridi who were to say the parting words to Haishin. The ceremony concluded, the seven of us started to gather our things.

"I'm sorry that this happened to him, Quivlie. I wish I could've met him, he sounds like he was a great person," I overheard Jaret saying to Quivlie.

Her answer stopped me in my tracks. "Death is not goodbye. It is 'until we meet again,'" she answered.

I turned to look to Tala's grave near the water. "Until we meet again," I said in valediction.

epilogue

quivlie

"Happy birthday!" we all shouted as Jack and Chris came into the room; Jack started slightly at the sudden noise. Lily ran over to her brothers, jumping onto Chris. The twins both burst out laughing as everyone went to say their hellos to them, Alison and Sari. The four of them had gone out to breakfast while Jaret and Lily had set up the twins' surprise party.

Paulto and I went to greet them after a few of the other guests did. "Happy birthday, you two," I said to them, Paulto repeating 'happy birthday' a moment after I did.

"Thanks, Auntie," Chris said, pulling me into a hug. I smiled and ruffled his hair.

Within a few moments, Lily, Paulto and the twins had run off to play with the two dogs that Jaret had adopted a few years ago. It was the twins' eighth birthday. Crackers bolted after the kids and the other two canines as Nemvar and Zaupa opened the door to the house.

"Ah shit, we're late, aren't we?" Zaupa sighed in exasperation as Crackers ran to play with the kids and the other dogs. The kids, all squealing in excitement, ran to say hello to Zaupa and Nemvar. Since Dot had moved in a few doors down from Jaret's house, Zaupa and Nemvar visited her whenever they were in the area, always stopping by to say hello to the kids if they were with Jaret, never failing to bring them interesting presents from wherever they travelled to last.

I glanced to the side as Nemvar held out his closed hands to Jack. When he opened his hands, a small lizard clambered up his mechanical arm, peering around the room quizzically. I smiled as the kids squealed in delight.

Sari walked over to me, putting her hand on my arm. She smiled at me. "How are you?"

"I'm well. How are you, Sari?" I answered.

She smiled again. "I'm pretty good, thanks. Shoot, one second," she started, seeing that Lily was looking into the fridge. She grabbed her adoptive daughter's shoulders and led her away. I heard her quietly suggest that she and Paulto go into Marley's room and wrap Chris and Jack's birthday presents.

Jaret had gone back to Traiton a few months after he got his apartment in Walkton, and returned with his friend Marley. Since Jaret found an apartment with four bedrooms for a surprisingly inexpensive rent price, Marley lived with him and the kids.

I felt a tug on the hem of my shirt, and I looked down to see Chris standing beside me.

"Can you help me grow my flower? It keeps dying," he whined.

I grinned. "Of course I can. Where is it?"

He smiled broadly and grabbed my hand, running towards his and Jack's bedroom. He scrambled onto a stool by the window, and he handed me a small pot, inhabited by a dull, wilting flower. I cradled the pot in my hands, and within a short moment, the flower started to bloom again, its leaves returning to a bright green instead of the pale, sickly jade that it was before.

"Were you remembering to water it?" I asked.

He nodded enthusiastically. "I remember, but then whenever we're at Alison and Sari's house, Jaret never remembers to water it for me," he answered, frowning in concern for his sickly plant.

I chuckled lightly. "That certainly sounds like something that he would forget. What if you bring it with you whenever you go back to Alison and Sari's house? Then you can always remember to water it, and it won't wilt again."

His eyes lit up. "That's a really good idea, I'll go ask Sari!" he exclaimed excitedly, running out of the room. I smiled and placed the ceramic pot back on the windowsill.

As I turned to leave the room again, I saw two pictures sitting on the nightstand close to the door. One was of the three children with Amelia and Charles. Lily looked to be only a few days old. Amelia was beaming, holding her daughter and looking happily at Charles. Charles was holding the twins, one in each of his arms.

I looked to the next picture and immediately recognized the day. It was two years ago, at Alison and Sari's wedding. Alison, in her typical fashion, refused to wear a dress, but Sari convinced her to wear dressier clothes than she usually did, and to not bring her crossbow. Jaret was standing beside them, Lily sitting on his shoulders, the twins laughing and standing in front of them. Alison and Sari both looked happier than I had ever seen them look before.

"You should come back, Quivlie," I heard a voice from behind me. I turned around to see Dot smiling in at me. "Jaret said that we are going to eat the sweet food soon." I smiled back at her. She saw the picture that I was looking at. "I remember that day. That was a good day," she said, turning back to go back to the living room.

I flicked off the light and closed the door gently, walking out of the bedroom. I felt the familiar melancholy twinge in my heart and my skin dulled slightly. I saw Jaret waving to me from across the room, so I smiled and walked over to him, following him into the kitchen.

"Cake time?" he suggested.

"Seems like as good a time as any," I answered. When he starting motioning frantically, my face contorted in confusion. I glanced behind me to see Alison walking to us.

"What's your issue?" she asked, grinning.

He jerked his head to the fridge. "Cake now or later?"

Alison shrugged, an incredulous expression passing over her features. "Now, I guess? I don't know, doesn't matter, now is fine," she replied, retreating from the kitchen as quickly as she could after answering the question.

"Alright, cake now, then. Could you get everyone to sit on the couches or at the table or something? It doesn't really matter where, I'll start lighting the candles," Jaret requested.

"Of course," I said, turning to walk back into the living room. I saw Paulto looking at me in confusion, so I motioned him over. I knelt down to face him. "Could you get the twins and Lily to sit on the couch in the living room?" I asked.

His skin brightened. "Is it cake time?"

I smiled and put my finger to my lips. "Don't tell Chris or Jack, okay?" I replied.

He nodded, racing off to tell them to get onto the couch. My eyes met Dot's, her face a mask of confusion. I gestured to the couch and she nodded, understanding. She tapped Nemvar on the shoulder, and soon the two Androids and Zaupa were walking to sit on the couch, Marley following suit as he overhead what was happening.

Within a moment, all of us but Jaret and Sari were seated on the couches in the living room, the four children all bouncing in anticipation.

After we sang the traditional human birthday song and served the cake, Lily had fallen asleep on the couch, despite the early hour of four o'clock. I looked around the room. Crackers was laying stretched out on top of Nemvar and Zaupa, drooling onto the couch; Alison and Sari were sitting beside each other on the floor between the two sofas, Sari's hand on top of Alison's; Jaret was sitting between Paulto and Jack on the couch, grinning as Chris retold what had happened at school the other day; Dot was sitting on the edge of the couch, petting one of Jaret's two dogs, and Marley was playing tug of war with the other. This was what mattered to me most of all. Family.

alison

I pushed open the door, and the kids all pushed past Sari and I. I turned and smiled tiredly at her. She gave a brief laugh, kissed me gently on the cheek, and followed the kids into the apartment. I sighed softly in happiness as I shut the door behind me.

"Sari, can we watch TV before we go to sleep?" Lily asked hopefully, looking up at my wife. Sari looked to me, raising her eyebrow in question.

"What do you say, Ali?" she asked.

I smiled and shrugged my shoulders. "To be fair, it is their birthday," I said slowly, drawling out the words.

Chris gave a small fist pump at his side, hoping that I wouldn't see him.

"Yes!" Jack exclaimed quietly.

"Alright, but not for too long, it's getting late," Sari said, sitting down on the sofa beside Lily. Jack grabbed for the remote at the same time as Chris did, and soon there was a wrestling-match happening on the carpet.

"Either you decide together, or you can all go to bed right now," I called from the kitchen, hearing the thuds from the other room. Immediately, the noises ceased and a moment later the crackles of the television started coming from the other room. I chucked softly.

After we watched almost half of a documentary about kailito deer, Chris and Lily had both fallen asleep, and Sari was halfway there too. Jack, however, was still entranced with how the small deer pranced about the deserts, never getting tired of the comical appearance of its large antlers and tiny wings. It wasn't long before he too started to yawn.

"Ready to go to bed, bud?" I asked.

He shrugged, rubbing his eyes. "I'm not tired, though," he said, yawning a second after.

"If you're not tired, then I don't have skin. Come on, it's almost midnight," I replied, standing. He nodded reluctantly, but didn't move from the couch. "Are you going to make me carry you?" I questioned. He raised his arms above his head and nodded. I grinned and reluctantly lifted him up. "Alright, because it's your birthday."

He yawned again and put his head on my shoulder. I gently nudged Sari's leg with my foot as I stepped around her. She looked up to me and smiled tiredly.

"Off to bed?" she asked

"Yeah."

"I'll get Chris," she said, stretching her arms above her head as she stood.

"Thank you," I said, starting to Jack's room. I could tell by the small patch of wetness growing on my shoulder that he had fallen asleep, leaving a puddle of drool under his face. I pushed open his bedroom door with my foot, and he awoke when I set him in his bed. He crawled under his blankets, and I tucked him in, kissing him softly on the forehead and bidding him goodnight before I went back to the living to return Lily to her bedroom.

Ten minutes later, Sari and I were getting into bed. As a light across the street turned on, a small beam of reflected light from my left caught my eye. Sari had framed a collection of fortunes from fortune cookies, including the one from the cookie that Pete had given me a few days before the earthquake.

> It is honorable to stand up for what is right, however unpopular it seems.

Even though I had scoffed at it then, I realized how important it had become to me over the past years. I kissed my wife goodnight and soon fell asleep, thankful for the opportunity to start my own family after losing mine.

Acknowledgements

Thank you to everyone who helped me in making this book possible.

To Eve, because somehow you flopping around on the floor gave me an idea for a plot.

To all three of my parents for supporting me with my desire to write.

To Dede, for being the first person to finish reading my book and for encouraging me through writing it.

Last, but certainly not least, a huge thank you to Chris! Without your help, I probably never would have finished writing this book, let alone have had it published. Thank you for helping me make one of my biggest dreams a reality.

CPSIA information can be obtained
at www.ICGtesting.com
Printed in the USA
LVHW090512191218
601039LV00001B/47/P